Praise for
MATTHEW I

MW00783577

"Bartlett has the ability to make the darkest horror sing like an angelic choir engulfed in flame, and you'll like what you hear." — Philip Fracassi, author of *Beneath a Pale Sky*

"Matthew M. Bartlett's use of the grotesque...is reminiscent of both E.C. Comics and the Grand Guignol...but at its core lies an antimisanthropy, a deep and true sense of grief that we are all so temporary and so ephemeral." —s.j. bagley, critic, and editor of *Thinking Horror*

"Matthew M. Bartlett has one of the most irrepressible, fiercely original voices in all of contemporary weird fiction - inspiring, horrifying, hilarious, and unforgettable." —Jon Padgett, author of *The Secret of Ventriloquism*

"Reading Bartlett is like watching the offspring of François Rabelais & Al Columbia frolic like demented wildlife, where people wear the faces of a Hannah Höch portrait while giggling macabre wisdom over obscene broadcasts from radio stations located deep within dark forests." —Christopher Slatsky, author of *The Immeasurable Corpse of Nature*

"Matthew M. Bartlett is an open channel to the darkness" —Michael T. Cisco, author of *Unlanguage*

"No, no, no, nononono, nope, I know better than to read the stories of Matthew M. Bartlett. They take root in my head. They squirm. They flex and creep through my delicate tissues. Yes, I've known better for years now, but I always come back for more. His work is truly unique in the crowded field of horror and weird fiction, and no author I've read follows the beat of their own drum so strangely and beautifully. If the feeling I get reading him is more infection than fiction, it's well worth the sickness. And the squirming. Bartlett is a master of the genre. Let him burrow into your brain, too." —Michael Wehunt, author of *Greener Pastures*

WHERE NIGHT
COWERS

MATTHEW M. BARTLETT

JOURNALSTONE
YOUR LINK TO ARTIST TALENT

ISBN: 978-1-68510-070-4 (sc)
ISBN: 978-1-68510-071-1 (ebook)
Library of Congress Control Number: 2022945834

First printing edition: September 30, 2022
Printed by JournalStone Publishing in the United States of America.
Cover Design: Mikio Murakami
Edited by Sean Leonard
Proofreading and Cover/Interior Layout: Scarlett R. Algee

JournalStone Publishing
3205 Sassafras Trail
Carbondale, Illinois 62901

JournalStone books may be ordered through booksellers or by contacting:
JournalStone | www.journalstone.com

Contents

MONICA IN THE HALL OF MOTHS
9

EFFIGIES OF FORMER SUPERVISORS
21

THE MUSEUM OF LAUGHTER
31

DR. 999
41

OH THE BEAUTIFUL STINK
52

PROVISIONS FOR A JOURNEY
60

CALL ME COREY
72

THE DARK MATCH
77

THE TWO-WHEEL SYSTEM
91

IF HE SUMMONS HIS HERD
99

LEEDS 2600
114

THE LONG-LOST PARENT
131

WE PASS FROM VIEW
143

THE STOREFRONT THEATER
156

DEEP INTO THE SKIN
163

GO TO THE DEVIL
175

THE MASTER OF THE HOUSE
186

WHERE NIGHT COWERS
198

MIKEYTOWN
206

PUBLICATION HISTORY

ACKNOWLEDGMENTS

ABOUT THE AUTHOR

WHERE NIGHT
COWERS

Monica in the Hall of Moths

Mónika, daughter of Father
Frost and Mother Furnace
Pure of heart, penitent and proud
wouldst thou enter yon Hall of Tane
Drest in a mantle of moths
Leaving behind thy quire,
Even as thy flowers dost chase thee?
   —English Folk ballad, circa 1504, untitled, author unknown

MONICA PASSED INTO the Hall of Moths three Decembers ago. We had just been seated at a table by the window at the Vietnamese restaurant in the cluster of strip malls just outside the city center, snow-gilded coats snug on the rack, menus spread out before us all but ignored as we watched people rush by, tinted blue and red by the neon window signs. A flame pogoed in a decorative glass cup. The radio played an Asian pop confection. A bespectacled, blank-eyed boy came around with a pitcher of ice water and upturned and filled our glasses.

I don't remember what exactly it was that Monica said, but I looked up at her, and all the color had left her face. Her hands gripped the sides of the table, thumbs red as berries. She leaned forward, the way she does when she's going to say something amusingly cruel about someone in the room, and I leaned in to hear it.

Red storm clouds surged into the whites of her eyes. Her pupils flickered as though mirroring faraway lightning. Then her brilliant, complex blue iris disintegrated to powder. For a brief moment, I saw a fluttering, winged thing behind that dissolving blue cloud. Then she pitched to her left and spilled out of her chair onto the floor. After that my memory consists only of disjointed flashes. One of the diners, a fat man in a grey sweater, rising from his booth, approaching me, leading me away by the arm. Pitying stares. The piped-in music going mercifully silent. Some of these flashes are false memories. In one flash, Monica is standing by my side, her cold hand touching, but not holding, mine, as we look down at the empty spot on the floor where she'd fallen. In another, I say to the hostess, *At least we know it wasn't the food*—we hadn't even ordered yet; this was a lame joke I made for Monica's benefit. "I can't believe I laughed at that," Monica says, and then she is on the floor again, looking curiously small and irrevocably still.

I remember her mouth hanging open, jaw unevenly set. I knew she would hate for people to see her like that, so I struggled to release myself from the grip of the customer in the grey sweater in order to cover her up, but he held me fast. I remember her shoes were off, like she'd been hit by a car. How did her shoes come off? Did someone remove them? Why would someone do that? They lay perpendicular to one another, a few inches apart, like some gnostic symbol or glyph. When I turned my gaze away, ghostly red images of them lingered in my vision, as though I'd looked at glowing coals instead of shoes.

I remember spying a small thorn on the floor after the EMTs lifted her onto their stretcher.

I remember I was howling.

I don't remember the ride to the hospital, but I must've gone in the ambulance, because I do remember retrieving my car the next day, driven there by who I cannot remember. I remember it was raining and grey, the roadways wet with the rain and the melting snow. I remember bursting into tears when I saw the car in the lot. I remember wondering whether I had the courage to lower myself into the driver's seat without looking over at the cruelly empty passenger seat to my right. I don't remember driving home.

We met through a mutual friend. We met when she answered my online personal ad. We met when we had a fender bender in a Food Mart parking lot. We met when we both slipped on the same banana peel. I gave her my number. She gave me her number. We slept together that night. We slept together after four weeks of dating. We remained virgins until we married.

It doesn't matter how we met, the details of our life together amount to nothing. Our trajectory is triteness itself, our story a carbon copy of countless others. They're out there now, ordering in restaurants, napping in apartments, couples like us. You drove by scores of them today, saw them as blurs in your periphery. In every way we were unremarkable. Her birth didn't make the world better, and her having entered the Hall of Moths did not worsen the world. She was a clerk at a veterinary office. She was a machine operator at a manufacturer of weapons-grade jack-in-the-boxes. She was a producer of silent television shows for a channel for the blind.

Her managers replaced her within days. Surely her replacement was just like her, with a husband just like me.

Shockwaves rolled out, as they do. Her mother, widowed ten years back, was devastated, shattered, or would have been, had she not been lost in the grey-white mists of dementia. Monica's friends and co-workers were shocked and saddened, but also secretly titillated. The death, the spectacle and the suddenness of it, was a break from the workaday, a jolt in the routine. Something new to talk about, to marvel at, to contemplate in the dark hours of night. They reveled in the excited camaraderie of detached mourning.

Friends of friends shrugged and briefly gave a side-eye glance at their own mortality.

I claim the worst. I earned it. I had to handle all the things she left behind: her clothes, her decades of accumulated this-and-that. I had to put my hands on everything, and everything had barbs that caught my flesh and sent tendrils in to weaken my muscles and corrupt my blood. After Monica entered the Hall of Moths, I became acutely aware of the passage of time. It propelled me away from Monica like I was tethered to the chest of a giant plodding through an endless field toward an ever-retreating mountain range. How I wished I could duck away from that relentless forced frog-march and tuck myself into the folds of a stray second.

The Hall of Moths is a children's book I read as a boy, written by someone named Burton Stallhearse, pictured on the back cover flap as not much more than a pointed nose and a thin, unsmiling mouth, the rest obscured by the shadow of a cowl. I remember the book's striking cover: a towering edifice rising from a field of poppies, bathed in the liquid blue of twilight, Roman columns topped by an architrave reading HALL OF MOTHS, the tall capital letters carved from the stone. I can close my eyes and see the yellow smudges of light from the windows. The curved wall of denuded trees that ringed the field. The ghostly moon riding triumphant on a chariot of clouds, like a god returned victorious from some celestial war. I can almost feel the weight of the book in my hands. Its contents are lost to me now, like a word just out of my reach, my mind bumping up against the concept of infinity, a ghost on the other side of a barred door.

I don't remember the story, but I remember the Hall. I dreamed of it many times, of its corridors and its rooms and its atriums and balconies. It is as solid in my memory as the coffee place I stop at every morning before work, the office tower to where I drag my lunch every day, the bar where I drink until they tell me it's time to go home. The maze-like corridors are as real as any of the squalid tenements that line the western edge of the city. I could find my way around without eyes: the high-ceilinged narrow corridors, fire reaching its hot-fingered hands out from stone sconces, the capacious rooms domed with chandeliers as large as cities, where the moths perched and preened, loving the light yet dimming the room with their fervent ministrations. It was always twilight in the perfumed rooms of the Hall of Moths.

Monica now dwells in the Hall of Moths. Three Decembers. Twenty-six thousand hours. I picture her eating sautéed moth wings for her dinner, accompanied by wine from the dust-clad bottles in the expansive cellar, tethered by strings of dust-coated cobwebs, their labels long ago peeled—a bad habit of Monica's, along with chewing her nails and picking at her face.

It never existed, the book. There is no such person as Burton Stallhearse. The Internet says so. I know better.

I'll tell you a secret: I still have the ghosts of her fingertips burned into my upper arm from when she pulled me back from stepping out onto a busy city street, the wind from a passing van blowing back my hair. I can feel the scars, the small shallow craters, ringed by thin semi-circles of raised skin. When I rub them I find moth dust in the whorls of my fingerprints. I touch it to the tip of my tongue. It tastes like dead skin and charcoal.

I do not know if she is the same person she was. Does she still laugh wildly, without self-consciousness? Do her pet peeves—unwary bicyclists, trilbies on women—still rile her up? Does she still have those familiar nervous habits? Does she whisper when her thoughts are too troubling to keep inside her? Has her time in the Hall erased her personality? Or, and I do not like to think about this, is she spread out on the floor of the Hall, all consciousness gone, blades of grass like IV tubes growing up into her body and filling her veins and arteries, dandelions like white clouds filling the chambers of her heart, moths burrowing into her brain to distort her dreams?

Her house was tall and many-storied, its dormers somewhere up above the treetops. And her garden was the envy of the town. Marigolds, crescentheads, bone-petals, and johnny jump-ups formed a lush expanse around the hall, interrupted only to admit a flagstone path from the rutted and pockmarked road to the entrance. The townsfolk walked out of their way to marvel at the colors, the scents, to watch the bees collecting nectar and the snakes slithering this way and that in the undergrowth.

She had trampled the garden in high June, but selectively, meticulously, only the least fair flowers catching the fury of her heel. Now, in October, she haunts the flagstone path, the Halloween tip of her cigarette leading her up and down, aimlessly. The only sounds are the soles of her shoes scuffing the stones, and the occasional long sigh of exhalation. Finally she uses her nails to squeeze the cigarette near its tip until the glowing ember—the cherry, her mother used to call it—drops into the dirt. She extinguishes the cherry with her toe, folds the butt, and pushes it into the pocket of her jeans. She grasps the sleeves of her sweater, hiding her hands.

The autumn nights are endless landscape paintings stuffed with dreams, no limiting frame in sight, no end to the panorama. In one dream she invents something that is like air, but you can hold it in your cupped hands, pour it into vessels, float in it like a bird rests on a tier of sky. In her favorite dream, she and a faceless boy spiral down through this buoyant air among a school of seahorses. – Stallhearse, B. (1937). *The Hall of Moths.* New York, NY: Scribner

Two months ago I drove by the Vietnamese restaurant for the first time since Monica's decampment. I thought maybe the doorway to the Hall of Moths might exist somewhere inside the building—in the kitchen, the stock room, the freezer, the office. My heartbeat drowned out the radio, muted the rain. When I reached the dreaded block, I saw that the building was gone; all that remained was a patch of dirt surrounded by red plastic fencing. The patch was surprisingly small— it seemed impossible to me that the whole restaurant, with its expansive dining room, its patio, its long bar lined with twenty barstools, had occupied such a small spot. I spied a sign taped to the fence and turned into the parking lot of the adjacent convenience store. I walked over to the fence, using my hand to shield my eyes from the rain.

COMING SOON, the sign read, and I looked at the graphic below and my whole body seized—it was a sketch of the Hall of Moths itself, as though someone had seen into my memory of that old kid's book and drew it with colored pencils. THE HALL OF MOTHS. A week later I drove by again. Construction had not yet started, but the convenience store and its lot were gone, as was the house that had sat on the other side of the restaurant. On a mound of dirt where the house had been, a crane sat tilted like the propped-up cadaver of a strange, large bird.

I no longer dream of the Hall of Moths. Instead I dream again and again of a day from my childhood. I'd hoofed it into the kitchen and breathlessly begged my mother to let me go tubing with my neighbor Jason and his father down at Devil's Province, where the Mill River meanders here, rushes there, a bubbling ribbon running through the state forest, families and couples riding inner tubes along its two miles, bobbing, spinning, hooting, and yelling through the rapids, splashing their hands in the dark waters and staring up between the tree lines at the stretch of sky that mirrors the river.

My mother frowned, her face darkening. A girl had drowned there just yesterday, she said, fell out of her tube in the rapids and was dragged under. "What are the odds," I said, "that someone would die two days in a row?" She turned away from me then and I sensed that she'd been lying—that no one had drowned in the Mill River since the flood way before she was born. I had managed to call her bluff before recognizing it as a bluff. I took her silence as permission and fled before she could say otherwise.

Jason's father, a broad-chested bearded giant, rented our tubes and orange lifejacket vests, and we rolled the tubes down the dirt path. Their smell reminded me pleasantly of that of a brand-new Halloween costume. As we walked down the incline toward the riverbank launch, he snickered and chortled, his large hand on Jason's skinny neck, surreptitiously making fun of the other families, Jason looking up worshipfully. Down at the launch, attendants—teenagers in red swimsuits, with ponytails and safety vests and flip-flops, not much older than I—told us the rules and helped us climb into our tubes.

I looked at Jason's father in his tube, knees up, large feet splashing in the water. He had donned a pair of large, mirrored sunglasses. He lit a fat cigar and stuck it under his mustache, flicked the spent match into the water. I looked away, at the rock-strewn shoreline, the thick tree trunks and dark woods. Ahead the river widened to accommodate leviathan stones like the crowns of giants, the restless waters bubbling up around and between them. The water's whisper rose until it became as the faraway sound of an excited crowd.

Jason waved from his tube as he spun into the rapids, knees up, feet kicking up and down in the foaming waters. His dad's expression was hidden under sunglasses. Their tubes drifted to the left of the first big rock, mine to the right, and then my tube began to spin and something pulled me right down through, folding me nearly in half. I kicked and held my breath as the underwater world rose to meet me. I felt my vest pulled off me as by a parent, and watched it sail away like a disembodied torso into the darker waters and disappear.

As I neared the bottom, frogging my feet wildly, flapping my arms, trying to drag myself upward, I spied a small table, around which four men sat in water-blackened suits. They argued bubbles at one another, jabbing at the water with knobby fingers. The man closest to me, the tallest of the four, banged the tabletop in slow motion and his glass bounced, teetered, and settled. He turned his head to me. His eyes had been chewed from behind their lids, and he grinned a toothless grin. Then he plucked a thin knife from inside his jacket and lunged across the table, stabbing the man opposite him in the chest.

A cloud of blood burst from the wound and billowed outward, obscuring the table and the men. The strong current carried me just past the red cloud's outer borders. I landed on my feet at the base of a gargantuan rock, the size of my boyhood house. A hole gaped on the side of the rock, and through it I saw blurred things swelling and undulating, bright colors flickering. I swam to the hole and through. Inside the rock, moths of a million varieties swam, and I swam among them. Bubbles of air sailed from my gaping mouth and expanded into amorphous, shimmering globules. The moths avoided them...but one moved just a stitch too slowly. That unlucky lepidopteran penetrated the side of one of the bubbles and, once inside, trembled violently with a seizure and fell to its undulating floor. As the side of the bubble healed itself shut, the moth dried up and disintegrated into a small hill of rust-colored powder. A giant white moth swam up to me then, as tall as Jason's father. It looked like an angel in intricate, dancing tresses. Its diamond-shaped space-alien face studied my face. It sniffed at my lips. I opened my mouth...

...and it was as though someone had tied a rope to my ankle and tugged. I was yanked out of the rock, past the still-expanding red cloud, up through the roiling waters, and to the surface. I pulled in great gulps of air, splashing the water with my hands, trying to find the voice to call for help. Something pushed up under me, lifting me out of the water. It was my tube. It cradled me like a large hand, carried me slowly through the still part of the river. A few yards ahead of me, Jason and his father spun gently in their tubes. It was as though nothing had happened. I stared up at the sun and let it dry me until I heard the roar of approaching rapids and, my mind still shuddering and reeling, managed to ready myself for the churn.

One Monday I woke on the Tuesday morning of a late Thursday. The bed was vertical, up against the wall. The bed floated an inch from the ceiling, upside down. The bed was as it should be, all four feet anchored. I slid to the floor in a torrent of bedclothes and pillows. The windows were on the ceiling and floor. Crawling to the horizontal doorway, I stepped on a window, breaking it into great shards like shark's teeth, cutting my heel quite badly.

I showered in hot steam, watching the blood swirling in the cold water that pooled at my feet. It took the shape of Monica's face. She looked desperately sad. It took the shape of a moth. It took the shape of a Vietnamese restaurant in a cluster of strip malls just outside a city center. It took the shape of an inner tube. Fear billowed in my stomach as elation swam like eels through my cerebrospinal fluid. I wondered how long it had been since I'd been to work. I wondered how many messages filled my phone like stones in a sewer pipe, like plaque in an artery. I put those thoughts into a strongbox in my brain and I locked it up tight and fed the key to the shower drain with all the other keys that caused the drain to slow, the pipes to clog, the water to pool at my feet.

The Hall had opened. I knew it, the way you know someone has arrived before the knock on the door—a stirring of the hairs on your arms, something different about the quality of the daylight. I drove there in a sun shower, each car on the thoroughfare crouching in its own nimbus of glittering light. I arrived to find the hall festooned in ribbons and fluttering banners. Unseen bells chimed and great black birds adorned the architrave and the ramparts. The rain had stopped, and morning wore the mask of early evening, dark grey with red underpinnings up high, everything sepia down low. The Hall emanated a bright white glow, cutting at the yellow.

I entered the Hall of Moths.

The capacious atrium walls were decorated at tasteful intervals with framed portraits of black-eyed moths in cloaks the color of straw, or of crinoline long neglected in some ancient armoire. They sat in jeweled thrones, reclined on silk-gilded chaise lounges, or stood in well-appointed libraries. The floor was coffee-veined marble; the copper-colored tin ceiling a panoply of bulging eyes, narrow faces, and pinwheels of ridged wings. A maze of ropes and stanchions emptied out at a reception desk not much larger than a podium, behind which a slender-necked young woman in a black dress sat, her hair tied up in a loose bun, her middle and index fingers parted just slightly, as though to accommodate the wish for a cigarette.

There are many varieties of moth: some as colorful as a pandemonium of parrots, some blacker than a goth's closet in a windowless bunker at midnight. There are sinister moths like the white witch moth and the death's head hawkmoth. There are corn-borers and imperials. The irksome oak processionary. The imposing Attacus atlas. The Hall housed nothing as dramatic as these; instead, within swarmed moths of the common household variety in such incalculable numbers as to form a great whispering fog through which I made my way, eyes squinting, pushing them aside as though swimming through fragments of yellowed feathers. Then *they* began to push *me*. Blindly I went, pushed left, propelled straight ahead, to the right, then the left. At times I nearly lost my footing on the floors, so slippery with moth-dust. But they righted me.

Then all at once the moths swarmed up to the ceiling, where they rested in many layers, the whispering of their wings quieting. Revealed by their ascension was a great ballroom lined with archways, each opening into a tunnel of grey brick terminating in deep shadow. Tall double doors stood a few yards ahead. They were of bronze, and in bas relief was depicted great fern-laden gardens, through which winged demons cavorted, thin and long-chinned. Many of the trees had miniscule humanoid infants clustered in their branches like budding fruits, and the demons were harvesting them, collecting them in sacks and depositing the sacks into big round baskets. With a great shriek of metal the doors swung slowly open, and a whirling, swaying funnel cloud of moths as tall as two men emerged and approached me. Somewhere in that fluttering cloud I saw a figure—my Monica?

Monica?

The rain had done something to the flowers.

It came down hard and importunate, light orange, like liquid rust, like dripping autumn leaves. It collected in the gutters and the flowerpots, the splash blocks and the watering cans, the potholes and the gutters. Monica spent the time in her bed, among her books. Moths flitted here and there. She pursed her lips and blew at them to get them off the pages. She read and slept, woke and read, lulled to sleep by the somehow gentle roar.

One morning she rose and went to the window to look out at her garden table. The rain had filled the teacups and spilled over into the saucers, dripped down through the grates, the effect was as a little array of decorative fountains.

And still the rain continued. The trees drooped and their leaves wilted and curled into tight damp tubes. Rooftops sagged. Cats crouched under carriages and dogs whimpered under forest deadfalls. Some of the townspeople swore the rain reeked of cabbage; others detected a burnt plastic smell; still others claimed the odor was that of spoiled yogurt.

When it did finally end, the sounds of downpour and patter were replaced by a profound silence, broken only by the occasional great rasping cough or burst of relieved laughter, people calling out from house to house. People emerged to rake the curled-up leaves and look up at the sun as one would a departed friend who had returned unannounced.

Monica rose from her bed and bathed. She sat in the great claw-foot tub, reclined in the cloudy water until it began to cool, then finally dressed and went to inspect her garden. At first the flowers seemed to have withstood the punishing, pummeling rain. They stood tall, their colors bright and vibrant, glowing and shining, leeching like radiation out into the air around them. But then she spied the most curious thing. A small throng of marigolds pushed through the larkspur and hyacinths, as though migrating, their yellow heads swaying, bumping violently against one another. Pink mouths opened to reveal yellow piranha teeth. They hissed and spat.

They emerged from the border of the garden and spread out, slender green branches like long, jointed arms, gripping thorns in tiny green fingers. Monica turned and ran back to the house, the flowers hot on her heels. They were screaming and screeching and wailing. She slammed the doors on them and fled to the attic. And there she sat, and sat, and finally went quite mad.

She never left the house again.

– Stallhearse, B. (1937). *The Hall of Moths.* New York, NY: Scribner

The thing that was not Monica emerged from that cloud of moths. Its skin hung in straps and tatters from its crown, covering its eyes, revealing only a pink snub nose and a tiny red line of a mouth. It wore a faded and wrinkled blue t-shirt with the words KING MOTH in peeling iron-on maroon, one word atop the other, a jeweled crown topping the words. Bloated hairless arms filled the sleeves, tapered down to thin wrists topped with fat hands but slender, almost feminine fingers. Crisp jeans, dark blue, held up by a cinched brown belt, dangled around its pencil-thin legs. Its feet were a mess of overlapping, malformed toes with pointed, bruised nails. It leaned forward to kiss me. I closed my eyes as its dry lips touched mine, and I heard the moths come down from the ceiling in their thousands. I felt them entering my ears, felt my head swell until it touched all the upper corners of the great room.

My therapist, Doctor Rittle, is very patient with me, though I test his forbearance with my dogged insistence that these things happened. There was no Monica, he insists, and there was *never* a Monica. There are no such thing as moths; I have simply invented a degraded version of a butterfly. There is no place called Vietnam, and if there were, they would not have restaurants. There are no cars, no flames in cups, no blue and red lights, no shoes laying side by side, no underwater men, no Hall of Moths, and no King Moth. Doctor Rittle is very insistent about all of this and will not be argued with.

There is no *me*, says Doctor Rittle, and his chair is suddenly empty, *and no you*, his disembodied voice continues, and I am back in the Hall in the twiggy arms of King Moth and my head is empty, hanging down against the back of my neck like the doffed hood of a sweatshirt, and he is carrying me and I can hear the thrum of his heart of wings and I can smell old closets and tucked away linens and I know that he is bringing me to my Monica, and now I can smell rich broth and hear the whisper of chopsticks, and Monica is there before me again, and her face is so *real* and *there* and yet so unreal, and we are just another couple at just another restaurant, and she again leans forward to say something, and I lean in to hear it, and I can see in her pocketbook that hangs from her chair a giftwrapped book, and I'm sure I know the shape and the heft of that book, I know the book so well I can see the cover right through the wrapping paper, and the sound of moths' wings fills the air and I can no longer see nor hear and I am suspended in water that fills my lungs and bulges behind my eyes and then everything is gone, gone, gone.

Effigies of Former Supervisors

GOD IS A corporation, incorporated when time itself awoke. Now, the campus-bodies that comprise his being are host to billions of workers. They move industriously between corner office and cafeteria, between cubicle and copier, conference room and courtyard, sales floor and stockroom. Some weep in his capacious washrooms; others whisper into portable phones in the cobwebbed corners of his warehouses. He pulls in paper and excretes pulp. He pulls in youth and excretes decrepitude. His windows are ghost-haunted mirrors. His contracts are forbidden grimoires. His workers must produce, see the closets packed with stacks and stacks of blister-packs, reliquaries of remedies to keep the whole mess in motion. He merges with other corporations in embraces grotesque and byzantine. Like cancer-bloated dragons in unholy union, they scorch the landscape with the leakage from their sore-riddled undercarriages. Overall, God supposes he can say that he is happy, fulfilled. He wants for nothing. He sleeps soundly. His snores, great and mighty snarls, startle his neighbors from their beds, but he sleeps right through their hoarse hysterics, the thuds of their fists on his walls. When he wakes, he hears only the pulse of the blood of billions through the arteries of his deep-sea heart. His managers are sadists and madmen. See their cadavers seethe with rancid pink foam in the high-ceilinged, fog-clouded confines of his Effigy Room. The harvest of pain, the bounty of bone and bluster. Come and see, come and see, come and see.

I
PERCY

He was a silo head atop a silo body, with a tumescent neck that did little to divide the two. He combed his brown hair down to form a ruler-straight fringe a few inches above his brow. Oval lenses magnified his dull blue eyes. His shoes had zippers up the sides. When I would arrive for the morning shift, even before I reached the back door, I could hear the brainless thump of the dance music he played at top volume before the store opened to customers.

With that music as background, he would lead me around the sales floor to outline his plan for the day. Dance-walking at random from fixture to shelf to window display to counter, some days he looked adrift and somehow forlorn, but determined to press on, smiling against it all, a stalwart marshal abandoned by his parade. Other days he exuded ecstatic excitement and abandon. His hands would twirl, go to his hips. He would shimmy and strut, his body listing from side to side arrhythmically, like a galleon in a high wind. *This is the big item to push today,* he'd say, thrusting his hip in the direction of the item in question. By the end of this daily grotesquerie, his green polo shirt would be soaked through with sweat at the armpits and the neck.

Percy was an ardent adherent of the efficacy of the add-on sale. *If they purchase this, suggest that. And that. And that over there. This item is by the register for a reason.* At closing he would fret over the average per-sale item count, calling me over to go over my receipts. "What happened here?" he would ask. I knew that the mystery of that sale, one of a hundred or so over the course of the working day, would haunt him, pull him from his sleep, fester in the folds of his brain. How could he stop the madness of the single-item sale? He would write everyone up. He would write up the world. First warning. Second warning. Do not make me issue a third.

On more than one occasion I opened the stockroom door to find him sitting in the cramped, angled space, cross-legged, weeping, surrounded by boxes shoved in awkwardly like mismatched puzzle pieces. I know that when I left and never came back, he wept. He had once asked me where I thought I would be in five years. Now he would never know. Or so he thought.

Percy danced to dispel the discarded things that leer and mock from the dark corners of the world.

His effigy lays draped over an ottoman in my Effigy Room. Its head is slightly sunken, its neck stitched up from some physical insult that must have occurred during transit. Its eyes are crusted as though with curdled milk.

2

MITCHELL

He was small, ginger-haired, pale, with freckles like pinkish clouds across his forehead. His trim beard tried and failed to deaccentuate his lack of a chin. He wore a leather coat with a sewn-in belt, and carried a matching duffel with a long strap and many pockets and buttons and flaps and compartments. He held the position of division supervisor, which meant that his presence was intermittent, and often harried. Once he'd swooped into the crowded confines of the shop, he darted like a cockroach trying in vain to dodge the glare of the kitchen light. His shoes were not designed for that amount of punishment, I surmised, which meant he would have issues with his feet in later years, assuming his heart allowed him to make it to his later years.

Once he'd surveyed the shelves and the seasonal signs, he'd head into the storeroom where my office was situated and go through everything, brow furrowed, looking for *issues*. He loved the word *issues*. I found some *issues* here I need to go over with you. I want to show you some *glaring issues* I found.

One day I went to work wearing denim, which was contrary to company policy. On my way back from a dismal, grease-soaked lunch in the mostly shut-down food court, I saw him sweep into the store. I ducked into a department store, where I bought a pair of khaki pants. I changed with haste in the pungent reek of the department store restroom. The pants were very long. I rolled up the cuffs so that they wouldn't end up underfoot, ground into the grimy floor.

I returned to the store with my jeans in the department store bag to find Mitchell sitting at my desk. He had pulled files and folders and forms from the drawer. They lay stacked on the surface of the desk. His face was anguished. Issues too many to count. "Your desk is terribly organized," he said. "How will you ever survive in the business world?"

The question entered my ear canal and fragmented like frangible ammunition. *The business world,* I thought. *The. Business. World.* Ho w would I sur vive. In. The Busine Wor

"I quit," I said. "I want my last check mailed to me."

I never did receive that check.

Mitchell scurried and scampered to evade the barbed tongues that slithered and licked from the furrows of the world.

His effigy is nailed by its hands to the wall of my Effigy Room to prevent it wandering. I keep its hollow interior stocked with fresh supplies of live insects to satisfy its need for movement.

3
MAURA

She was large and lumpy, with a pudding-basin hairstyle and a bulging, watery accumulation of chins. She favored flimsy, garishly designed dresses and shoes that exposed a grotesque tangle of red toes. Her brows arched cruelly over small eyes in a nest of wrinkles.

When she was terrified, and she was often terrified, especially in meetings, she would, apropos of nothing, issue a bland witticism and follow it up with a loud, raucous laugh. No one else would join in. She appeared to be unaware of the fact that she was the only one laughing as she looked around the conference room table at everyone as though we were all sharing a moment of rich, debauched hilarity. She would, after a time, trail off into helpless trills and titters, and the meetings would hitch forward.

One afternoon I received a call from my landlord that there had been a fire in the apartment above my own, and the building had been declared uninhabitable. The firefighters had opened all the doors, and my housecat could not be located. When I informed Maura on my way out of the office, she reacted with annoyance and impatience. When would I be back? Could I possibly come in for part of the day tomorrow? Could I let her know as soon as possible? She really needed me there.

Maura screamed and laughed to frighten away the monsters in the halls and the monsters in the walls of the world.

The hands and feet of her effigy are stapled to the ceiling of my Effigy Room. She hangs there looking down upon the other effigies, an overgrown cherub monitoring her charges. I sewed the hem of the dress to her calves for modesty's sake. Would that she had afforded us the same consideration.

4
CONNIE

She was of medium build, trim, with lank brownish hair and reading glasses that dangled from her neck, tethered to a leather cord like the carapace of a captured insect. She favored dark-colored skirts and suit jackets over a silk blouse. A slight strabismus lent her a deceptively flighty, fatuous aspect. The company sent her in to damage and dispirit departments that had previously been getting through the work of each day with little interference.

"They called me the Dragon Lady," she said of the previous department she'd upturned. She said it with a prideful grin. In the same monologue she claimed that the company moved her from place to place because she was "good at managing people."

Upon leaving a meeting, she would turn the lights off while people were still rising from their chairs.

She would tell us that our department was under a black cloud.

She told me that she was surprised I had ever been promoted.

She told me that I made too much money.

Within a week of arriving at our department, she set up meetings with each of us in order to determine the nature of our weaknesses and flaws. She did not care for me. I was unprofessional. In fact, my unprofessionalism bordered on a kind of characteristic, inbuilt insubordination. Moreover, I was slothful, she said, having observed exactly none of my working day. She told me that she would "light a fire under my feet."

I don't care for a stranger commenting on my feet, in any context.

I wished terrible things upon her. A car accident on a lonely winter road, one that caused the jagged interior of her vehicle to tear her open from knee to armpit and let the deep freeze and the slow bleeding compete to remove her from existence. I wished upon her cancers of the brain and bowel, or the tongue. None of these things took her in the end. Once our department had been reworked in such a way that two factions were created and subsequently pitted against one another, she moved on to do further damage elsewhere.

Connie disrupted and destroyed in order to propagate an image of herself separate from the horror she encountered in the mirror.

For a time I kept Connie somewhere other than my Effigy Room, but a wave of humidity forced my hand. It sits crumpled like a wounded spider in the corner. Its face is a mask of cobwebs. Its eyes bulge. Its tongue hangs down past its chin. It is a dragon brought down and desecrated.

5
STANLEY AND NICHOLAS

Stanley, a tall stick-figure with a carefully tousled coiffure, came to the company after his ouster from a professorship at an unremarkable college a few towns away. An investigation of unknown provenance had preceded his departure. One gets the idea, reading the account of the matter published in the local press, that many details have been softened, glossed over, or omitted in their entirety in order to protect readers with more tender sensibilities. What we knew of him was arrogance and pettiness costumed by a soft southern accent and laconic manner.

He was amused by the mantle of authority placed upon him, and he entertained himself with the capricious cruelties his unearned position allowed him to wield.

He scheduled frequent two-hour meetings in which he gave undue weight to the absurd hypothetical questions posed by the smaller-brained staff members, allowing tangents to derail an already unwieldy agenda. These meetings inevitably dragged into a third, and sometimes a fourth, hour. He twirled time around his fingers like twine.

Stanley saw in our colleague Nicholas a kindred mind, for Nicholas often took his side, slyly ingratiating himself. Finally, Stanley recruited the younger man to work with him as co-manager. Nicholas: squat, broad-chested, with a thick, ruler-straight set of brows to match his rectangular, thick-framed glasses. Soft-spoken, and projecting quiet rationality and a measured demeanor. These were mistaken by the lummoxes in upper management as competence and capability. They assented to the promotion.

Our department consisted of two factions meant to cooperate in order to achieve the desired results. The woman who managed the faction of which I was a part was let go under the guise of "reorganization." Stanley managed the opposing faction. Nicholas had been a neutral party working with both. Upon his promotion he paired with Stanley to oversee both factions. My faction, newly bereft of its own leader, no longer had any say, and no hand in dividing the workload.

Prior to the official start of his managerial tenure, Nicholas shaved his hair into a mohawk, to prove what he considered to be his artistic, rebellious nature. This display of insecurity served as a warning, for, of course, within days he had shaved his head villain-bald and begun to establish himself by enacting policy changes that were as damaging as they were abrupt.

His favorite method of subjugation was to ask the opinion of the staff regarding his idea for a policy change and, when the opinion was overwhelmingly against his suggestion, with backing evidence to prove its inherent unworthiness, he would, in mocking, peevish tones, defensively restate his original plan, which he would then proceed to implement.

The two managers held many closed-door meetings in which they ridiculed and caricatured staff from my faction and set plans in place to oust any workers who attempted to challenge or confront them. This was achieved by a combination of a) making our work difficult and exacting and b) plying us with time-consuming, monotonous tasks that required no skill in order to harass or bore us into resigning our positions.

It was nearly a year ago that they turned their regimented treachery in my specific direction.

As the pressure my tormenters put on me increased, expanding at one point to include interminable meetings with the stolid and disinterested human resources manager, so did my online surveillance of the two.

Gaining access to their virtual lives was simplicity itself. Using a false account and scanned photographs of a long-dead friend, altered with professional image editing software, I first connected to their connections on social media, and interacted with them agreeably and solicitously. After I time I sent requests to Stanley and Nicholas, who both without hesitation accepted my friend requests. I engaged with them minimally while collecting data. Of Stanley I learned little. He was reticent, closed off. I knew that his scandal had cost him his marriage to a gaunt, stern-looking woman with whom he still had tenuous and volatile ties, and that their union had produced a daughter, a comely young blonde whose allegiances were still in flux.

Nicholas was far more careless. I discovered his amateurish attempts at literary writing and poetry. His blank verse was atrocious, his rhyming verse embarrassing. He wrote paeans to furniture outlets, meditations on snack foods. His wife wrote erotic poetry lacking in eroticism, the product of a stunted intellect combined with a middling imagination. She painted a picture of herself as daring, brash, provocative. If you hadn't seen her, you might think her tall, spike-heeled, long-legged, and voluptuous, with high cheekbones and smoky eyes. Instead she proved a pale, pointy little thing, all knees, nose, and elbows. A collection of twigs assembled and wrapped in a freckled and bruised casing.

In any event, and more importantly, Nicholas's status updates and posted pictures indicated a clear map of his daily patterns. They were so fixed and precise that I felt a strange admiration for him. Come to find out that he is not the only one for whom this is true. It may be, in fact, an as yet undiscovered trait of those who pursue management, and even of those who find it thrust upon them.

Nicholas and Stanley combined their powers to dispel the loneliness of tyranny that otherwise might weaken the will and introduce doubt into a system not accommodating to it.

The two switch parts like interchangeable child's toys in my Effigy Room. They switch limbs, organs, even heads. In one's stomach, the other's hands might rest. One's foot might distort the other's mouth to nauseatingly nasty comic effect. Other bits and parts move one to the other according to my mood.

6

ME

I was removed from the company's campus by physical force on a chilly October morning, not long after I had arrived for the day. I should have known it was coming, after the final meeting with Stanley and Nicholas, and the faceless human resources manager, wherein they produced printouts of emails and records of my supposed transgressions. They recounted past conversations, innocent at the time, in a fictional framework so that they now seemed sinister. The past several months they had been amassing evidence, framing it, hack authors collaborating on their opus. I saw that I had been manipulated. Outfoxed. My fate was sealed, as surely as the door to my secret room.

As two of the huskier building managers hustled me out to my car under a dark and cloud-streaked sky, I remained stoic, offered nothing in the way of resistance. It occurs to me now that I was already planning the construction and implementation of my secret room, and the assembling of my effigies.

In fact, that has become my new vocation. I am, as the phrase goes, my own boss. My savings and my pension serve as my salary. They are a timer ticking down, giant red numbers I've stored in a locked quadrant of my brain as I toil away.

7
EFFIGIES OF FORMER SUPERVISORS

Something awakens me. A sound? A physical jolt? I don't know; I sense only an uncanny atmosphere of aftershock. I sit up in bed. The sheets are wet with my perspiration, and I peel them from my body like removing a vast swatch of dead skin. I detect a faint glow from somewhere in the house. It reaches through the open bedroom door and stains the ceiling.

The silence now is freighted. The anticipation goads my blood.

Finally, well past the point of excrucation, I hear a loud thump, followed by the shattering of glass. I feel a strange mix of relief and terror. My bedroom brightens just a touch; combined with my eyes becoming accustomed to the low light, I fear I can see entirely too much.

The insurrection must have started weeks before. I'd thought the recent new proliferation of night sounds was merely the product of the paranoiac nature tattooed into my blood by years of subordination and supervisory subterfuge. A whisper. A snicker. A mirthless chuckle hiding behind a thunderclap like a fiend hid in a cloud. Something slithering on the carpet. Other physical signs I dismissed as an accumulation of mental effluvia. A drop of something gelatinous on the kitchen tile. A pinprick hole in the wall. A shadow that could not be dispelled by direct light. An effigy slightly askew one day. Another one with a torn sleeve or a hiked-up shirt. A strange look on a bloated face or a slight shift in a should-be-dead glance.

I should have known, of course, that mutiny was the only possible outcome. I was a cliché as old as time: the successful revolutionary become tyrant. Berating them and beating them, placing them hither and thither at my whim. I had not formulated a *good business plan.* My *purpose* had been unfocused. I had seen myself as untouchable, others held to my account, without their own will. My product was revenge, and revenge will be my fate.

A cabal approaches: bodies, stuffing, straw, and stitches, caressed by creeping, swirling tendrils of ectoplasm. Their long shadows crowd the light on the ceiling. That light begins to flicker and swirl, and I hear a sound like the snapping of twigs, and then a pop, like a knot in a log bursting. A dark referendum has been reached. I did not meet nor exceed expectations. My performance was unsatisfactory. My lot is further disciplinary action, up to, and certainly including, termination.

God is a corporation; a rat-king mind; a sprawling network without center nor borders. In such a conglomeration there is no place for the trifle called MERCY, no piddling DECENCY. The harvest of pain, the bounty of bone and bluster. Come and see, come and see, come and see.

The Museum of Laughter

The Museum of Laughter: Killing the Audience
pulls together four overarching themes:
1.   Laughter compromises the respiratory system
2.   To coerce a laugh is an attempt to cause harm
3.   The successful comedian fails in this attempt
4.   The successful comedian harms only himself

Not long before my cousin died, we coated him in lard. He went downhill
fast.

BIRTH IS A dark ritual in which the Being in transition from Not-born to Newborn is the subject of worship: the Traumatized God. The cult has assembled in a secret room to greet this unknown Being; outsiders are verboten. Giant figures, their faces obscured by masks, stand ready to be anointed with the blood of the Mother-Host. Tray tables bear an array of occult instruments, sanitized and hermetically sealed. The Being is pulled forth and into piercing light and is greeted by the figures, who utter strange, inexplicable sounds. The tallest, at the forefront, completes the first phase of the ritual when he wields a blade, pulling up the living tether that connects Mother-Host to Newborn.

Newborn boy.

The newborn's baffled shrieks are met with reverie and worship. He has been summoned and, as the electronic prophecies foretold, he has arrived.

Now he must be cleaned, swaddled, placed into the arms of she who provided his first sustenance. His eyes close. Sleep takes him. He awakens not long after in a strange new place. People in funny hats, squinting eyes, mouths bent upward with mirth, kneel to worship him. They bring offerings. They bring overpowering aromas. They quaff ceremonial libations. Their distorted faces swoop and loom. Through it all his ears are assailed by a strange new litany of sounds: percussive, convulsive noises bursting from their wet pink mouths.

HA HA HA HAHA HAHAHA HA HA HA HAHAHAHA

Frightened, he imitates the sound.

It sounds like: *ha ha ha haha hahahaha ha haha ha ha*

It says, unsure but hopeful: *I am one of you.*

It works. They are delighted.

They coo and again bark out this strange language. The boy barks back, grins and bleats, even as he secretly pines for his chamber of muffled sound, its warmth and wetness.

But it is gone, closed to him.

He is no longer welcome there.

Moving is one of the most traumatic events through which a god can live. The change of environments causes in the demented a particular bafflement and stress. They call it *transfer trauma.*

Transfer trauma.

Traumatized God.

Funny, right?

A will is a dead giveaway.

It's easy enough for a traveler to miss the gap in the trees. The only indication of its presence is a modest mailbox, once white, now brown with rust, mostly engulfed in a cloud of tangled vines and crabgrass and impaled on the thin, gnarled stump of a long dead tree. Capital letters, each in a leaning reflective square, spell out THE MUSEUM OF LAUGHTER. The Ms are upside down Ws.

The gap is just wide enough, its ceiling of foliage sufficiently low, to admit a small car. Leaves will slap at its windshield, roots will challenge its suspension, will make for a bumpy, uncomfortable ride. A long ride too. Just when one begins to wonder if the trail has an end at all, the faraway laughter starts, a chortle from somewhere in the depths of the forest, something mud-choked and febrile, strangely reminiscent of distant thunder. Before long it comes from all around, cruel and wanton and mad. Just as a wild, screaming titter sounds loudly from under the car, the trees thin, and the gap empties out into an expansive, kidney-shaped lot of packed dirt, lined with a low rock wall, and intermittent tall poles atop which loudspeakers prove themselves the source of the laughter. At the far end of the lot the house stands like an anomaly, a mistake, something that should be on an historic street somewhere. Tall and white, ringed by a porch busy with rocking chairs, pumpkins piled in straw, and wooden boxes with splintered slats, its domed turret just grazing the cupola of leaves.

My uncle's funeral was widely attended by people who wanted to make sure.

You found it in the Classifieds, an ad mixed in with the notices. Museum of Laughter, 1 Museum of Laughter Road, Leeds. That's all it said. You picked up an area map at the Gas & Chew. No such road. You mentioned it to your dad, who said, "I've heard of that, off Rural Road 3, leading out to the hill towns." He adjusted himself in the creaking recliner and popped another in a parade of Natty Ices. Food of the Gods. You lit out on a dreary nothing-to-do Saturday several weeks back and missed it entirely, drove to the nearby town ("If you hit Westerfield, you've gone too far"), stopped at a gas station with ancient pumps, rolling digits and rust and peeled-away logo, used the restroom with the tilting floor and the warped mirror and the nostril-assailing ammonia smell, a mini-funhouse in and of itself, grabbed an off-brand grape soda and some jerky, and drove back home.

This time, mid-October now, you watched for the mailbox, driving slowly, other motorists swerving around you, some hitting their horns. You spotted it right away, a glint in the foliage. You turned in, your heart beating fast, like your first visit to a brothel.

The front door opens into a kind of antechamber, with a white couch, a shallow counter below a curtained window, on that counter a pot of plastic flowers and a leather-bound guest register (brand new, still in an opaque plastic sheath, tassel tucked neatly in the middle pages, alongside it a similarly sheathed click pen). Inoffensive music involving woodwinds emanates from a set of small white speakers.

The music fades. Just when total silence is attained, a hungry growl of static sounds, then a feedback shriek caroms through your ears. "Neural paths," states an authoritative voice, the voice of '80s film strips in darkened classrooms, a figure in shadow seated behind a large oak desk in a double-breasted suit and thick-framed glasses, fingers entwined, speaking into a tabletop microphone, the scene shot in shadowy, noir-ish black & white. "Neurons throw axons along a synapse. Lights flicker in the hypothalamus and subthalamus. Truncated vowel-like utterances sound involuntarily every 210 milliseconds. Give or take. Diaphragmatic convulsions wrack the body. Sputtering, coughing, even wheezing as the respiratory system is challenged..." The voice goes on in this way until you spot the small doorbell by the interior door to the right of the curtained window. You ring the bell. There is no sound except for the whisper of wood on carpet as the door swings open.

The stutterer died in prison before he could finish his sentence.

The door opens into a long, brightly lit hall with gleaming wide-panel hardwood floors under a steel-grey runner. Built into the white walls at intervals are small television screens. On each screen a mouth convulses and spits. Lips shudder and pull back to reveal gapped teeth. Tongues ripple. Metal fillings clack. Saliva floods in from hidden ducts. Nostrils flare and eyes squint, the skin around them crinkling. Heads throw themselves back violently. Jowls shimmy and shudder. The mouths warp. Lips split. The silence is disconcerting.

You bark out a laugh, as involuntary as a hiccup. Then another. Then you guffaw percussively, each bark punctuated by a thud from somewhere in your chest cavity. You double over, grab your stomach, the laughter morphing into a deep, low chuckle, then rising, wavering, to a tittering falsetto. You shriek and wheeze, go to one knee, a hysterical genuflection. You cough and cough, and finally a greyish globule sails from your throat and lands in the center of the door leading out. On the screens, all the mouths are still. The cameras pull back to reveal glowering faces, all focused on you. You feel strangely chastened. Laughter starts to bubble up again in your stomach, and you flee the room.

The next hall is wider; on your left runs a wooden railing, over which, looking down, you can make out unlit display cases, crumpled papers, empty binders splayed open like bats on display, black trash bags full-to-bursting, chunks of plaster, fast-food wrappers, and hard-to-identify thises-and-thats; to your right is a series of dioramas, roped off, each depicting a scene with the floor tilted upward at a 38-degree angle for better visibility. In the first diorama, every item, including the figure prone on the floor, is in shades of grey and white, mimicking a pre-color photograph. The prone figure is a man of medium build with dark hair and a beard. He has a white towel wrapped around his waist, a handkerchief tied tightly around his upper arm.

***

After a beat or two a man with a cheap white wig and scab for a face oozes from the wall into the silent hallway. He carries a red cloth. With jerky, almost robotic movements, he wipes the guest's discharge from the door. He places it, swaddled, in his upward-held palm and then he sinks silently into the floor, singing softly. The echo of his voice lingers and then is gone as well.

***

Human laughter may have had its start as a communal expression of relief at some peril having passed, an indication also of trust in one's confederates.

***

Excerpt: Killing the Audience
An Educator's Guide

Your students will laugh. You will laugh. This is expected. Asthmatics will not be admitted without inhalers on hand. Those prone to hernias are encouraged to wear trusses. The museum will not be held accountable for any injuries incurred from laughter, nor of any deaths, though death due to laughter is rare. The painter Zeuxis died after painting Aphrodite—an old woman had insisted on modeling for the painting. Pietro Aretino, the Italian satirist, died of apoplexy laughing at a dirty story told by his sister. A Thai ice cream truck driver died laughing in his sleep. And the Greek poet Philemon died a hero's death: laughing at his own joke.

Assuming you and your students are not injured or killed, the act of *conscious laughter* will awaken in you a *deeper understanding*. Like that of the Neo-charismatic churches, this *holy laughter*, if prolonged, may in fact lead to harmless yet profound dissociation. The walls may fall away and the landscape crumple to the ground like backdrops painted on curtains, cut down by unseen hands. The students may be convinced they are in a small clearing at the center of a vast landscape of strange-shaped objects towering into an uncertain sky. They may see long-limbed, grinning things in recesses and cubbyholes that mock their cries with bird-like calls. They may become convinced that this curious, cruel audience has been watching them from birth, ridiculing their clothing and hair, replaying their foibles and errors, the foolish things they've said and done, for the entertainment of their demoniac race. This is a temporary condition.

A battery of psychological assessments is recommended prior to your visit. (see Appendix B)

Students with pseudobulbar affect, which can cause laughter or crying unrelated to emotions, are admitted for free if they can show they are not medicated for the condition.

What do you call a dead fly? A flew.

Excerpt: Contract with Klenze Kleaners

Exhibit 1: The bearded figure may be removed and placed on a gurney; this is a two-man job. Please remove and launder the white towels in which he is wrapped. The tiles must be mopped with water only, no chemicals nor solvents, and must be fully dried before the figure is replaced. Do not remove nor wash the handkerchief around the dummy's upper arm; the stains are theatrical. The same goes for the shower stall and toilet. The walls themselves are stained to represent the dinginess and desolation of the scene. Staff will inspect this and all of the dioramas to insure their fidelity to the original installation and to the source photographs. Notes on triennial cleaning of all wax figures will follow. (see Appendix C)

Exhibit 2: The face-up figure on the carpeted floor must be moved by a team of four; use the large gurney. The belly is removable, affixed to the base with Velcro straps. The marks on the belly and torso depict an array of bruises and thus must be washed lightly in soapy water; abrasives may compromise the coating. The purplish face is also theatrical. The legs are fixed in a diamond-shape, they must not be adjusted nor manipulated in any way, as they are fragile and prone to breakage. The foam obscuring the mouth and nostrils is part of the figure; though it looks moist and pliable, it is merely designed to look that way, and is firmly attached to the head. However, as with any protuberance, it is at risk of breaking if the figure is not handled with caution. The remainder of the room must be cleaned as any room might: the furniture dusted, the glass polished, the carpet washed. Clothing, sheets, and blankets may be removed from the floor, but not washed, as the stains are theatrical. Marks on the carpet indicate their location and color; please see Appendix F for diagrams of replacement of clothing, furnishings, and detritus in all of the rooms, especially Exhibits 2 through 6. This is important and violations may void the contract. (see pp iii-iv)

Exhibit 3: The figure in the seated position is held up by a belt wedged into the hinge of the door; therefore the door must not be moved. The shoulder may be shifted slightly in order to remove any scuff marks from the molding. The figure and the clothing in the closet need not be cleaned. The pocketknife need not be cleaned; please check it for rust. If any is detected, please notify management.

Exhibit 4:
This is our most complex exhibit. The bed with the brass bed frame, full of blood, blood splashed up onto the headboard and wall. The tangle of embroidered silk sheets and thrown back down comforter. The man with the sleep-tousled hair, glazed-over eyes, with the slight smile on what remains of his face. The scattered pillows. The nightstand with its pill bottles and books. The open bathroom door, revealing the sink and vanity, on the black and white tiled floor a spray of blood-soaked blonde hair and fragments of tile among clumps of brain matter, a hand, manicured fingernails painted red, clutching air. The brass must be polished once a month and the dresser and television dusted, but otherwise this exhibit must not be touched nor cleaned. The flies are not to be killed. Any breaking-down of the figures is natural and must not be countered.

Where do suicide bombers go when they die? Everywhere.

Yelp Review
This place was funny as hell, the worst museum ever. It's a good thing there's no fee, only a donation box. I threw in a buck, figured I'd throw in more if I had a good time. Worst dollar I've ever spent. I've lost dollars and had more fun. The attendant who led our group through was a big weirdo, bald and tall and potbellied and stooping. He was wearing, like, 1970s pajamas. He was barefoot (which is gross). You could, I swear, smell my man's deformed feet as he led us around. He didn't narrate at all; he just giggled and snorted and

whispered to himself. The headphones they gave the group just played static. The dioramas looked awesome, I have to admit, but they smelled like old laundry and mold and bad meat. Half the interactive displays didn't work. The lights fluttered like they did at my uncle's place before the electrical fire. The floors were splintery and the carpets had the remnants of cat puke on them. The windows were smeared with dried soap. The part where you stand in the giant laughing mouth was the worst. There were no warning signs posted. The "tongue" was wet and hard to stand on—especially when it started moving. The teeth were sharp. Whatever they made the "tonsil" out of was ruptured and leaking something yellow-grey and lumpy. A little girl fell under the tongue, and when we left, the parents were still trying to get her out.

Did you hear the joke about the dead kid? It never gets old.

In your waking dreams, the mailbox has teeth. Not the white, perfect triangle teeth of Saturday morning cartoons, but chipped slabs stabbing out from inflamed red gums, stained with plaque and who knows what, the toothy mailbox is an oblong eyeless head atop a vine-strangled neck and it lunges from the shrubbery and takes a bite right out of your side. It tugs your purple ropes and you feel your insides tear and loosen, tumble and spill.

There are only waking dreams now.

Every time the black blanket of sleep starts to pull its warmth over you, a thought blooms in your grey garden, a tickle in your throat, a sliver in your spinal column, and you bark. Chortle. Helplessly laugh all hoarse and hysterical, crying and wheezing, pulling at the skin of your neck, jamming your fingers into your mouth to clear a path, your fingernails cutting into the tender pink flesh. And then the adrenaline does the rest. Later, bloody-mouthed and bloated-eyed, you clamber from your damp bed. Your heart sputters, arrhythmia, misfiring, your vision blurs at the edges. You check the mirror for signs of stroke. The sagging eye. The drooping cheek.

Your doctor schedules a sleep study. The one-story stucco structure smells of powdered teeth and a corruption of mint. A diffident brunette woman, skeleton-slender, avoiding your eyes, glues paper circles to your body, wires snaking into machines. You watch the muscles move below the pale skin of her arms as she releases from a sealed plastic bag an opaque snorkel-mask, which she places over your face and affixes to your head with Velcro straps. Cool air with a hint of mint flows into your nose and mouth. It's quick, the spiraling down, the ceiling a swirling blue-white. For a brief time, blessed blackness. The taste of infinity for the starving man. Then *bam*, you're up, yanking off wires, bellowing. You tear the mask from your face. The wires are affixed to the mailbox, which stands obscenely next to your bed, leering. You tear the glued circles off your skin, pulling out hair. It struggles to simultaneously pull you to it and pull its roots from the floor. Once you're free of the wires, you flee the room. The attendant's chair is empty. An uncapped pen rests on a notebook paper adorned with sketches—cruel caricatures of your slack, sleeping face. A drop of blood, a translucent red bubble, sits on the counter like a button begging to be pressed. The wall of monitors shows masked people in blue-lit beds, convulsing, grabbing at their stomachs. They blink and sputter and jagged lines of static bolt across, and the beds are empty, masks dangling from corrugated hoses, covers thrown back.

You flee down a long blue hall of indoor dusk toward the blackness at its end and emerge on a stage. A red X marks your spot, just before a microphone stand. The house lights are down, and you're in the center of three overlapping spotlights: green, blue, and red. The crowd are clad in pajamas. Some grip stuffed animals to their necks. Others sit, daring you to make them laugh, arms crossed, cigarettes jutting between their fingers like tiny smokestacks. The smoke gathers at the ceiling like dry ice. Through the panoramic row of windows beyond the audience you can just make out the halls and displays of the Museum of Laughter. A bespectacled tour guide leads a group of rambunctious children toward the dioramas. They hop and skip, bounce in their shoes. Their heads whip back as they laugh.

You turn around to leave, but a wall-wide screen is sinking from the ceiling, cutting off any possible exit. The flickering of a projector lisps above the balcony, and on the screen, three profusely maned lions descend on a man, their massive paws slamming him to the ground. Cut to the effigy of a figure in a curly haired wig being raised up on sticks as a forest of lighter-wielding hands set alight the hem of its pants. Then a teenage boy crouches at the window of a building cloaked in flames, smoke billowing out behind him. He leaps. Cut to a blanket-swaddled toddler in a dunking booth falling shrieking into a glass tank filled with rotting tomatoes. You turn back to the crowd, baffled. Are you supposed to make jokes about the events on the screen? Your stomach churns and dizziness takes hold.

In the silence of the auditorium, someone in the back rows clears his throat. "Well?" a voice calls out, closer. You pick him out, right at the front of the stage: a fat man with a moustache and a bad wig. He's wearing pajamas with tigers and lions on them. A glowing red circle rests at the side of his mouth: the lit end of a fat cigar. "Come on," he says. "Insult me! Here, I'll get you started." He affects a mincing falsetto. "Look at you, you disgusting pig. Look at you there, with your mouth on fire. Cancer face! Blubber butt! Jammies-man!"

Someone groans and shouts, "You suck!"

You stutter a retort. "I haven't said anything yet. That was him!" Your finger trembles as you point at the fat man, who looks left, looks right, shrugging his innocence, palms up.

"What's the matter?" a woman's voice, shrill and hectoring, off stage left. "Can't sleep? Who's bad at *sleeping*? Do you have trouble *eating* too?"

She has the tone and rhythm of a comedian, you note, but the material is lacking. Still, she has a funny voice. You start to laugh. Something lands on the stage in front of you with a click. Something small, white and red. A mint? You bend to look at it and someone breaks into sarcastic applause, as though you've deliberately bowed without having done your act.

It's a tooth. Another lands next to it. You put your hand up to your mouth and pull it back to look. Blood. Your teeth rain onto the stage. You run your tongue across emptied-out gums. You feel your face distort into a grimace. The crowd bursts into sudden laughter, whistling and yelling *whooooo*. They stomp their feet until the spotlights under you shake in time with the beat. Something loosens inside you. Oh no. Oh no, not here. You're soiling yourself. You can feel the coldness behind you, sliding down the backs of your legs. You look down at your shoes. A thin purple rope slips from your left pant leg and coils like a snake. Then the right. A searing pain bounces around your stomach like a pinball, and an ache awakens in your backside and immediately starts throbbing. The crowd are standing now, even as you sink to the stage. Something pours from your nostrils and over your lips, covering the teeth on the stage, shoring up against the coiled innards that have come out. The last thing you see gives you a curious surge of hope. A red sign. Capital letters.

It says "EXIT."

Funny, right?

Dr. 999

Clovis Dr. 999's NL-id Blends Micellar Moisturizing Milk (DISCONTINUED)

Bad hair can inhibit or even obstruct your spiritual growth. Industrial detergents, enervating dyes, chemicals with unpronounceable names. They weaken your powers, sap your energy, leave you dry and desolate. Isn't it finally time to be rid of the lank, lifeless hair that's been holding you back? Inspire your hair, and make clear your path, with the essential nutrients and life-giving cultures infused in Clovis Dr. 999's NL-id Blends Micellar Moisturizing Milk. Clovis's water-rich complexes gently nourish, cleanse, and purify to restore balance to every filament, every follicle. Formulated without harsh parahydroxybenzoates, free of their troubling estrogenic effects, this non-toxic, dye-free, all-natural, organic, environmentally safe moisturizing milk will enrich and enliven, reconstituting and rebuilding the very structure of your hair, resulting in impossibly soft and radiantly lustrous hair. Heal and calm your hair with Clovis Dr. 999's NL-id Blends Micellar Moisturizing Milk. Your hair will thank you.

About the Product
- Conditions, rejuvenates, and hydrates with Dr. 999's Super Secret Formula
- Manufactured with high-grade materials
- Balances natural scalp moisture
- Gentle enough for everyday use
- With added Orisha Obatala and Abra Melin Annointing Oils

- Not tested on animals

Product details
Size: **12.6 oz.**

- **Product Dimensions:** 3 x 2.4 x 6.1 inches; 10.4 ounces
- **Shipping Weight:** 13.8 ounces
- **Domestic Shipping:** Item can be shipped within U.S.
- **International Shipping:** This item is not eligible for international shipping. Learn More
- **ASIN:** B0108MRORI
- **UPC:** 894382738   822142170089   885310346846 820909809803   6336871897230   633911651278 63332181040159807404150287   633911605264   885353857293 8835098087003885453
- **Item model number:** 76505201

Product reviews
CarrieFurbush1966 (one star)

Bought this conditioner from a seller called "ConditionLife" located in Leeds, Massachusetts. Shipping to upstate New York was next-day. The item arrived without any protective packaging—I found the bottle on its side on my front step, with no mailing label nor postage that I could see. I examined the bottle and found a number of oddities. The ingredient list was smeared and illegible, except for "galega officinalis infusion" and sodium laureth sulfate, which actually dries hair out. There was no UPC code or registered trademark symbols. Bottles of conditioner usually have a website or a phone number. Not this bottle. There were numerous misspellings as well. "Botianical." "Frargrance." "Lusterous." Opening the bottle was extremely difficult. The cap's hinge had an extraneous ridge of plastic that required careful work with a penknife to undo, and ultimately I had to disconnect the cap from the bottle entirely. The odors released when I peeled off the safety seal were earthy and unpleasant in a hard to define way, with an undertone of an astringent-like pungency that assailed my nostrils and actually made me a little dizzy.

Upon first using the product, I found it overly watery and bubbly. It stung my hands and scalp, not in the kind of pleasant, cold-feeling way that dandruff shampoo does either. There was slight blistering on my palms afterward, and my scalp felt rubbed raw. I found that using colder water lessened that effect slightly. Trying to towel-dry my hair caused a terrible burning sensation, and the hair dryer was even worse. I had to settle for combing my hair very gently and then letting it air dry.

My hair looked AWFUL, all day. Co-workers commented on it. Clients were unusually reticent. I think this conditioner actually cost me sales! Moreover, my hair *hurt*. It hurt to touch. It hurt when the wind hit it. I began to think strange thoughts. I felt overheated and feverish. Shadows loomed high and wavering on the walls and at times the very desk at which I was sitting seemed miles away. When I reached out to grasp the edge of the desk, my arms elongated until they were thin white threads sailing off into a blurry distance. I left early and took an Uber home right after work. The driver, in dark sunglasses and some kind of greenish jumpsuit, seemed to be staring at my hair in the rearview mirror, his lip curled in disgust. I went immediately inside and shaved my head. Then I ran it under ice-cold water until everything resumed some semblance of normalcy.

I poured the remainder of the conditioner down the shower drain, and ran the hot water on full blast in order to get it as far from the house as possible. After about thirty seconds, the water and conditioner began to bubble back up, filling the tub. As I was turning the knob, I heard a terrible squelching noise behind me, and I turned to see bubbly black water pouring from the toilet and the sink. I immediately contacted a plumber, who informed me that the clog was not in the pipes inside my house, but in the sewer line for the whole street. His crew had to access the street's sewer main through a basement pipe using an industrial toilet snake the size of a bazooka, and after seventeen hours of work, the man they'd sent informed me that the pipes were destroyed, corroded, and unsalvageable. They had crumbled like chalk, he said, his eyes wide, his hands shaking slightly. Their toilet snake, too, had been broken beyond repair during the process. I was informed the cost to replace it would be added to the charge.

No one on my short dead-end street can flush their toilets or run water in their showers or sinks. I've been contacted by the city and by local environmental agencies about contaminated groundwater and corrupted soil. They're accusing me of deliberately sabotaging the sewer line. The letters are hostile and threaten monetary damages and even jail time. Jail time!

Needless to say, I do NOT recommend buying this product. I Googled the company, and got no results at all. After numerous unanswered emails, I telephoned this site's administrators to find contact information, and kept being put on hold, only to have the connection drop. This happened more than forty-one times in a three-hour period. Now I'm getting phone calls that show No Caller ID, and when I pick up I hear high winds and in the background a woman weeping or faraway voices chanting.

As an alternative I recommend buying a high-priced conditioner at any local salon. I see no value in this product, only heartache, prodigious expense, and legal entanglements that will sap your time and money and keep you up nights in terror of the indifferently cruel and punitive machinations of city bureaucracy.

RapScallion_Green0110 (two stars)

I am bald what do I even need conditioner for. Conditioner is just a way for these ripoff artists to make money off of gullible people. Shampoo is enough. Their was a cracked in the bottle and the contents leaked in the packaging. It was a mess and a lot of the product unsalvagable. Hey how come my Dean Koonts book never showed up, please email me at Ronny93475334@hotmail.com and issue me a refund immediately or I will contact the Better Buisness Buroueu and the FBI.

Mary Lacey-Neverchange (three stars)

My hair is long, down to the backs of my knees, and is very straight and fine. The ends are wont to get frizzy and dried out, and in the colder months in New England, static is a major problem.

Pros:
1. Not gunky or greasy or slimy.
2. Dispenses easily. I use a drop at a time, six drops total, which is four more than suggested in the instructions. I called the number on the bottle to make sure this was okay and the friendly customer service representative reassured me that it would cause no lasting harm. Each drop is probably 1/16 to 1/18 of a fluid ounce. I apply to the ends only, by which I mean, from the neck down.
3. Can be used on hair that is dry as well as wet. I apply it with my hands and then use a hairbrush to ensure even distribution. So this will also reach a little to the "non ends" of my hair.
4. Even using more than the prescribed two drops per day, this is a very economical purchase.

Cons:

1. OMG I hate the smell.

2. The design on the bottle is ugly—why not flowers or a meadow or a pretty lady instead of the weird 3-D symbol that changes depending on the angle you look at the bottle? I covered it over with a blank white label because it was literally giving me vertigo.

3. The trampling of the flower garden outside the bathroom window.

4. The calls from the customer service representative to check up on my hair are nice but a little intrusive and too personal, and sometimes she calls very late at night. Not to mention the promises to "come around one day soon."

I will need to gather more data before I can report on the long-term effects. I will try to keep using it every day for a year and report back.

PeterPeter45678 (four stars)

I love this Conditioner! I am not usually one to write product reviews on sites like this, although, to be fair, I have written some negative reviews, for detergents that don't work or snack chips with an unpleasant aftertaste or some gadget or appliance that doesn't come with all the parts promised or else doesn't work as advertised. It's such a release to call out an inferior product, or a rip-off, to prevent others from having a bad experience. In these busy times, when it's all work and TV and hastily eaten meals and trying to squeeze in time to stave off the encroaching filth in the home, and then to bed for six restless hours, it is rare to find a spare minute to do something that injects a positive energy into the world.

But what a disservice to companies that make a superior product. People are never moved to leave positive reviews. Look at Yelp! It's all complaints, most of them overblown, and insults. Why? Because it's easy to complain. It's fun. Complaining fills the body with endorphins and self-righteousness and excessive pride. It feels as though no one is ever moved to write a review when they have a generally decent experience, never mind an excellent one.

Which brings me to Clovis Dr. 999's NL-id Blends Micellar Moisturizing Milk. I've been looking for a conditioner that gives my hair that soft, floaty feeling, without being oily or drying out my hair or causing it to lay limp on my head like a washcloth. I've tried everything from your fancy salon product to your bargain bin one dollar Job Lot special, and the result has always been a resounding Nothing Spectacular.

I had never even considered buying conditioner online until Clovis Dr. 999's NL-id Blends Micellar Moisturizing Milk popped up unbidden in my "suggested products" list, along with the usual roach sprays, pickle chips, Tom Clancy novels, mouse traps, adhesive removers, party balloons, fly strips, and all the various other things I have to buy online because they don't have them anywhere near where I live. It was strange, because the mysterious algorithms of such sites usually hone in on something in your searches or your general web browsing history, and I had never done any internet research on hair products to speak of.

I was on unpaid leave from my job due to a minor protocol violation, the exact nature of which one of my contract clauses prevents me from revealing, when I received this conditioner (well-packaged in bubble wrap and unbroken cardboard, and undamaged), and I confess that a significant period of time elapsed before I first used it. At the time I had little interest in personal cleanliness or grooming, and was content to let the mice prattle about, the roaches gather and scatter, the parasites feed at will, to let everything fall into disarray. When I received the call that I was okayed to return to work after the oncoming weekend, though, I had to turn things around in short order. I did the apartment first, three straight days of no-sleep tidying, sweeping, vacuuming, mopping, scrubbing, really getting down in the muck and grime and mold, getting into the dark corners and under the fixtures and the this-and-that. The refrigerator alone took four hours to empty and clean. Then I had to get rid of the cobwebs and position air fresheners and open all the windows to let air in once again.

When that was done, I feared I was too far gone to ever get my own self clean again. I stunk up the place, that's no lie. A heat wave had begun too, with oppressive dew points and triple-digit temperatures. I took a three-hour shower, watching with amazement as the weeks of grit and dirt and dried sweat pried themselves from my skin, mixed with the cool water, and swirled down the drain. I washed my hair with melon and rosemary infusion, digging my fingernails into my scalp, lathering, rinsing, and repeating more times than the directions...directed.

Then it was time to use the new product. Clovis Dr. 999's NL-id Blends Micellar Moisturizing Milk sat on rubber-coated wire shelves screwed into the wall, along with an array of razors, antacids, astringents, decongestants, bismuth subsalicylates, cotton swabs, cotton balls, hydrogen peroxide, bar soap (I am a Dove devotee; see my review of their all-natural soap which immediately cleared up an aggressive groin rash that had plagued me for months), toothbrushes and pastes, painkillers, Listerine, et cetera.

Even the bottle, among all the typical junk of self-cleaning, is of an elegant shape, subtly similar to the classic hourglass figure that draws male to female like a flower pulls in a bumblebee. It just feels right in the hand, like it was made to be grasped lightly around the midsection, and even the plastic—I don't know what they used to give it such a pleasurable surface, a kind of sheen or something, your hand just wants to touch it—is strangely similar to the touch of goose-pimpled flesh, yet somehow smooth. I know that doesn't make sense, but that's the best way I have to describe it. Anyway, it's that kind of attentiveness to seemingly unimportant details that sets Dr. 999 apart—with such care put into appearance and the very feel of the packaging, the consumer can't help to be extremely eager to see what wonders await in the product itself.

With my right hand I gently held the bottle—that sensation!—and squeezed just slightly. A warm bath of scented liquid pooled in the hollow of my palm. How to describe the aroma? It smelled like a cloud might; like the soft breath that wafts down to your nostrils when a woman's tongue teases the rim of your ear as a bee explores the rim of a lily; like a bell tolling in the depths of a deep wood; like a child's first taste of a strawberry (although there was no strawberry scent); like standing up in the back of a pickup truck rolling just a little too fast along a ruler-straight country road on an April sometime past midnight, peepers singing their soothing song, pumpkin fields on either side of you (though there was no pumpkin scent), the comforting heft of an axe in your right hand and your feet still clumped with drying mud; like a leaf tossed about in the upper reaches of a tornado that has drawn blood; like a cat catching a moth in its teeth; like the cry of the betrayed toddler; like a brand new luxury car; like a plastic Halloween mask purchased on the cheap on November first; like the infected ear of the noble elephant.

I snapped awake some unknown amount of time later, my hand still cupped at my chin, my arm aching. The water had gone completely cold, to the point of being icy—I think that's what woke me up. I was holding the bottle between my calves, which caused my legs to tingle sensually. I chuckled—it was a husky, raspy sound, nothing like my usual laugh—and I lifted my hand over my head and let the manna of Clovis Dr. 999's NL-id Blends Micellar Moisturizing Milk saturate my hair, and with both hands I worked it into my scalp. The sensation was unlike any I'd ever felt before.

Imagine a storm cloud in the crown of your skull, darker than the inside of a witch's hat, and it rains a silk rendered somehow into gelatin down through your brain, rolling down through your neck along your spinal column, limning your ribcage, gilding your pelvis, sending its rolling rivulets down your arms and legs, into the tips of your fingers and toes. It was a feeling of being loved, and not only physically. It had, how shall I say this in a manner that doesn't send the censors scrambling for their red pens, the same effect as a certain blue pill as well.

When I finally with great reluctance rinsed Clovis Dr. 999's NL-id Blends Micellar Moisturizing Milk from my hair, my whole body tingled, almost like the sensation of being tickled, or of fingernails being lightly raked over every millimeter of the surface of my skin. Invigorated, turned-on, roused and aroused, I dressed and went in to the office. What a work day! I impressed bosses, co-workers, and clients alike with my increased acuity, my sharpened memory. Am I attributing this all to Clovis Dr. 999's NL-id Blends Micellar Moisturizing Milk? No...and yes. I feel like it mixed somehow with my natural chemistry to bring out the best I had to offer. Here's the proof that's in the pudding: my supervisor apologized to me at the end of the day for having to put me on leave. If he'd had it to do over again, et cetera.

I even took Lily and Carrie from accounting home to celebrate with me.

Every which way.

***

After, I considered allowing the ladies into my shower, but I felt the need to keep Clovis Dr. 999's NL-id Blends Micellar Moisturizing Milk all to myself, despite what I was fairly sure of the delectable effects it might have on their lovely young systems. There would be time for that though. I sent them packing, recommending the Look Diner for their hearty dinners and super-strong coffee, and I took a shower that lasted from just past dinnertime until the darkest hours of early morning. That time I did not employ Clovis Dr. 999's NL-id Blends Micellar Moisturizing Milk. I dozed in the tub, woke, and showered again, this time filling my hand twice with Clovis Dr. 999's NL-id

Blends Micellar Moisturizing Milk and rubbing it all over my head, my face, and my body, pushing it into my ears and nostrils, pouring some down my mouth, and even applying a generous portion to my rear portal, if you will. I missed work that day. They were all the more grateful to have me back the next day. And why not? I was making them beaucoup money.

***

The weeks sailed by in a kind of milky, silky miasma of energy, relaxation, orgasmic pleasure, and extravagant meals. I kept up with the cleaning, trimmed the hedges, mowed the lawn, even trimmed the trees that lined the street, though they were not mine to maintain. I excelled at my job, accumulating accolades and bonuses and tokens of appreciation. One was a gift card to this very site.

With that gift card I bought ten more cases of Clovis Dr. 999's NL-id Blends Micellar Moisturizing Milk. I stacked them in the pantry. Some nights before my shower I knelt before that totemic tower of cardboard and I prayed in a strange language previously unknown to me. It had just...come to me.

That night a neighbor banged on my door, complaining of the noise at the late hour. I kicked my front door open, hitting him square in the forehead, sending him tumbling down the porch steps and sprawling on the walk. I was in the altogether. I showed him my brand-new Sig Sauer P226 Legion RX pistol. It never jams, I told him, not even the slightest hiccup. No surprises. As reliable as fall following summer, and barely any recoil to speak of. I explained my extralegal acquisition of the weapon, its lack of a serial number, rendering it virtually untraceable, the devastating effect of its ammunition on the human body.

He may have known that if I hurt him, I would be almost immediately implicated, my timely capture inevitable. Obviously, his family would tell the police his last act was to come to my house to complain. He may have considered ballistic tests, GSR testing of a suspect's skin and clothing. If he considered any of these things, he didn't bring them up. Clearly, he was suitably impressed.

***

Update: It's been a year since I first purchased that one seemingly inconsequential bottle of Clovis Dr. 999's NL-id Blends Micellar

Moisturizing Milk. About a month after I wrote the review above, eight months having passed since that first propitious purchase, its true effects became known to me. After a shower on a Sunday morning, I looked in the mirror to discover that my hair had formed itself into a multitude of thin arms. I had first thought them snakes, as though I had become a Medusa-like figure, but then fists uncurled at their ends. The arms elongated, stretching up to the ceiling, gripping it with what I can only assume was a preternatural biological adhesive of some unknown species. Then the arms shortened, lifting me right off the floor and, glue-tipped fingers sticking and unsticking, propelled me around the house, leading me to the front door and dropping me there.

I opened the door and stepped onto the porch. Overcast sky, a light wind whispering through the leaves. A voice, many voices, whispered in my head, overlapping, finally coming together. It directed me to my neighbor's house. I slipped through the unlocked front door and my hair-hands once again gripped the high ceiling, pulled me up, and sent me, legs swinging, into the living room. Below, my neighbor and his daughters sat around a card table, engaged in a game of Scrabble. He was letting them place words untethered to the main gameplay, out at the farther edges of the board, allowing them misspellings and strings of letters that were not actual words. This awoke in me a kind of rage. Looking back, I'm not sure exactly why. My hair-hands disengaged from the ceiling, dropping me down right onto the card table. It collapsed under my weight, sending tiles flying. The girls shrieked. Their father cried out. I stood like a superhero, my hands on my hips, one foot on my neighbor's head. I ground it into his ear until he screamed. My hair flew about my head like great, life-giving grain, like the glory of a victor's battle flag in storm winds, like the sails of a mighty galleon. Then it curled itself into thick tentacles, wrapped around my neighbor's throat, and lifted him into the air. His kicking only caused the hair-noose to tighten. I lowered him to face me and watched as the life leached from his eyes and his tongue popped out of his purple face like a shy gecko finding its way out of a letterbox. I then slammed him to the ground.

His children had fled. The rest of the house was empty. I exited through the front door, my hair back to normal. Well, if normal is silky and lustrous and manageable and imbued with as yet only minimally explored power. My heart was beating like war drums, pulsing in my wrists and legs, my whole body wracked with the thrumming and humming of my excellent heart. I again prayed to my totem that night and took a seventeen-hour shower. My bonuses were just about covering my excessive water bill. Somewhere in there I heard the sirens, then the heartbeat of a helicopter. I never saw anything about it in the paper or on the news. No one talked about it at work. A week later I saw that the neighbor's windows were boarded up, the weeds encroaching on the driveway. I found this very gratifying.

***

Since Clovis and Dr. 999 parted ways and the conditioner was pulled from the market in the midst of a war fought with lawsuits and countersuits, with sabotage and newspaper editorials and public recriminations, my hair has become the stuff of legend. It's talked about worldwide, in hair salons and brothels, in trailer parks and mansion compounds. I am priapic, godlike. My hair sways and sings, dances on the air, forming curious shapes. It sings songs in forbidden languages. Children are in awe of me. Men envy me. Women eye me with curiosity or outright lust. People send me gifts. Packages of all different sizes pile at my doorstep. Some contain cash money, wrapped in rubber bands. Sometimes the bills are sopping wet and falling apart. Other times they're brand new, sequentially bundled, the ink still damp. I travel the world. Many hands have touched my hair and my hair has touched many bodies.

In the spring of this year, I arranged through certain entities with whom I'd made acquaintance to meet Dr. 999. He lives in the fabled inverted caves in a protected region of the Ngari Prefecture in Tibet. He is surprisingly small, bespectacled, Caucasian. His hair is glacier-white and gorgeous. At night he basks in unthinkable, terrible pleasures, and during the day he toils in his laboratory with a silent coterie of masked assistants, devising a new formula which will, he claims, put Clovis Dr. 999's NL-id Blends Micellar Moisturizing Milk to shame. After his work is done and we've sat for dinner and wine in the cool, capacious caverns that form the outer edge of his environs, we touch our coiffures to one another, and he passes along his many secrets.

Oh the Beautiful Stink

SIX WEEKS AGO, driving down a sun-splashed suburban street to the supermarket, I saw a young couple and a boy approximately six years old leading an old man down the sidewalk, the boy holding the man by the wrist. On the old man's head sat a colorful, conical, pointed birthday hat. He was clad in a light blue sweater vest and white linen pants. His eyes were covered with a black blindfold. The trio, clad in catalog-perfect pastels, pleated and pressed and perfectly fitted, grinned and guffawed, while the old man's slack mouth and upraised brows betrayed discomfort, possibly terror.

You forget large swaths of your life.

In the same sense that I am already in my bed tonight, unable to sleep, watching headlights draw white-blurred shapes on the ceiling and drag them down the walls; in the same sense that I am already sitting at my work desk, heart rat-a-tat-tatting, unable to perform the basic functions assigned to me by my employer; in the same sense that I am already sitting on an examination table, clad in a hospital gown, being shown impossible pictures by a goblin in a white coat; in that sense and all reasonable senses and tenses I am already deceased, a dead person, a non-person, a void that does not howl nor swirl for it is nothing and I am nothing, and so I was before and shall be again, and then for an eternity.

The past is a shadow thrown behind me by the sun, the future is the glare that blinds me. There is only the present, and the present teems with trouble.

A gift? For me?

The trouble with the pastels-clad couple and the boy of six (or so) leading the old man in the party hat down that winding, tree-lined, cufflink-clasped street is just one example.

There's also the trouble at the supermarket.

The bottled water that turns out to be translucent, malodorous gelatin of unknown origin. The eyeless, sun-bleached human heads, shaved and shrink-wrapped and mixed in among the cabbages, ears flattened, mouths sewn shut with corn silk. The hundred-legged bugs hiding in the banana bunches, spindly and dull red, with tubular bodies, pincers, and long stingers—their reportedly painful sting leaving cruel distention and discoloration of the skin where the stinger penetrates. Behind the glass doors of the frozen foods section, behind the packages, something pale and nauseous white slithering and bunching like some alien earthworm.

My friend Samuel is an overnight stock man there and said there was something off about the meat manager, that he whispered to cutlets, pulled apart roasts with his fingers, eyes rolled back, singing to himself in some rotten language. Samuel swore up and down that the meat manager had nothing to do with the malodorous gelatin of unknown provenance, the shrink-wrapped noggins thrown in with the cabbages, nor with the long red bugs, nor with the worm behind the frozen goods. The insistence with which he expresses this belief causes me to suspect Samuel himself is behind these things, or that he knows who is.

How good a friend is Samuel, after all? How close are we, really? I don't know the secret places in his home, nor in his brain, what may crouch and plot in the dark folds and murky corners. I know he reads books whose covers are dark smudges, whose interiors are inscrutable, written, it seems, with the smeared bodies of insects. I know that on his nights off he wanders through the town collecting strange trinkets whose locations he finds on a disintegrating folded map he carries with him at all times.

I haven't witnessed any of the above troubles, save the terrified old man being led by the couple and the boy, who might be seven and might be five, down the long, drawn-shades suburban street, but I have become aware of them by overhearing co-workers and others...though I have also, I now recall, seen the trouble with the postmen.

Their little boxy trucks all now bear a round, black sticker near the gas cap, the number **999** emblazoned on it in a bold purple font. They bounce down the streets spilling letters and packages from the open back doors. The postmen and women themselves walk in a desultory, lazy gait from house to house without their sacks, taking nothing, leaving nothing behind. They all whistle the same disquieting tune. They all have a scar just above the bridge of their nose. Some stand outside certain houses at night holding oversized red knives in their hands. Sometimes they slice at the air, their faces distorted by scowls.

Oh—I have also seen firsthand the trouble with the television. For example: the screen displays the contrived set of a situation comedy: a large living room with green walls, chairs and couch facing the camera, four people quipping at one another to a soundtrack of canned laughter. My eyes sweep to the darkened doorways at the back of the set. They are in danger, these chattering people. Something shifts behind the red curtains on either side of the picture window. It will reveal itself if I don't turn the channel, an unthinkable thing, any pretense of form just a vehicle to convey teeth as sharp as X-Acto knives, and it will pull them into its wide mouth and its barbed tongue will puncture them, softening their bodies in preparation for chewing.

I turn the station.

Two women, a blonde and a brunette, in raincoats, hoods down, stroll along a wet city sidewalk, holding coffee cups and discussing matters of criminal law in broad, expository terms. The camera faces them, the cameraman presumably walking backwards, then the scene switches to a camera following them. For a time they walk, the camera bouncing slightly behind them...and then a long-fingered white hand reaches in from off-screen, followed by a long white arm stained with red flecks and blue bruises, and grabs the brunette by the hood of the raincoat and yanks her backward.

I click again.

A large family—ages ranging from infancy to dotage—sits around an umbrella-crowned glass table on an expansive deck on a bright blue late morning. They look vaguely Scandinavian. Behind them a cheerful in-ground pool glitters out of focus. The family blurs as the pool resolves into sharp focus. Something long and wriggling and black swims across the bottom toward the family. The focus returns to the people seated at the table, all talking animatedly, though the sound is a muttering, incomprehensible voiceover. In the lap of a middle-aged man sits a toddler, whose face creases, then goes purple-black and crumples inward. The camera zooms in on a bowl of potato salad, in close, until all is a yellow-white blur.

You forget, an announcer croons, *large swaths of your life.*

In the same sense that I am in my living room chair, damnably awake, watching headlights draw white bodies on the walls and smear them across the ceiling; in the same sense that I am already sitting in the restroom at work, heart thump-a-thrumming, unable to countenance the numbers trapped in cells on my computer screen; in the same sense that I am already a pile of sticks in a hospital bed watching uncomprehendingly as harridans shriek on the television; in that sense and all reasonable tenses and senses I am already a thing, a lifeless mannequin, a not-person, a void, a zilch, a nothing, as I was once, long ago, now devoid of potential. A forever void dragged along the ceilings and walls.

The past is a shadow thrown behind me by the sun, the future is the glare that blinds me. There is only the present, and the present teems with trouble.

What is this terrible, beautiful gift you have given me?
Open it.

Five weeks ago, driving aimlessly, the radio blaring sweet, busy static, I saw a young couple and their boy leading an old man down the sidewalk, the youngest holding the man by the hand. The old man wore a colorful pointed birthday hat and a black blindfold. The trio laughed hysterically, stumbling and throwing their heads back, while the old man's mouth seemed to indicate despair or horror.

Let me shake it first. Give it here. Hm. It has the weight of life. See how it resists?
Open it.
Open it up.

I'm at lunch with Samuel. He wears two pairs of glasses around his neck, donning a different pair depending upon whether he's reading or staring into the distance. He has a hard-to-place accent that I consider an affectation. Samuel has called me because of trouble with his wife Trixie. He sips his water, plucks the thick glasses from his nose, starts to lift the thin pair, then lets them drop. His pupils pulse, unused to the absence of a filter. "I've discovered that Trixie is made of rubber." He is speaking in a whisper. He leans forward, cupping his hands around his mouth. "Rubber all the way through."

"How did you find out?"

"I cut her," he says. "In the night as she slept. She didn't feel it. Didn't even flinch. I pulled the skin apart. There was...no blood. Nothing. Smooth. I slid my finger in. There is a particular chemical smell even still." He thrusts his index finger at my nose and I pull away, though I smell nothing except the mayonnaise from Samuel's sandwich, which smells as though it's gone over. He slams his open hand on the table. "Rubber."

As he continues in that vein, I note that our waitress is hovering nearby, wringing her hands. She has put the bill on the table but we haven't touched it yet. People are milling, waiting to get in, to be seated. They crane their necks, stare pointedly at our empty plates. The waitress tries to force eye contact with me. Finally, I turn and look. She rolls her eyes back and opens her mouth, revealing a translucent bug crouching on the back of her tongue like some great prawn. Its eyes are black beads on thin stalks and its carapace is expanding and contracting as though it's drawing breath. She closes her mouth again and her eyeballs roll back down. She winks at me and backs away slowly into the kitchen.

I know her. But I do not know from where.

I drop two twenties onto the bill and we leave to the sound of raucous laughter from the kitchen and the other guests.

Four weeks ago, driving to the flea market, I saw a young couple and their boy leading an old man along the shoulder of the main thoroughfare, walking through the dirt and the cigarette butts, the youngest grasping with his small hand two of the old man's swollen fingers. The old man wore a light blue sweater vest and too-large linen pants, rumpled and sweat-stained. On his head tilted a polka-dotted birthday hat and a black blindfold. They were practically dragging the old man, who beat at them ineffectually with his free hand, which was paralyzed and claw-like. The three, clad in cargo shorts and superhero t-shirts, chuckled and chattered, while the old man's slack, drooling mouth betrayed confusion and panic.

I don't want to open it yet. I'm savoring the anticipation.

There is the trouble with silence and ambient noise, both of which have been banished, and with screens, which have proliferated. I unscrew the gas cap, leave it dangling by its plastic thread, insert the nozzle into its waiting aperture. Over hidden speakers an unhinged teenager emotes insipidly over an artificial drumbeat, while on the pump a screen shows a weeping, disheveled man carrying the limp body of a child through a lingerie store. Surrounding the man are banners and signs showing women in garish lipstick violently shoving their breasts together, their faces severe, their expressions furious. All the brassieres are sets of eyes, staring impassively. The skin of the dead boy's face jounces. The man gibbers and drools. All around me elderly inject their cars with nozzles, their faces as stern and serious as those of doctors as they stare at their own screens.

It's getting dark. It's getting late, so late. Open it. Use this blade.
That's a sharp and shining blade. Too good a knife to use to free a gift from its confines, even a beautiful, terrible, hideous gift such as this. Open it.

Yesterday I saw two adults and a boy dragging a blindfolded old man down a long street. The couple was holding the man up by his upper arms, needling and ridiculing him, the boy trailing behind, kicking at the dirt. The old man's legs shuffled; his feet clomped down, then dragged. His conical birthday hat had fallen and was now covering his mouth, lending him the appearance of some strange bird. He began to collapse and they hefted him back up. He had soiled himself, apparently multiple times.

What if, I wonder, it's me? What if I am responsible for the troubles? You never know, do you? You forget large swaths of your life. What if my freezer, the cellar freezer, is full of heads that I prepare and bring to the supermarket? What if I ordered strange bugs from sites on the Third Web, and placed them within the bunches of bananas? What if the waitress burps up strange translucent worms when we couple, and I smuggle them into the supermarket to try to freeze them, to neutralize them? What if I am the meat manager? You never know, do you? You forget large swaths of your life.

Sometimes the water in the bathtub backs up. What has fallen off my body and into the pipe? It burps and the water goes pink and swirls down.

Walking to the market today, I saw Samuel's face in the smudged, graffiti-strewn window of the newspaper box. I knelt to see more, but could discern only gloved hands on his arm like fat spiders, and an uncharacteristic calm, settled expression on his face. I found myself jealous. Samuel's diffuse struggles were over; now the scope of his particular trouble had been limited, a thin red stripe he must follow, no more choices to make, no more choices to unsettle his sleep. I searched my pockets for change and sliced my finger on the razor I keep in my front pocket. What lay under the skin was more complex than I'd expected. Organs, clumps, veined things, snatches of stuffing, wiry hairs. Something back there moving, slithering, and bunching. I used the thumb and forefinger of my other hand to open the wound further, wincing against the pain, to see more. A blurred Samuel stared up at me from his smudged window, his palms against the glass, so very pale and white.

The past is the shadow thrown behind me by sunlight, the future is the glare that blots out my vision. There is only the present, and the present bursts with trouble.

We forget large swaths of our lives.

Tonight the dark and silence shatter as my bedroom door slams open, splashing the light from the hall across my room. In the doorway loom the couple, their pastels mud-smeared and torn, their boy, his expression hungry and anticipatory, his hair a tangled mess, and the old man, whose linen pants are stained yellow at the crotch. Flies buzz around him singing their unsettled songs. The man draws from his pants a long, gleaming red knife and places it in the old man's right hand. The woman peels the man's blindfold from his eyes, which bulge like the throats of frogs. His eyes light upon me, frozen in my bed, and bulge further. Drool lolling from his lips in gelatinous tendrils, he says to his family, "A gift? For me?"

It resists the blade.

Push. Slide it back and forth. Saw.
Oh, it glistens as it spills. Oh, the beautiful stink of it.

Provisions for a Journey

RICKEL STOOD IN the closet, naked, waiting. Mothballs and odoriferous shirts. Dank underthings in fly-blown hampers. Sour sweat. Stifling heat. He wrinkled his nose in displeasure and shifted his weight. Something, the hem of a sleeve maybe, tickled his hand and he swatted at it, released an exasperated exhalation, and then closed his eyes, willing it all away. Somewhere in the house a clock ticked. He let the sound hypnotize him. After another hour, the ticking was briefly supplanted by the sound of a key being nosed into the lock downstairs. It might as well have been the sound of shattering china. Rickel's eyelids snapped up as energy flowed into him and spread to every extremity. There in the darkness he readied himself.

Rickel was always the last man Mr. Whitenose would send. The first fellow, MacDaniel, was tall and insinuating, with cruel eyes and outsized hands. He had a way with the language; it typically took but a few turns of phrase to talk recalcitrant whiners into abject compliance, and on those occasions MacDaniel wouldn't have to put those hands to use. The second man, Waterston, was broad, imposing, and could turn on anger as readily as you or I might don a hat. He was the man who ratcheted up the threats, tightened the terms, administered pain like it was medicine. MacDaniel and Waterston were in their early 30s, godless ex-cons, rough and hungry and game for violence, non-lethality preferred but not required.

By contrast, Rickel was north of 50 years old, rumpled, thin to the point of apparent frailty, and wore a perpetual look of exhaustion. He had never seen the inside of a prison, had never fought with his fists. He had never driven a car, never held a gun, and the only knives he ever wielded were unfolded from a cloth napkin and accompanied by a fork. When he spoke, people had to lean forward to hear him. On assignment, though, he never spoke.

Mr. Whitenose had pulled Rickel from a grey job in a grey business in a grey city because Mr. Whitenose saw in him something no one else did.

Mr. Whitenose knew people.

Footsteps on the stairs now, the whoosh of the door brushing along shag carpet, the creak of a man sitting down heavily on the edge of a bed. Rickel grinned in the darkness of the closet. "Well," spoke a voice thick with phlegm, sounding almost jovial. "You might as well come out. I haven't got what he needs, and I don't expect to get it any time soon."

Rickel kicked the door open. On the edge of the bed sat a man, bald, porcine, clad in slacks, a white t-shirt, and suspenders. He was kicking his blucher-clad feet back and forth like a kid on a swing. When he saw Rickel, really saw him, his feet stopped. Rickel moved quickly: he hit the bed in three steps and sealed the man's mouth and nose shut with his hand. Ignoring the meaty fists pummeling his sides and beating on his back, he chewed away the man's eyelids and sucked the eyes into his mouth, his teeth sawing at the tendrils. Rickel's palm absorbed the screams. Then he ate the man's nose away, spitting out the cartilage. Finally he pulled away his hand and went for the tongue and lips. That done, he settled into the real work.

When it was finished, he extricated himself from the red wreckage and went dripping out into the narrow hall. Across from the top of the stairs he found the washroom: tiny, cramped, only a sink, a toothpaste-spattered mirror, and a stand-up shower stall. He pushed aside the rubber curtain and ran the water hot over his body. Steam billowed around him. Chin to chest, he watched everything swirl down the drain. The bits that wouldn't fit he ground down with his toes until they would. He did not hear the door open downstairs, did not hear the footsteps on the stairs. He did not hear the voices talking in unison.

***

Clean and dry and pink, he went back to the bedroom and pulled his case from under the bed where he'd stashed it. He pulled out his street clothes and dressed hurriedly. As his thick fingers buckled his belt, he paused, pointed his nose toward the ceiling like a cat. His nostrils twitched and then dilated, the hairs within separating and pointing out straight like the legs of a hermit crab. He'd detected a new odor in the house, something sharp and pungent, some sort of spice, but singed and smoky. He could not place it, but it disagreed with him greatly. The bodily odors in the closet would have been preferable.

He stepped back into the bedroom to determine whether he could locate the source of the odor. All was as he had left it. Except...on the floor in the doorway sat a silver coin a hair larger than a silver dollar. He picked it up. Under it was a flat, black beetle. It scurried out of the room, clicking and chirruping, and vanished. Rickel suppressed a strong urge to follow after the thing and stomp it into oblivion. Instead he held the coin up to his nose and sniffed at it. Odorless. He held it out in front of his face. It bore a symbol something like a 4 and something like a capital A. He spun the coin around. The opposite side bore the image of a nondescript man with five eyes ringing the front of his face. Rickel supposed he could have overlooked the coin earlier. He slid it into his trouser pocket. Then he affixed his hat to his head, descended the stairs, and exited into the grey and the drizzle of the April afternoon.

***

Rickel much preferred the dining car to the passenger carriage. He did not care at all to have for a view the back of a seat, nor to strain his neck just for a look out the window. He was in luck today too, as he had the car to himself. He sat at the table, an untouched cup of coffee cooling before him, and watched the backsides of lowly towns roll by: disused car lots, leach fields, abandoned gardens, litter-strewn alleyways, the scarred and unkempt backs of shops and restaurants. He pulled his phone from his pocket. Odd that Mr. Whitenose had not yet called to ask the status of the job. Typically he called within a half hour; this time, nearly an hour and a half had gone by without a word.

The train rumbled along, its windows looking out on blight and graffiti and light from the low orange sun glinting off powdered glass. Rickel put his head back and savored the memory of the afternoon. Two of his back teeth felt tight. He poked around with his tongue, summoned a flood of saliva to the affected area. Finally, digging with the long fingernail of his index finger, he was able to work something out from between the two teeth. The coppery taste of blood filled his palate. He swallowed. It made him sleepy, and so he touched his head to the cold window and dozed. He did not dream. The door to the dining car opened, and in walked two gaunt, bearded men with deep-set eyes and crooked teeth. They paused just behind Rickel and whispered to each other. Neither carried baggage of any kind. Both lightly touched the back of Rickel's hand, and then they exited the car through the opposite door. Rickel did not stir.

***

The call from Mr. Whitenose never came. Two evenings later, as dusk crept in from the trees, Rickel tried the number from a graffiti-strewn payphone at the far end of a car wash parking lot. Between electronic bleats a voice vaguely female informed him that the number was no longer in service and suggested politely that he recheck the number and call again. Typically contracts with Mr. Whitenose were permanent, or had a very pronounced (and quite literal) termination clause. This was unusual. Unprecedented. Rickel puzzled over it for a time, and after an accumulation of weeks, and then months slipping into years, it faded from his mind.

***

Timothy despised kids' birthday parties. He didn't care much for children at all, for that matter. One child, okay, one child was necessary to move the family and its interests into the future; maybe a second in the event something terrible befalls the first, devil forbid. Hence Stanley, and hence the new, slight bulge between Juliette's breasts and waist, Garret if it's a boy, otherwise Mariah. Quiet, or at least able to be made quiet, Stanley lived the bulk of his noisy, frantic life in the soundproof basement rooms where his toys lay scattered like totems, and books with cardboard pages sat worn and ignored, all looked over by a sixty-inch LCD screen crowded with bug-eyed cartoon characters and babbling avatars. Just the sight of them made Timothy tired.

Parties brought more children. Stanley's classmates. Neighbors' kids. Strangers. Impossible to quiet. Chattering in some jarringly dissonant language he never cared to understand; their words were colors without substance, noises that blared from video game consoles and hand-held gadgets. Ugh, the snot-caked nostrils. The mucous-clotted eyes and wet mouths. Timothy was certain that if he squinted hard enough, he'd be able to see green spores in the air between the brats, little bobbling bubbles bulging with germs. If not for Juliette's insistence on propriety, he'd have insisted on renting surgical masks...and portable toilets.

And on top if it all, he'd now been charged with the maddeningly vague task of picking up some kind of game or activity for Stanley's fifth birthday party. He did not relish the idea of hunting around some over-lit superstore, walking endless unkempt aisles of garishly colored trash and insipid ad-copy. Now, driving on the long road between the shoreline compound and the grotesque pseudo-city of superstores and showrooms and emporiums, the road whose path roughly paralleled that of the interstate, he spotted, of all things, a novelty shop. He had driven this road a thousand times before, and had somehow missed seeing the building. It seemed out of place on the winding, tree-lined residential road, a bowed-roof shack just a little too far back from the curb, almost in the woods, as though the forest was slowly gathering to surround it.

He pulled over and peered at the shop. The sign over the door read "Ben's Novelties and Magic" in red letters lined with yellow dots meant to signify lit bulbs, but now so faded as to appear extinguished. The yellowed blinds at the windows were drawn, but glowed with faint, dust-dimmed illumination from lights inside. There was nothing else to indicate whether the shop was open.

He pulled up onto the lawn and parked the car between two dead oak trees, annoyed that there wasn't even the *pretense* of a parking lot. And if there had ever been a walkway, it had long ago sunk into mud and been erased by weeds and pinecones and decades' worth of unraked leaves. A bird bounced on a branch, twittering madly. It sounded like a typewriter on helium. Timothy felt the absurd urge to shush it. He ascended the squat, broad wooden steps, pushed open the door, and entered.

The interior resembled the vandalized attic of a retired theater costumer with a compulsive hoarding disorder. A row of gape-mouthed masks lined the upper walls like a serial killer's collection of trophies, faces of old men, of women in garish lipstick, bearded faces, chubby-cheeked faces, faces with noses like fists, the swollen faces of cherubic infants. A dozen rows of clothing racks filled the center of the shop, many of the items having fallen from their hangers and piled underneath the racks and into the aisles between them. At the wall to his right, a variety of costumes—clowns, cowboys, policeman, priests—sagged from hooks like exsanguinated, deflated cadavers. The place smelled like an untended ashtray full of mothballs and half-smoked cigarettes, with a pine-tree air freshener on top of the whole mess. From a small, dust-cloaked speaker next to an ancient cash register, calliope music groaned and bounced, distorted as though played on a heat-warped vinyl record. There was no clerk evident.

Then he saw it. On the counter among the action figures and dolls; the marbles and jacks and pilled, wilted stuffed animals; the wigs and hats; the piles of faded invoices and receipts and parking tickets. It was the strangest thing he'd ever seen, five-feet long and feathered, with a curled tail and a profusion of black pipe-cleaner legs, two muscled plastic arms stuck out from its sides, claws at the end, finely detailed, with small "teeth" like the claws of a crab. A tag tied to the left front leg read "pinata" without the tilde over the "n." No price was listed. He lifted it by its squared-off, furry chin and looked into its empty eyes. A strange, pungent odor assailed his nostrils and he winced. Then he jumped back, cursed. A man was rising from behind the counter as though on a platform. The man was prodigiously bearded, the beard hairs, brown and white and grey, here and there tangled into dreadlocks. His nose looked like someone had pinched it permanently shut, the nostrils quotation marks. His eyes stared from grey hollows, blue eyes, small of pupil, faded as though kept in the shop window over the course of a sun-scorched summer. A horrid grin stretched across the man's pallid face, and Timothy thought of a coroner hooking his fingers into a cadaver's mouth and pulling back the lips to force a smile.

"How much?" said Timothy.

The man's grin widened.

***

Juliette sat at the kitchen table, Stanley across from her, little hands gripping the glass of milk. He sipped at the straw, his little cheeks sucking inward. He smiled at her with his eyes, and her heart broke just a little. Then he puffed out his cheeks and exhaled, causing the milk to bubble in the glass, attain the edge, splash down onto the table. "You stop that *right now*," she said, pushing back her chair to grab a roll of paper towels from the counter.

"I had the straw the wrong way around, Ma, that's all," he said, his voice a mimicry of remorse. He upended the straw, popped it back into the glass, sipped. "See?" Shaking her head in exasperation, Juliette reached over Stanley's shoulder and swiped at the spill. Her hand hit the glass and it tipped, hung for just a second as if deciding whether to topple, and then did, sending milk cascading over the table onto Stanley's shirt. He jumped back and Juliette shrieked at him, a torrent of curses and excoriations and invective. Stanley ran as from a mad dog, bellowing, bawling, and Juliette surprised herself by bursting into sobs that failed to abate for nearly three full minutes.

When she was done, a strange urge gripped her. She wanted to stand up, walk over to the granite counter, and slam her belly against it over and over again, killing the thing growing inside her, the little curled-up parasite she didn't even want. One was enough. One was too many. Maybe she would be one of those mothers you read about, drives her car into the woods, stabs her kids to death, buries them by a bubbling brook, and drives home to concoct a story about a masked man, an armed kidnapping. But then what? Timothy would want another child, and adopting was out of the question. She knew from experience not to ask. She'd seen the bruises her sisters-in-law had tried to hide at innumerable family gatherings. Even in a one-piece, you can't hide bruises that big.

What about leaving Timothy?

That was a laugh. It was worse than the mob, this, worse than Scientology. You simply don't get away. Not even in death do you get away.

***

The kids swarmed up the gentle slope of the green lawn in strange patterns that reminded Rickel of a murmuration of starlings. Their chatter wasn't much different either, starlings, or honking geese, twittering sparrows. It was a strange foreign language, maybe not so much birds, he thought, but more like the unfathomable patois of some alien species. He adjusted himself in the lawn chair, looked up at the sprawling branches of the oak tree under which he sat. The wind rustled the leaves, redistributing the sunlight. Rickel pulled from his jacket and donned a pair of sunglasses big as a Cadillac's windshield. He looked back down to see his grandson, little Stanley, standing before him. Striped shirt, little denim shorts, sandals that looked like toys, he stood, fists on hips, belly thrust out, like a miniature bookkeeper preparing to admonish an underling. His eyes were red rimmed, and he looked very serious indeed.

"How old are you again, kid?"

"I'm five."

"Not five and a half?"

The kid scrunched up his face. *Very* serious. "I said *five.*"

"Go play with your friends."

"Are you alright, Grandpapa?"

"Right as rain. Right as the rats in the rafters."

The kid puzzled on that for a moment, then grinned, spat a spastic, machine-gun laugh, and trotted off to rejoin the swarm. "Rats in the rafters! Rats in the rafters!" he yelled as he ran. Rickel looked after him. He was so much smarter than the other kids. And he brooked no nonsense. He was five years old, no more, no less, and wouldn't be contradicted. He walked with a purpose, carried himself like a man. A phrase Rickel had gleaned in high school, *self-actualized*, arose in his mind. Stanley was destined to do great things. Rickel could see it in the kid's eyes too: a kind of gravity, single-mindedness. It had skipped a generation. Way it works. Way of the world. At that thought, Timothy, the kid's father, Rickel's son, emerged from the house, carrying some sort of giant insect.

Rickel started. He stood, stepped backward, grabbed the chair and swung it around to get it between him and the abomination in Timothy's arms. He lifted his sunglasses to the top of his scarred head. "The fuck is that?"

"Dad, language. Are you...are you all right?"

Rickel's eyes focused and he saw that the thing in Timothy's arms was not a giant insect at all, but some kind of large stuffed animal. Still, it was an ugly, ragged thing, covered with tattered scales of brown and grey, patches of fur in tangles and knots. The thing's eyes were painted white spots, its mouth a furrowed black groove that resembled the lips of a toothless cadaver. Just over the eyes, embedded in the surface of the fabric, sat a silver coin bearing an emblem that looked something like a capital A and something like 4. Rickel furrowed his brow. An ancient memory swum up from deep in his grey matter, but failed to surface. A coin...but damned if he could summon the memory of when and where it come into his possession; he remembered only trying to sell the thing to antique shops and to numismatists, only to find his prospective buyers alarmed and frightened. Where was the blasted thing now? Frustrated at the loss of memory that increased with every year, Rickel turned his attention back to the hideous stuffed animal. Who on earth would bring that thing to a kid's party?

Timothy.

Rickel shook his head.

"What's the matter, Dad?"

"Not a blessed thing." Still, he stayed standing, put his hands on the back of the chair. He could smell the thing now, an odor of spices and beetle-strewn earth. Another memory burbled to the surface, something stronger. He saw in his mind's eye a fat man swinging his feet on the edge of a bed, awash in red light, a look of alarm in his eyes. Nothing more.

Timothy wound a rope through the loop on the piñata's back—it had a *spine*, Rickel noted with distaste—and flung the string over a branch. He pulled it up, tied it in some ungainly knots. The children began to gather, their eyes large, their chatter muted. They were looking at the piñata with cautious trepidation mixed, curiously, with something like reverence.

Juliette came out from the kitchen finally. Her eyes were red at the corners and her mouth was small with suppressed fury. Rickel noted that she was keeping a careful eye on the piñata, the way one would cautiously monitor a muttering man carrying a machete at his side. He felt a fleeting kinship with her at that moment, pitied her for casting in her lot with Timothy. Such potential, squandered. She should be somewhere else, anywhere else, in some city, in charge of things, with some other husband, some different son to coddle. Stanley should not be clasped to his mother's breast. He should be utterly free to explore and learn about the world he would one day make his own.

Juliette held tightly in her hand a rainbow-striped stick. She handed it to Timothy, who waved it up and down. "Nah, this won't do," he said. "Hold on."

He jogged into the house, came back a moment later with a shining metal pipe.

"That's going to be too heavy for him," Juliette said.

Rickel rolled his eyes beneath the shades.

***

Stanley did not care for the piñata at all. First, it was ugly—it looked like some mangy creature who ate garbage and killed pets for fun. Second, it stank of attic and of wet dog and of closed-off crawlspace. If there was candy somewhere in the thing's innards, he wanted no part of it. No...the fun would be in busting the thing open until it was in pieces and then, maybe later that night, smash the pieces to powder and set the whole thing on fire using Daddy's lighter. He was good at lighting fires. He once lit up the dried grass and leaves in the expansive field behind the middle school, a blaze that lit up the night sky for miles, and the unsolved fire that reduced to ash a good third of the Vernal Rushes Condominiums, displacing many, killing three? Well, that was Stanley, not so little Stanley, not so stupid Stanley.

He regarded the thing with disgust as he hefted the pipe. His dad came up behind him, pulling a handkerchief from his pocket. He knelt to wrap it around Stanley's head, and Stanley held up a small hand. "No, Dad," he said.

"It's not fair if you can see it…"

"Dad? No."

Timothy stared, and then nodded, not quite knowing what to do with himself except tuck the handkerchief back into his pocket.

The kids gathered behind Stanley, now silent. Stanley swung hard, hit the piñata on its side with a loud thud, like a bat hitting solid flesh. Then he passed the pipe over to his left hand, hit the piñata on the side of the head and, showing off a little, he'd admit it, tossed the pipe back and swung again, striking a flank. A low growl came from somewhere. For a moment Stanley thought an airplane was flying low overhead, but the sky was clear and bright and empty. Then he swung once more, hitting the piñata in the throat, breaking it open. Beetles poured out, thousands of them, in clumps and clusters, big ones too, flat and many-legged. They scattered as the assembled crowd screamed. Some kids ran. Some stomped on the beetles.

The thing's eyes went red, and its squat arms elongated, legs like those of spiders grabbing wildly, claws snapping. It yanked the pipe from Stanley's hand and before anyone could react, swung it at Stanley's head. It hit just above the left ear. The sound was a mortal one. It echoed through the neighborhood, resounding farther and farther, bouncing off distant houses. Stanley slid to the ground, muscles failing. There was a flash of open skull, of brain, then blood flooded the wound, jetted into the air. Stanley's left leg kicked, and his hands clutched at the sky. His eyes showed whites and blood gathered at his nostrils and lips. A dark stain spread on the front of his shorts. He was gone. The sound still echoed.

Timothy fell to his knees on the beetle-strewn lawn and put his hands over his eyes. His mouth was open in an O, but no sound came out. Juliette shrieked and fumbled for her cellphone, forgetting how it worked, how to wake it from its dark-screen slumber, how to get to the phone keypad, what number to dial. *I didn't mean it*, she thought wildly, over and over, a mantra that wouldn't stop. *I didn't want this. I didn't mean it.*

The other kids stared gape-mouthed. Some began to bawl, little sirens, rising and falling, underscored by the fading echo of the bat's strike. Rickel was up in an instant, a howl thrumming in his neck. The thing was swinging the bat wildly in one gnarled, black claw, growling like a cornered cat. With the other it tried to free itself from the tree branch, pulling and snipping at the rope. As Rickel approached, the world swam and went orange. Nausea flooded his belly. And then everything went sideways.

He was looking down from the tree upon his family, upon himself. His arms were long, white, muscular, with claws at the end. He saw them as through a fish-eye lens, curling in from his blurred periphery. He looked down and there was Stanley, alive, intact, a curious look distorting his features. He was holding a metal pipe. Stanley swung, the pipe bypassing Rickel's arm, connecting with his ribs. Paroxysms of pain throbbed in his side and in his head. That can't be Stanley, he thought. Stanley would never hit his grandpapa. "Stanley," he cried. "Stop it now, stop it. I love you, boy. Put down that pipe 'til I give you a hug."

If Stanley heard, there was no indication. The pipe swung in again at the end of a blurred chubby arm. This time it caught him in the throat, splitting the skin. He felt his insides pour out, felt himself choking, spittle seething at the ducts. Rickel grabbed the pipe away and swung, connected. The boy fell dead. Rickel watched as the children shrieked, as Timothy crumpled, as Juliette screamed. An old man came looming in Rickel's periphery, his face a mask of rage and despair. The man looked familiar. The rope holding Rickel in the tree snapped, and Rickel descended upon the old man. He took the man apart there on the green lawn under the dazzling sun as the beetles gathered around to feast.

***

Juliette ran under the deck past the piled firewood and the barrels and the hoses coiled like sleeping snakes. It took her three tries to open the latch of the tall gate, her hands trembling, her body twitching with jolt after jolt of terror and elation and emotions for which she as yet had no name. She fled up the driveway, where the garage sat silent and serene in contrast to the nightmare behind her. She typed in the code and the garage door groaned as it rose.

A clicking sound behind her. She turned. A large, flat beetle had followed her, was closing rapidly, pincers opening and closing. She turned to duck under the garage door and shrieked.

The tall man stepped out from the shadows. He walked past her, toward the beetle. As she watched, hands over her mouth, he stepped on it, ground it into the dirt with the toe of his shoe. Then he turned and regarded Juliette. He had very large hands. A long beard hung down from his chin and into his overcoat like a tangled scarf. Five brow-less eyes ringed his face, two above the nose, one on each cheek, one under his long, thin-lipped mouth. Each eye blinked in turn. He cocked his head in the direction of the house. Juliette could hear the sound of flesh being torn from muscle. "Good boy," the man said, as if to himself. "Such a good, good boy."

He stepped to the side, gestured to Juliette. She walked to the car door, slid inside, pulled the key from above the visor. The man watched her as the engine growled, and she drove out and off, down the street. The car turned off the main road. The engine sound faded. Eyes blazing, the man approached the house. The crushed beetle pulled itself from the dirt and followed.

Call Me Corey

C ORRINE SAT PRIMLY, one arthritis-hooked hand crossed over the other in her lap, and watched the rain-blurred city roll by beyond the expansive windows of the senior van. She sat where she always did when the seat wasn't taken: two seats behind the driver, facing the center of the van, purse at her side, walker in front of her like a rickety shield. Today she had the van mostly to herself, a rarity. One old coot in a trilby and a woolen *paletot* sat in the very back, holding a black cane between his knees, both hands gripping it at chest level. Dark glasses obscured his eyes. Normally the van was crowded with stooping men with cinched belts and old biddies clutching pocketbooks, chattering inanely, off to medical appointments and markets and who knows where.

Getting here had been an ordeal, every piece of it. Swinging her legs out of the warm bed, throwing the covers back. Relieving herself. Bathing her old body, a tedious and dreadful chore, drying off in the steam-filled bathroom, stepping into the chill of the bedroom, pulling on her old, familiar dress and sweater. She had done all those things and she had pushed her walker through the carpeted halls, past the institutional art and the bulletin boards and the half-finished jigsaw puzzle on the big table, past the shelves of large-print books, out to the porch, where a rickety elevator shuddered and creaked down to the walk where the van waited, exhaling impatient puffs of cobalt blue smoke.

With no one blocking the windows, they served as a movie screen; today's feature was a smeared and blurred montage of neon-bruised storefronts, empty lots, apartment buildings with barred windows, city buses, figures in coats and hats caught up in the rush of a mid-morning weekday. She looked down at her shoes, lined up her feet neatly, one aside the other. Today was Dr. Grant. His name was there in her daybook, in her spiky, blocky hand, ball-point blue, pressed hard into the paper. He was to look at her feet, which had of late begun to swell in the evenings, to ache when it rained, propelling needles of pain up into her knees.

The van turned off the main street, passed still and silent tenements, three-story houses with plywood for windows. On a weedy sidewalk a thin, long-bodied dog walked unsteadily on its hind legs, teeth bared, ears up like toast points, determination in its eyes. It held out its front paws like a tightrope walker. *Good boy*, she whispered, unaware that she was speaking. *Good, good boy.* She watched the dog's procession for as long as she could before the van turned onto another road of decrepit houses and overgrown yards. She saw a rat on a windowsill chewing out the stomach of a rag doll. She saw a little girl in jeans and a smudged green raincoat sobbing into her fists in a fenced-in front yard. She saw a billboard above the highway advertising caskets made of hard candy.

The driver's face in the mirror was porcine and expressionless, his lips pursed in a silent whistle. He pulled the van over at a disintegrating curb in front of a boarded-up gambrel-roofed house. A rusted tricycle leaned, half sunk, in the mud of the front yard. A candy bar wrapper flapped like a winged thing trapped in the leaning chain-link fence. A muted buzz started, grew louder, like that of a hornet, and a power-wheelchair toting a twisted up white-haired lady appeared in the driveway, then buzzed up to the van. The driver activated the lift, and in a flash the old lady was on board and seated across from Corrine. As the driver pulled away from the curb, the newcomer smiled. It looked like a grimace of pain.

"Good morning," the lady sang. Her eyebrows were painted on a touch too dark and a touch too low, lending her a comically sinister aspect. Her cheeks sagged and her hair, white as the snow in the eaves of a church, shone under the LED lights. Two small Band-Aids locked arms on her cheek.

Corrine nodded, looked past the woman at the houses, the trees, the squat little school, the overgrown shrubs, the garages and sheds.

"Can't talk or won't talk?" the lady said, her sugary tone gone sour.

Corrine smiled, but it didn't touch her eyes. "I'm not much for chatting," she said.

"Oh, that's fine," the lady said. "I'll do all the heavy lifting." Her tone shifted from kindly old lady to schoolmarm. "I am *Arlene* and I'm from *Chelms*ford. My son never calls me, I hate cats, and my doctor tells me I'm more cancer than woman. I am 89 years old, not 'years young,' and they say growing old is not for sissies, and so I'm no sissy, because I'm growing older by the second."

She paused. A shadow crossed her face, then she grinned a hard grin. "Statistically, I'm dead."

Then she brightened again, scratched at her knee with a crooked, long fingered hand. "I used to be a brunette, I used to be sex-mad, and I once knocked a woman out cold for touching my husband's shoulder at a cocktail party."

Corrine said, "You're a real firecracker."

"She *speaks*! Heh. Not anymore, lady. Maybe a stepped-on old bottle-rocket in the dirt of a public park. But I had a good time. I surely did."

The bus turned again, passed Turnbush Elementary School. A jungle gym, its colors faded, glistened in the rain. Giant metal animal heads with handlebars for ears nodded to-and-fro, to-and-fro behind a rusted chain-link fence, their oval eyes mournful, weary from decades of silent acquiescence. Birds lined the roof in a companionable row, some flying off to the powerline and back, reporting to the others what they saw from that superior vantage point. The van turned onto a rutted road of winter-torn concrete and gravel. Above the interstate, traffic seethed under a looming billboard that depicted a cartoonish devil running toward the viewer, reaching out with a three-dimensional claw. HE'LL TAKE THE HINDMOST, the billboard claimed in a lightning bolt font. Somewhere someone screamed.

Corrine leaned forward in her seat. The bus driver honked his horn and swerved slightly. "Arlene," she said. "My name is Corrine, or Corey, that's what everyone used to call me. When I was a girl, I was abused by my father and his friends from the Knights of Columbus. They took me each in turn, and then two or three at a time. They smelled of cigars and sweat. They tore my flesh, and broke my spirit. I was a *toddler*, Arlene. They tried to break me, to ruin me for men, and for women. But I'm not milquetoast, Arlene, and don't you ever mistake me for milquetoast."

"I've lived eighty-five years in service to Satan."

Arlene's painted-on eyebrows rose an inch and she opened her mouth to speak.

"I'm not done," said Corrine. "I've caused mighty trees to grow from the ground and subsume the bodies of violent men. I've seen the fabric of this world pulled apart like skin, looked into the illimitable. I walked through savage blood orgies in certain houses in a certain city, my hair soaked with breast milk from the devil's handmaidens, my feet sloshing through God knows what. I've danced in midnight mausoleums with the dusty dead."

The bus jounced twice, as the driver rode up onto the curb at the edge of a great field, beyond which a river snaked and mountains rose like the haunches of half-buried gods. The van bounced along over hillocks and wheat stalks and catchweed and thistle. The ladies gripped the posts nearest them. The driver hit the radio, and ragtime music filled the van.

"I've been a good old wagon, but I done broke," the driver shouted.

"Yes indeed, yes indeed," said Corrine. "Oh, Arlene, you dear thing. Have you ever tasted the boiled flesh of infants? Rutted with red-fleshed devils in fang-lined caves on islands of muscle? Would that you could hear their screams of pleasure. It was like your fingernails torn off and dragged across all the chalkboards in the classrooms of Hell. You want to talk about cancer? I eat cancer for dinner and shit out the common cold."

"Okay," said Arlene.

"Okay what?"

"Okay, Corrine."

"Call me Corey."

A bell dinged once. The ladies looked back at the old coot in the trilby and the overcoat, who had just pulled the stop indicator. The van shuddered to a halt and the man rose, checked on and around his seat for personal belongings, exactly as the sign behind him directed.

"Creeping Jesus," Corrine said.

Arlene said nothing.

The man shuffled up to them, lifted his hat. The top of his head was bald, scorched, torn away in places. Something was feeding in there, or many things. The chewing was audible over the ragtime music that still bubbled around them like fizzy pop. "Ladies," the man said, and stepped off the van. The sewn-in belt of his coat caught in the door and he was spun around, grabbing at the side of the van for purchase, finding none. As the driver rolled off, the man was crushed under the back wheels. The driver backed up over the man, then rolled forward again, then back.

"I'm terribly sorry for the delay," he said with a voice like top-shelf rye. "If you have any complaints, you may call the customer service number and utilize our feedback system. It's in the book!" Then he pulled from the front pocket of his vest a tube of paint and an artists' brush. He squeezed a glistening glob of black paint onto the bristles and daubed it onto the rearview mirror, swishing the brush back and forth, back and forth, as Corrine and Arlene watched. Then he turned a lever and the side mirrors folded inward.

"There is no sin," he said, letting the tube of paint and the brush fall to the floor of the van, "and all is as it seems."

Arlene said, "I'm going to be late, damn you, damn it all."

Corrine said, "Ride it out, honey. We're in the hands of the devil now, in his infinite pride, under his watchful gaze. We're not late. We're early."

"All," said the driver, "is as it seems." He started up the engine, pumped the gas, and continued through the field, speeding up now, the van jouncing and jolting mightily. Thunder stuttered in the darkening sky. The riverbank approached, rocky, lined with benches. The river was orange murk, bubbling. The van filled with the reek of blood and alcohol, ammonia and charcoal. The ragtime music fell away into static.

Corrine pictured Dr. Grant's waiting room, people flipping through magazines, the young blonde at the desk calling out her name, no one answering, calling it out one more time. The smell of the office, carpet cleaner and anxiety. The shelves of file folders, tabs of red and blue and green. The bleating telephone. The tiled ceiling and the easy listening music. Dr. Grant's swollen hands and his disarming, tight-lipped smile. "Yes," she said. "I'm ready. I'm here."

The driver piloted the van between two of the benches, over the rocky edge, and into the river. For a while it floated along. Then it began to sink.

The Dark Match

AND THEN SEPTEMBER alighted, bringing with it a welcome cooling, but also throngs of earnest and eager students who enlivened the small river-bordered city with color and life and noise and heat. So vulnerable and small, so dangerously open to the world, frail and foolish and capricious, compromised by chemicals, undermined by pheromones. After thirty-four autumns, I could not bear to watch another round; further, I could not bear to participate, to propagate the dark imperatives of the city fathers. Being especially attuned to the evils in the city, but finally feeling something like empathy in my heart, on a fragrant early September night, blood and perfume in the air, after sitting awake for hours in horror and despair and desperate indecision, I fled in the purple pre-dawn with only what could fit in two small suitcases and a shoulder bag, like a refugee from a violent lover. I suppose that I did love the town, and also that the town might in the end kill me, and hence my departure in darkness, with two small suitcases, stuffed full, and a shoulder bag, fat as a tick, the three of them crammed with violence into the hatchback of my small car, and they and I went east, with only the sound of the wheels and the motor's groan, as my last act in Leeds had been to tear the radio from my car like a black-clad surgeon excising a cancerous thing, and stomp it into the ground, and then bathe it in kerosene and set it alight, and I drove until the clouds lightened and then the sky did as well. Even beyond the borders of the city I felt exposed, felt bolts of regret shoot through my fingers. I avoided the glances of other drivers for fear I might see His horrid face, and after several hours I exited the highway onto bright and crowded streets, to the place where the land stopped and the ocean began, the town of Hulse, which I remembered from my youth, from a family vacation, only in fragments, like a slideshow under strobe-lights glimpsed through a scarred and soaped-up window, like opening your eyes up underwater and then snapping them shut from the sting.

The town was a rugged barnacle on a long bowstrip of land that stretched out into the waters of the Atlantic Ocean. It was a degraded and neglected beachfront town, not yet dead, but struggling for breath, lined with boarded storefronts and plastered with pleading realty signs; a failing arcade whose machines still bleated and bleeped and blinked at one another in the half-light; a few bars and restaurants and sagging hotels with snarled vines climbing their staircases. Upon my arrival, smelling the sea air and the fry-o-lator haze, I felt an instant symbiotic kinship to the place, more so than with the town I'd fled, for the evils here felt to me mundane, and perhaps tamed somewhat since the time in the early 1900s when the state seized control of the town and flushed it of its gambling halls, pickpockets, con-games, and riff-raff, dispatching the corrupt administration that looked the other way or else leeched away the profits into their secret coffers.

I moved my suitcases and my shoulder bag into a furnished efficiency apartment above a convenience store, the kind that sells cheap cigars and variety packs of smut magazines bound in plastic and salty snacks, candy bars, sugar drinks, and beer. The efficiency itself had a low tiled ceiling, stained brown in places, so low that I could reach up and touch the tiles, and bright white walls painted over so many times that the square footage had likely been compromised considerably over the course of decades. The furnishings consisted of a sagging bed, a particle-board desk, and a short counter with two electric coils under which a small boxy refrigerator roared with the confidence of a locomotive. The bathroom, not much larger than a broom closet, had a stand-up shower with a rubber curtain, and a sink and toilet designed, it seemed, for a child. It was one of the few apartments in the facility with its own bathroom; despite my dwindling reserves of savings, this was the one luxury I allowed myself.

In the mornings I descended to the street and watched the waves draw and redraw foaming lines of white, towering as they neared the sea wall, or else walked along the shore as the water pulled the sand out from under my feet, dragging pebbles and shells back into the ocean. After a time, the sun would spill its glow over the expanse of ocean as the faraway lights at the blurred horizon faded, revealing hulking shadows and towers too far away to characterize. Joggers bounced by alone or in twos, through or past the pennant-topped pavilions; the occasional man walking his dogs, earbuds jammed into the sides of his head, lips singing along to some unknown song. I'd stroll the silent promenade where benches sat like open hands, stare across the road where under the dim security lights of the rotunda stilled carousel horses waited quietly, eyes and mouths agape, and seagulls lighted on lampposts and picnic tables to squeal their shrill imprecations before coasting down to toddle drunkenly along the shoreline in search of fish.

Yes, I would stay here in this seaside town until I found work or until my money ran out, and I would die here, let my jagged shell be just another among the array of seashore husks, die in peace across the state from the town of my birth, a town whose sourness and sickness had dulled my senses, eroded my moral fortifications, and made me complicit in its crimes, a town where I had done terrible things, caused good people misery and fear, agony and loss. In the end I had taken the coward's path, choosing flight over insurrection, but I was alive, and might never again see His face look upon mine. In the end I had broken my covenant. That did not bother me particularly. I was never very good at keeping promises.

***

November, afternoon, low tide, the rhythmic crashing of the waves far off, and the odors of sulfur and putrescent algae from the tidal pools among the rocks along the eroding sea wall. The ramps and stairs dotted with pinched cigarette butts and wads of chewing gum, overflowing waste baskets, now bereft of bees, sitting on the landings. I walked the sidewalks again, kicked stones along, relishing my newly acquired peace. The unease, the pervasive fear that I might not have escaped the range of my old town's dreaded signal, had all but faded. I passed a storefront painted white, FASCINATION scrawled in red paint above the windowed bi-fold doors, held fast with rusted padlocks. I cupped my hands to one of the windows. Sepulchral arcade games cloaked in cobwebs surrounded an old unpainted carousel horse, pale as exposed bone, its eyes wide and nostrils flared. Prize tickets in rolls and piles lay here and there among ancient tokens and bent nails. Bare footprints in strange patterns disturbed the dust on the parquet floor.

I saw in the window's smeared reflection a man stopping, staring at me, and my heart quickened. Would he beg me for money? Brace me and rob me? Maybe stick a knife between my ribs? I felt a strange thrill at the idea. I turned my head as if to scan the shoreline and he raised one hand slightly as if considering whether to wave. He wore a bathing suit that depicted surfers riding waves the garish oranges and purples of a sentimentalized sunset, and a faded aquamarine tank-top whose arm holes sagged to his protruding bronzed belly. The skin of his arms was dark, dark brown and textured like burlap, pilled with skin tags, and dotted with blackheads. Pinkish streaks, scars from ancient battles, lent him the look of a retired street fighter. His longish hair, straight and white-blond, bounced as he approached, a grin splitting his face alarmingly close to the jaw-line.

"I mean no harm, buddy, I mean no harm."

I turned to face him. Wrinkles crisscrossed his forehead, lined the sides of his face like streaks of rain down a dust-covered window. His nose was a fat fist, his eyes a surprising, brilliant blue.

"Before this was a Fascination parlor, it was the old location of the arcade. Before that, though, it was an exhibition hall," he said.

"Was it?"

"It was. A different time, buddy, a time long gone...but some things linger. Some things never leave, no matter how much the storefronts change." He paused, seemed to consider something. Then he said, "Do you have time for a story, friend?"

I smiled. I imagine it looked unnatural—fearing it might appear as the grin of a lunatic—but it felt fine nonetheless. "I do," I replied. "I have all the time in the world."

He bowed his head, reached out and laid his palm on the door like a benediction. He closed his eyes tightly, then opened them, wiped at them with his palm, and cleared his throat noisily. As he proceeded to unspool his tale, he capered and gestured, mimicking the actions of the people of whom he spoke, affecting voices, posing animatedly, stooping here, pointing a tobacco-stained finger there.

"My parents moved me here when I was sixteen. I had scraped together a friend or two where I grew up, down in New Jersey, and I resented being uprooted without any say in the matter. I was an out-of-control kid anyway, moody and smug, and I thought I knew everything about everything, more than my parents, at least, I was sure of that. I was like any adolescent, I guess, ugly and awkward, crude and full of self-hate. I had acne on my face and neck, severe, to the degree that no ointment could hold it back. I felt like a deformed creature, both inferior to the new kids around me, but at the same time superior, smarter, more cunning. I was cruel to those who loved me and rude to strangers, and I couldn't picture any kind of future for me here...or anywhere. I didn't appreciate all this, the beach, the ocean. It was just a big bowl of stinking water, and the sound of the waves was just static, a radio between stations. And the stupid tourists every summer with their blaring car stereos and their cruel-sounding accents, dragging around bawling children, and their litter and noise...

"Despite myself, I managed to make some new friends, not at school, but here at the beach, bad kids, you'd probably call them—I just called them 'the boys.' They had dope and could sneak rum from their parents' cabinets or get stupid tourists to buy them six-packs. We'd sit on the picnic benches and rank on the tourists and the townies, curse them out, do mean little imitations of them. They were alright, those guys. They were funny, they could split your gut. You had to be funny if you were ugly and the whole town hated you and looked away in disgust when you went by.

"Anyway, I would leave the house at night; my parents knew it, and they also knew that there was nothing they could do about it. The cops had plenty to keep them occupied, and didn't have the manpower or the patience to go chasing after a brat like me. Some nights the boys would join me. Johnny Wicker. Nick Flick. Freddie Sharp and his fat brother Ford. We would sit on one of the benches and complain about the stupid tourists and the terrible music of the time and the stuck-up girls and the sticky sidewalks. We'd carve our names into the benches, tear the seats off the toilets in the restrooms, break our beer bottles on the boardwalk.

"One Thursday night it was nasty humid and hot, I was tired, but I couldn't sleep. My father had something against air conditioners, and the old box fan we'd had since I was in diapers was all coated in dust. You could put your face right up to it and barely feel a breeze. I left the house, walked along the quiet roads, went down to the beach, and put my feet in the water to cool them. I heard a commotion over the sound of the waves, so I walked back up to the street and saw a bright, shining light among all the chained-up, shuttered stores. I got closer, and saw a huge crowd leaving this hall, right here where we're standing now, hooting and calling out, slapping each other on the backs. I walked over to see what was going on. 'Burnmouth County Grapple all night long and the next day too!' a bloated bald guy in athletic shorts called out. 'Granny Marbanks is the sootiest! Hotter than clam piss! Hotter than beach fire!'

"A mustachioed man in a seersucker suit hollered back, 'Granny Marbanks is a dusty, fusty, musty old trollop!' and the two started circling each other, rolling their fists around. They were smiling though, big, toothy smiles, and laughing as they traded insults. *Fatty. Mustache-man. Dirty tramp.* I wanted to be a part of this. I vowed to come back next week and as I turned to leave, a tall man with straight white hair and the...the *widest* mouth I've ever seen—wide like a puppet's mouth— stepped out of the shadows and into my path. He leaned over and put a small, folded piece of paper in my hand, then he closed my fingers around it, like my grandmother used to do when she gave me some old coin or trinket. He held a long, pale finger up to his lips. A wedge had been cut into the middle of the fingernail so that it looked like a capital M. There was blood caked under it too. *Shhhhh,* he said, and he walked those long legs away down the walk, went into the rotunda and sat on a carousel horse, where he began moving his hands around like he was conducting a diabolical, invisible orchestra. Shadows rose up and started moving around in there all around him, shadows that were wrong, that didn't make any sense, their shapes, the way they undulated.

"I unfolded the paper. It said, *Stay for the after. Amateurs strut their stuff. See the Dread Count Marcio and Grim Dave compete for the Night Belt and the Dark Hour Championship! All-out Mayhem! Complete Abandon! Civility and comradeship go by the wayside in this all-out, winner-take-all, loser-take-wing match of a lifetime!*

"I pushed my way through the exiting throngs. Their faces were perspiration-shiny, pink with excitement, swollen with drink. The men's pupils were pinpricks. The women were hard-faced and thin-lipped, their voices raspy and breathy. They averted their eyes as I passed, clearing a way through to the mostly empty hall. It reeked of perspiration, aftershave, and some burnt spice that I couldn't identify, like cayenne and clove and ash.

"Six rows of folding chairs surrounded the hexagonal, rope-lined ring on four sides. The ropes were black, the ring and platform bright, blinding red, as were the curtains that hung from the perimeter. Television cameras on wheeled stands draped in black tarps huddled together in the far corner like giant, hooded monsters. The walls were cement block, with a line of framed posters of groups of costumed grapplers, little round hairy men in tight leotards, tiny-waisted musclemen with large mustaches and wild eyes, ladies with wild, frizzed-out hair and sunburned cleavage, chests held up like a shelf by their bustiers. Someone somewhere began to extinguish the ceiling lights, row by row, leaving lit only the row directly above the platform

"I heard raucous laughter, and two bearded wrestlers in garish purple and gold leotards and capes emerged from a darkened corridor across from the entrance, wiping their faces with frayed, threadbare white towels. Their pompadours were tall and shiny, one black as coal, the other platinum blonde with streaks of bright red. They grinned at me as they passed by, and the gaps between their teeth...they could have used buoy rope for dental floss. One of them goes, 'Sure you're in the right place, boss?' and the other elbowed him sharp in the ribs.

"It hit me quick—I felt all flushed and overheated, my ears burned and my mouth dried up—my face must have been as red as the ring. I turned to get the hell out of there, only to see a new crowd coming in. This bunch was quiet, creepy quiet. Their eyes sagged, from some of their lips unlit cigarettes dangled like they were glued there. They looked like they weren't supposed to be there, or were fugitives, afraid of being discovered. They were dressed formally, like for a dance or a fancy party, but I saw mis-buttoned shirts, torn blouses, open zippers, frayed hems, mud stains on collars and on cummerbunds. My first thought was that they looked like the ghosts of a mass-murdered opera audience. And they smelled like low tide.

"What really bothered me, though, was their faces and their hair. A lot of them looked like they were wearing dampened wigs. Some of their skin was flabby and...it didn't look like living flesh, and the dark circles under their eyes were so black I thought maybe they were the eyeholes of masks. At least one guy had rubber hands, and I saw a lady whose lips looked like just those wax lips you can get from one of those supermarket vending machines for a couple quarters.

"They started to take their seats in silence, and once the aisles were clear of all but a few limping stragglers, I headed toward the exit, only to see that workmen in blue jumpsuits had closed the doors and were blocking them. They had neutral expressions, but somehow the way they stood, legs slightly apart, arms crossed, and the way their jaws were set, they looked menacing, ready for a fight. So I veered off and went over to the concession stand like that's where I'd been headed all along.

"The letters on the menu board had been rearranged. They said things like HOT HAMS. FRIKKIN CHIGGERS. FUGGETS SCREAM.

GRULED CHESTE. FRENCHES FYR. NION STINGS. I ordered a coffee. It was warm, but I drank half the cup in one gulp.

"There was shriek of feedback. I almost spat out my coffee—no loss, by the way—and then came the amplified *thump thump thump* of a thumb tapping the crown of a microphone. I turned my attention to the stage, where there now stood a very short, very fat man in a purple tuxedo with a red cummerbund and tie. A silver pendant hung at his chest—an oval ringed with eyes, and some kind of strange symbol in the middle, something like a 4, something like a capital A. He had a gleaming bald head and a waxed mustache that had to be wider than the span of his arms if they were outstretched. He was sticking out his belly like he was proud of it. The mic was squeezed into his fat sausage-fingered fist. He cleared his throat, prompting another yelp of feedback. The crowd didn't wince; they looked morose but focused, like they were at a child's funeral, and were expecting the child to climb from his coffin.

"'Harrahya, good Sirs and Ma'ams, Ring Rats and little loves, my lambs!' As he said this, the lights dimmed, and his pendant cast a beam of yellow light upwards, changing his jowly face into a gaunt and drawn demon's scowl.

"The crowd responded in perfect unison. '*Harrahya! Harrahya! De Deo Caeli, Harrahya!*'

"'Vox in Ventum!'

"'*Vox in Ventum! Moventur fluctus eius! In foribus portarum abominatio!*'

"'Good 'morrow, good marrow, and greetings. I am your dashing host, your most debonair guide, your master of ceremonies, Cotton Beresford Skent, Doctor of Clobber, Professor of Put-Over, winner of too many awards to name! My mantel runneth over, as sure as blood will run over the edge of the stage tonight! I welcome you all to Eighth Hand Productions' presentation of the match-up of the season.'

"'A few notes!'

"The crowd came to life now, booing, raising their hands in the air with their thumbs up, and then angling them down. They were yelling 'Get on with it!' and 'Go home, Skent, go home!' and 'Drop dead!' and their voices were low and bubbly, like they were gargling.

"'I'll be brief! Here goes! No referees! No rules! Let us shower in blood and drape the innards of the loser about our necks like gold! Safety be damned and to Hades with decorum! Now! Without further ado, I present tonight's combatants!

"'From Parts Unhallowed, his mother a cadaver and his father an undertaker, his sister a wraith and his brother a werewolf, the Beast who dwells in the Halls of Death, The! Dread! Count! MARCI-OOOOOOOO!'

"Music began pumping from the sound systems, relentless guitar chords backed by swooping violins and insistent, militaristic percussion. Count Marcio bounded from the corridor in an explosion of dry ice, shot through with purple lightning bolts. He was tall but pudgy, crammed into a pink leotard with the collar cut low to reveal a jet-black thatch of chest hair and nipples like copper pennies. A black cape fringed with pink ribbons flowed behind him. His hair was in a wet mullet, spiked tall on top, draped down in the back, oily as his razor-burned baby face. He pumped his fists and the crowd cried out, arms shooting up into the air, mostly middle fingers, a few in fists with the index finger and pinky fingers raised. He bounded up a short set of stairs and rolled under the bottom rope. He leapt up, arms raised, exhorting the crowd to whoop with him, then he danced around the perimeter, whooping and howling, pointing out at members of the crowd, taunting one, giving thumbs-up to another.

"'And now, from the wild and thorny back roads of Leominster, Massachusetts, let's welcome our challenger, born in a parking garage and raised on a pig farm, the bringer of pain, the withholder of mercy, an enemy of emotion, a stranger to compassion, Mister! Grim! Daaaaaaave!'

"Yellow light shot out from the corridor now, bright and blinding. I held my palm up to my forehead to shield my eyes. The music now was throbbing synthesizer, climbing and falling, backed by stuttering electronic drumbeats. As Grim Dave emerged, the light softened and went red. Dave was wearing a mask that I think was meant to be the head of a raven, big black feathers, polished black beads for eyes, a plastic beak that stuck out over his nose and mouth, and a cape that looked like wings, but what struck me right away was how skinny the kid was. Rib-counting thin. His arms were like twigs, and you could see the bone structure of the hinges in his elbows and knees. He was the palest thing I'd ever seen too, and hollow-chested, with a belly like one of those Ethiopian kids from the commercials. He was preening and jutting his chin to-and-fro, to the crowd's awed approval, but he couldn't get up onto the stage without help. A few people from the crowd had to push his skinny ass up onto the platform. A slack-faced man lifted one of Dave's legs up and hooked the wrestler's foot up onto the platform, as one of the ladies gave his crotch a very enthusiastic squeeze, and he cried out as he skittered away and scrambled to his feet. Whole place went nuts and he stuck out his pipe-cleaner arms, his fingers in Vs for Victory.

"Skent looked back and forth, chest puffed with pride under crossed arms as the wrestlers circled him.

"'Gentlemen!' he called as he backed up to the ropes, spreading his arms wide. 'Begin!'

"The two men circled each other, and without warning Count Marcio lunged forward and grabbed Grim Dave's twiggy arm above the elbow. He spun Dave around, then put one hand on the man's long neck, the other on his lower back, and rushed him over to the corner of the ring closest to my seat, where he bounced Dave's head off the padded turnbuckle, and then repeated the act at each corner of the ring. Next he frog-marched Dave to the center, where he lifted him up one-handed by the feathers and then slammed him face-down to the mat with a thud that echoed throughout the hall. The crowd leapt to their feet, kicked over their chairs, moaning with disapproval as Count Marcio went over to the ropes to hurl insults at a lady who was shrilly booing him. The moaning turned to cheers as Dave executed three quick push-ups, clapping his hands under him, and then used those terribly skinny arms to raise himself up.

"He approached the preening Count Marcio from behind and leapt up onto his back, slapping at his head, then exaggeratedly wiping his hands on his briefs as to get the oil off. Marcio plucked the kid off his back like pulling out a tick, pulled him over his shoulder, and held him vertically, head down over the mat. He lifted Dave as high as he could by the ankles as the crowd howled, and then dropped him on his head. I had to put my hand over my ears to drown out the screaming of the crowd.

"Marcio, drawing energy from the rage, picked up Grim Dave's now-unconscious body by the waistband of his shorts, and flung the man out over the crowd. His neck bone must have been snapped right in two when he hit the mat—the way his head flopped this way and that as he flew, I'll never forget it. Dave's body bounced off the counter of the concession stand with a terrible mortal thud, knocking over the napkin dispensers and the condiment tray as the clerks dove out of the way. Then Count Marcio strutted to the center of the ring, stuck out both his middle fingers, and did a knees-up victory dance, feet slamming into the mat as he spun in a circle, blowing kisses to the audience.

"I was in shock. I had just witnessed what I was sure was a murder, and the crowd was starting to stand up, to grab the folding chairs in which they'd been sitting. They were going to beat Count Marcio to death, I was sure of it. I scanned the crowd for Skent, hoping he would appear to restore order and to check on Grim Dave, but he was nowhere to be found.

"Then the lights started to flicker.

"Grim Dave rose up from behind the counter, wings blurring behind him, and hovered in midair. His bent neck was one big bruise, his face was like a corpse's face, slack and sightless, and his left hand hung at an unnatural angle from his blackened wrist. He held up his right hand and razor blades shot out from his fingertips, splitting them almost in two. His eyes blazed red and he roared as he flew up into the rafters. Count Marcio followed his progress, his jaw slack, his shoulders up in a shrug. Dave descended in front of the Count and slashed his hand down along his face.

"The Count turned away and stumbled over to the ropes. His right eyelid had been split in two vertically, one part hanging by a thread of skin. His nose sprayed blood in pulses down into his chest hair. He spat a tooth into the audience in a torrent of blood. Dave remained expressionless as he leapt onto the Count's shoulders, slashing at the back of the man's head with his razor-tipped fingers. I moved back to the wall by the doors as blood sprayed in great looping arcs into the crowd. In the strobing lights, it looked for all the world like they were trying to catch the spraying blood in their mouths, leaping and snapping like sharks.

"The Count reached back and grabbed Grim Dave's jaw and started squeezing even as Dave bit wildly at the webbing between thumb and forefingers. With a squelching sound, the Count pulled Dave's lower jaw—and the tongue with it—right off and flung them to the mat. It...it didn't stop Dave at all. The Count went to his knees and Grim Dave started..."—here the man gulped, and swallowed a few times, looking as though he might burst into tears—"he started tearing Count Marcio apart.

"Finally, Skent, the fat little emcee, came running out of the corridor, pudgy legs pumping, and leapt sliding into the ring. He pulled Grim Dave up off the pieces of the Count's body and lifted his good arm by the wrist to declare him the winner. The audience roared, and then fell silent. They started to hum, and then to chant, their voices rising and falling. Grim Dave beamed at them, a horrific sight, all top teeth and everything below them torn away to the clavicle. He went around to the back of Skent and reached around to manipulate Skent's face. He pinched Skent's temples and pulled upward, shaping the announcer's skin into long and twisted horns. Then he palmed the top of Skent's head and raised his hand as high as he could. Skent grew as tall and slender as a mantis under Grim Dave's cupped hand. The pendant at his neck began to glow again, and his features rearranged themselves, the flabby cheeks going taut and sharp, the nose lengthening, the pursed mouth stretching wide over glowing—and growing—white teeth.

"He pointed at me—*right* at *me*—and I got the strange sense that something was expected of me...to chant along with the crowd...to make a threat or to scream...or maybe to bellow out a jubilant exultation. I stood up, not knowing yet what I was going to do, and heat spread through me again until everything swam and tilted. I felt like I was on the deck of a boat in a terrible tumultuous storm, and I slid to the floor and passed out. The last thing I saw were the faces of the crowd gathering in an oval above me, looking down. Masks. They were all wearing sagging masks, and their hands were rubber hands. The eyes that looked down from the holes in the masks were as empty of expression as marbles. There was nothing human in them.

"I woke curled up on a bench that used to be right where you're standing. It was a cool morning, too early for joggers, the coming day's light only just a pinkness over the horizon. I stretched and stood, and then it caught my eye. Down on the ground in the sand and cigarette butts was Grim Dave's jaw, the tongue still in it. I found a popsicle stick, purple at the tip, and used it to lift the edge of the jaw. A pinkish substance, like gelatin, was oozing from the torn hinge. The tongue looked real enough, dried out and cracked, the little surface bumps all whitened. The teeth looked real too—I saw a silver filling, some plaque, a bit of spinach caught between two of the teeth."

I had been frozen in place during his speech, paralyzed with dawning horror. He looked at me, and must have felt pity. He had more to say, a lot more, I was certain, but he hurried through a foreshortened denouement:

"I left the damned thing there and went home. For the next week I avoided the area altogether. I loafed around further down the beach, or else went downtown and hung around the convenience store, or the greyhound track, or the ice cream place. The next Thursday, though, I came back here right after school. Skent was inside, back to normal, chubby and round, sitting on a folding chair in trousers and a white tank top. He was eating a fat sandwich from a clamshell

Styrofoam container sitting on a chair opposite him. He chuckled when he saw me. 'Didn't think I'd see you here again, kid.'

"I said, 'I want to wrestle. Not the late-night show though. The evening show.'

"And that's what I did, 'til they shut the place down. Trained. Trained hard. Built myself up. Came up with a gimmick—Sergeant Charlie—and a signature move, a couple of catchphrases. I won more matches than I lost. I made some friends, good friends. The crowd loved me. And I always left the arena before everyone else. I never saw the people from the late-night show again. They're still here though, brother." He pointed up at the windows of the houses on the green hill that rose up over the line of shops, the start of the mainland, beyond which lay the downtown and the chain stores and the highway. He pointed at the massive apartment building that looked like kids' alphabet blocks scattered down the small peninsula at the west end of the shore. Their lights fluttered and blinked, shadows moving around within. And he pointed down at the sea. The moon peeked out from behind a cloud, and in a wink everything looked different to me, all leaning, shimmying shadows and skewed angles. The waves whispered out a rhythm and the fluttering pennants snapped in time. The lights out across the ocean blinked and winked and the faraway towers and hulking shadows swayed like worshipers in the thrall of some imbecilic, savage god. Everything was hints and insinuations and I felt it in my pores, in my cells, in my axons and dendrites, in the open spaces inside me, and in my secret chambers and catacombs where slumbering demons were snapping awake, stretching and yawning. Something was here, and had been awaiting my arrival.

Sergeant Charlie grinned at me. It was a grin shot through with weariness and sadness. "I guess the reason I tell you all this is that this is not a place to run *to*."

And he walked off, whistling a strange and jaunty tune.

And I staggered back along the inside curve of the town's long and beckoning finger, toward my efficiency apartment with its sagging low bed and its gangrenous ceiling tiles, where my unpacked bulging suitcases sat with my shoulder bag fat as a tick, where the walls grew inward with decades of paint, and vines slithered along the gates and the walkways, under the many winking eyes of the houses on the hill, and the utility poles like great hungry gallows towered into the purpling sky where the high streetlamps exhaled black smoke like blasphemous censers, and high above that the stars were rearranging themselves in the sky and I could almost *feel* the staticky clicks and hisses in the wind and the putrefying algae in the tide pools and the lashing of the waves on the shore beating in time as my footsteps echoed and multiplied and I looked behind me and I was leading a great, foaming army of masked cadavers in seaweed-strewn white glowing gowns, ripping away their prosthetic limbs and spilling rank seawater and slippery things from their gurgling guts, out of the sea they came in legions, heads cresting the water, ascending to the sea wall and up the stairs and the ramps, hissing and spitting and bubbling, and I raised my fist skyward and they raised theirs and I knew the seaside town would fall under the dark dominion of the city fathers and I was among them, reborn and refreshed and renewed and...

The Two-Wheel System

IN SID HETU'S body, blood courses through soft pink caverns, past a black cell turning its neighbor black, through windowless wet chutes to his brain, where synapses fire like ordnance; axon, dendrite, *neuron*; in diagrams a neuron looks like a ghostly eye growing in a tree. He is trying, the creature named Sid Hetu, to explain to the prison doctor the fundamentals of the Two-Wheel System.

It is so simple in his head, before it is confounded and corrupted somewhere between there and his tongue: day wheel is *day wheel*, white, maybe, or off-white, molded plastic, hamster wheel, touch wheel, love wheel. Night wheel is *night wheel*, gunmetal, reflecting his feet as they hit its curved surface: challenge wheel, dark wheel, kill wheel. The risk, of course, is in the precarious leap, a leap over a bottomless chasm, from day wheel to night wheel. Sid Hetu has made that leap, by his count, sixty-four times, and each one he has managed to survive.

He has been through it, he really has, fungus and thrush, wilt and wound, to get to *here*, and now he *is* here, here where he might reveal *all*, let the world know that he exists, finally and fully, and that they must now acknowledge him and fall before him, and the pictures are in his head but the words, which have always been a difficulty, are once again failing him. Maybe it is the lights in this clinical, green-grey warehouse that houses the shunned and the cast-aside. The bulbs are too dim; they make everything sallow yellow, sickly green, pale and muted and insubstantial.

"Day wheel is happiness?" Dr. Liebl asks, trying to be helpful, and Sid Hetu puts his face in his big pink hands, his hair, straight and white-blond, hanging over the whole picture like a curtain. "Doctor," he says. "Oh, Doctor, I wish I could make you understand."

And he tries again, tries to tell it the way the radio had told him, had told the creature called Sid Hetu, just a toddler, of the Two-Wheel System, left there, left naked, hungry, no blanket, no pillow, by his eternally distracted mother, with only the radio for company. He could still summon in his mind that authoritative voice, resonant and reasoned, in the dark of night, and he had absorbed the information, but now could not convey it, and the doctor kept trying to simplify it into opposites, into categories, into blackest black, brightest white. Sid Hetu could not make the doctor see the fact that—for just a short time, maybe once every eight years—day wheel WAS night wheel, and that? That is when momentous events occur.

***

Let's move back, eight weeks back, to where Sid Hetu is in his house, just another suburban house on just another suburban street, the yellow raised ranch where his mother had died in her bed struggling for air, now his house. He is seated in the living room, above the basement dungeon. *Why would the newspaper call it a basement dungeon?* thinks Sid Hetu, back with us for just a moment in the present in Dr. Liebl's office. *It's just a basement.* The word that Sid Hetu does not know, a word that many of us do not know, is *oubliette*.

Sid Hetu, eight weeks back, as we have said, is in his house, in the living room, sprawled in his flyblown recliner, its horizontal legs resting in the grooves that the combined weight of the recliner and of Sid Hetu have dug into the braided rug above the trapdoor that leads down to the *oubliette*. Below the trapdoor are the things he had gathered at the height of day wheel, *the dog days of day wheel*, he liked to call them. Sid Hetu leans forward, stomps with both feet on the floor. The things shriek, confirming their continued existence. Sid Hetu feels relief, though he knows that there aren't many days left before night wheel, and that the things in the basement, the things that he had collected during those whimsical, halcyon, merry-go-Sidney dog days of day wheel, will have to be dealt with. And what if, Sid dares conjecture, what IF the next time day wheel turns to night wheel, day wheel and night wheel are to merge, for just that one short period of time? What if the next time is THE time? Sid Hetu thinks that is a very likely scenario.

***

Now we're going five weeks back. Dr. Liebl is for the moment just David Liebl: faded green t-shirt, madras shorts, bare feet, toes gripping the rung of the stool at the kitchen bar. In David Liebl's body, orange juice, eggs, toast merge, are flooded with saliva, the bolus slides through esophagus, pharynx: bolus to chyme, muscles contract and expand, pummel and punish.

May Liebl, her back to David, scrubs at a dish, blue liquid and flaked yolk swirl, bubbling, into the metal sink and down through the drain into darkness. "Got a weird one today," says David.

"Do I even want to know?"

"The thing on the news, over in Haverhill..."

"No! *That* man? With the dungeon? He is honestly *the* most terrifying man I've ever seen. Those terrible *eyes*. Is he awful in person? Did he tell you about it? Is he even coherent?"

A shadow falls over David Liebl's face. His heavily veined hands brush back a swath of grey hair. "There are things they didn't say on the news. What they found. The...*condition*."

"That bad, David?" May laughs, a nervous laugh like wind chimes, a laugh that irritates David, though he dares not say so.

He doesn't answer. Images careen inches behind his brown eyes. Full kitchen bowls, smeared walls, the things on the door of the filthy refrigerator, affixed with magnets and nails. Furniture white-grey with fungus; rolled, flattened tubes of ointments, unguents, and salves. Darting silverfish and the maddening chorus of flies. Clustered, swollen mushrooms the color of bruises sprouting from disused light fixtures. Synapses launch like rockets; axon, dendrite, *neuron*; in illustrations the neuron looks like a ghostly eye staring from a treetop.

"That poor family," says May, and she pictures them, a grey-haired father in a sweater vest, a woman, brunette, in a blue blouse and leggings, holding a family portrait before them, seeing the faces of their children, their children's chubby pink hands, and knowing the brutal physical reality of what had become of those faces, of those small hands, of what those tiny minds, not yet developed, the minds, truly, of innocents, must have had to countenance before they were cut short, extinguished, forever and ever gone. The reality of it, May thought. The *reality* of it. She holds up her hand and looks at it, really looks at it.

"That poor family," says May again.

***

Back to now, in Dr. Liebl's office Sid Hetu has leapt again to night wheel, on night wheel he runs now, shadow wheel, plague wheel, kill wheel. Above and around him the black stars sparkle and shoot, launch and soar. His body is intertwined knives, razor and blade, red hot glow at the thousand edges. The terrible things that fly at him from the dark are neatly sliced and fall in chunks, bouncing off the inner surface of night wheel, falling into the darkness, landing in mortal thuds somewhere far down below on playgrounds, rooftops, roads, and gardens, on parks and car lots and beaches. Dark wheel, kill wheel, night wheel. Challenge wheel, death wheel, gunmetal and blood wheel.

"Open your eyes, Sidney," says Doctor Liebl. The creature called Sid Hetu opens his eyes. He grimaces, his paper-white cheeks turning pink. It's too dim in here, too dim, thinks Sid Hetu. Sallow yellow, sickly green. Inside, Sid Hetu's knife-legs churn as night wheel rolls faster and faster, faster flickering starlight on the gunmetal sheen. Already day wheel is coming, thinks Sid Hetu. Day wheel is coming FAST. The cycle is contracting, the transitions more frequent, and Sid Hetu does not know why. Or maybe he has just forgotten: this happens before night wheel and day wheel, just for a short time, are one. And that? That is when momentous events occur.

Dr. Liebl watches as Sid Hetu deflates like a pink air mattress in blue sheets. Everything streams out of Sid Hetu's eyes as he slumps to one side. The doctor jumps up, clipboard clattering to the floor, applies to the side of that pale neck two ruddy fingers. In Sid Hetu's body, the heart expands and contracts, valves open and close like alien mouths: nodes, bundles, fibers—that sound, the sound that comforts an infant, counts down a life. Sid Hetu has left the room, left the building, but Dr. Liebl knows in some atavistic, animal way that Sid Hetu is *somewhere*. And Dr. Liebl is scared.

***

Nineteen years back: it is one of those summers New Englanders know well. The days are weighed down with haze, blaring yellow-hot and cruel; in the afternoons, everything turns orange and still, and the thunder comes, and the rain, and before bed the sun returns in blood-red robes to cook the dampness until it blackens into night. Sid Hetu, just a boy, reclines on a singed brown hillock, legs spread wide so that no skin touches skin, so the red doesn't come back at his tender hinge. Looking down over his white chest to his toes rising like faces above the hill of his pink belly, Sid Hetu can see the many microscopic things that make his body home. They live, war, dance, fight, orgy, die, and are reborn on the surface and inside of the thing called Sid Hetu. Sid wills them in their legions, in their many millions, to lift him, and lift him they do, up, up, and up Sid Hetu flies, into the clouds. Day wheel is night wheel, yes, yes.

***

Thirteen years back: an October of oranges and yellows, suburban street, everything smells of burning leaves, porch pumpkins leer from nests of Indian corn, the days are sepia-tinged, the dusks bluer than blue. On the edge of the street, at the leafy curb, Sid Hetu is killing William Cobb. His pale pink fists are full of Cobb's brown hair as he bashes the back of the unlucky boy's head against the curb's edge. He grabs his switchblade from his pocket, one hand still gripping bloody hair, and he slices at the flushed face of William Cobb, drawing wicked red lines that open and spread. Sid Hetu is cackling. Then his head whips up at the sound of sirens. Sid Hetu looks back down at the dying face of William Cobb, a blue-red triangle with eyelashes and teeth and a trembling pointed chin. Sid's eyes narrow and roll back, his hands fly from him and trace inscrutable designs on the air. Inside William Cobb, vessels widen to allow the blood, unclotting, to flow back in. Skull fragments adhere to flesh and hair, fly together and rise to meet the back of his head. Blood leaps from the pavement, shedding its cargo of grit and gravel as it returns into the open cuts. Muscle and tendon knit and swell, skin follows, red lines, pink lines, white lines, no trace. Sid Hetu flees and William Cobb, dazed, bewildered, in shock, gets up and walks unsteadily home. Day wheel is night wheel, see, see?

***

Seven years back: Sid Hetu slides through the industrial brown corridors of Leeds Memorial Hospital. He passes rooms with curtained enclosures, door after door showing ancient feet, heavy veins; visitors squirming in uncomfortable chairs, waiting for the right amount of time to pass before it is appropriate to escape into the daylight. Sid Hetu glides by, and machines begin to bleep and bleat in an insistent cacophony, colored lines—green, red, blue—draw mountains on black screens, and then draw valleys. Toothless mouths reach for air and grasp nothing. Blue fingers fumble ineffectually at call-buttons. The ward darkens; Sid Hetu barrels down a stairwell, into a shadowed garage where cars hunker like great beasts, and into the maze of neighborhoods and playgrounds as a discordant chorus of sirens rises behind him. Night wheel is day wheel, oh my.

***

May Liebl thinks herself inviolable. When she was a girl, a very young girl, there occurred a grievous transgression by her mother's brother, after which he wept and pleaded and begged for her discretion and she, fearing even then, as a girl, as a very young girl, what she knew would follow if she did not take a decisive step to stop it, and that which would follow was THREATS, capitulated, and afterwards she boxed up the memory and she wound the box with sturdy tape and she stored it illimitable fathoms down within herself.

And so she was with her house, her stronghold. Every door locked, every hatch battened, all the windows latched, peephole in the front door poised to expose potential intruders, Jehovah's Witnesses, magazine subscription salesmen, petition-touters, all seen in the fish-eye lens, noses bulged out as though sniffing for prey. And so she was with her body. She encased it in girdles, buttoned it up into grey suits, fastened everything tight at her wrists and ankles, admitting only the good doctor, but only with her strict guidance and at her direction. And so she was with her mind. Unproductive thoughts and needless worries and unwelcome challenges were banished and exiled like deposed tyrants.

May Liebl thinks herself inviolable. No one is inviolable.

Cortex is a word from Latin meaning "bark," as the bark of a tree. Through the bark of the tree of May Liebl's brain, through the *cortex*, into the frontal lobe, cells spring into being, supplanting the cells that May would have thought her own. Like a black flower the profusion of cells unfurls, jetting thorned tendrils into the hippocampus, into every lobe, under and around the myelin sheaths, pulling them aside, undressing the axon, nuzzling the nodes of Ranvier, spiraling down the spinal column like supercharged worms. The knees of May Liebl give way and she goes to the floor in a tangle. Her eyelids flutter. Her fingers and toes clench, unclench, stretch. Her stomach heaves, sending bile up into her throat, scorching her esophagus. Bubbles form at her lips, and one lets go. It hovers on the air, floats across the room, touches the corner of an end table, and dies in a noiseless burst.

And so it is that the creature called Sid Hetu awakens, feeling light, feeling insubstantial, a stranger in an unfamiliar body in an unfamiliar house. Blinking rapidly, he looks out past unfamiliar lashes through a stranger's eyes at a room pristine and clean and suffused with sunlight. Somewhere a woman is screaming, a high, wavering noise, ceaseless, like a warning siren. He flexes his mind, closing some spectral door, and stops it, or, rather, mutes it, renders it a faraway whisper. He uncurls the body of May Liebl and rolls it onto its back. It moves so easily in contrast with his ungainly mortal bulk, a bulk that sits nearly lifeless somewhere in a dim and dank prison examination room, sallow yellow, sickly green. He stretches the body's slender limbs, its fine fingers. He moves those fingers to undo the knot in the body's hair and lets it fall to the floor. He shakes his head, feels the hair move beneath him. The phone rings, a shrill electronic bleat.

***

"Hello?" the voice of May says into the phone.

"May?" says Dr. David Liebl.

Sidney Hetu cannot help it. He laughs and he laughs. He screams and he cries. "Doctor," he manages to say. "Oh, Doctor, darling, do come home."

***

Dr. David Liebl believes in the physical systems that govern the body. Dr. David Liebl believes also in the physical systems of the mind, the impulses it sends to the body to put it in motion. The physical, and only the physical. Axon, dendrite, neuron: systems that are known, systems you can look up in any book in any language and they will be the same. They are solid, they are inviolable, they are universally known and accepted.

David Liebl pilots his Lincoln Town Car through the streets of Waltham at unsafe speeds, weaving through the other traffic, leaving in his wake raised fists and fingers, shouts and curses and expressions of deeply felt ill will. His foot pushes on the gas pedal, shoots over to nudge at the brake pedal when turning. His hands grip the wheel and his teeth chew on the inside of his cheek. What was wrong with May? Why did she address him as Sid Hetu addresses him, as *Doctor*? David

Liebl's mind is telling him that he can no longer trust the physical, and that he must accept that, and that he has to act accordingly. That nothing is inviolable. David Liebl does not want to hear it.

***

Today, right now, as you read these words: David Liebl has arrived at his home. His Town Car is on the lawn, its blinker flashing brainlessly, its door open. Walking into the darkened bedroom he calls to May, calls to Sidney, "Tell me now, Sidney. Tell me about night wheel. I'm ready now, son. I'm ready to really listen." He flips the switch but the room stays dark. He turns and outside the room the house is suddenly ablaze with light, every light on, glowing fiercely in their sockets, causing brown spots to metastasize like carcinoma on the lampshades. Somewhere in the house a bulb shatters, then another. David backs into the dark room and sits on the bed. May appears in silhouette, framed by light that pushes past her, reaching white fingers into the room. She holds in each hand a chef's knife.

"Night wheel is gunmetal," says the creature called Sid Hetu. The creature called Sid Hetu, costumed in the body of the woman called May, approaches Dr. David Liebl, the cowering man on the bed. It tells David Liebl everything, everything, in words as clear and lucid as a drop of untainted water that drips from the curl of a leaf, magnifying the clouds. It has taken so long to get here, fungus and thrush, wilt and wound, day wheel and night wheel, soft pink caverns, cells blackening, synapses firing, May's arms whirling, blades slicing. The creature called Sid Hetu runs and runs on day wheel night wheel now, white and gunmetal, love wheel and kill wheel, legs churning, heart beating, nodes, bundles, fibers, blades whirring, mortal thuds, night wheel day wheel turning rolling turning rolling as the creature called Sid Hetu finally explains to the doctor fully and with terrible lucidity the fundamentals of the Two-Wheel System.

If He Summons His Herd

ARK MYTHS AND suburban legends roam like living things through the halls of Leeds High School, whispered in stairwells over bubblegum-tinted tongues; scrawled on the wall of the secret room above the auditorium stage; argued over in the shaded courtyard adjacent to the cafeteria, buoyed on grey-brown clouds of cigarette smoke. There's the Weird House up on Tremens Terrace, haunted by a trio of cannibalistic fiends with a taste for wayward boys. And the coven of teachers, including Mr. Gauthier (Chemistry) and Miss Knell (English), who cavort with a charred-skin devil in the glass-walled natatorium after dark. And the secluded hollow in the lonesome wooded hills that stretch for untold miles beyond the eastern border of the school grounds, where a pale, eyeless thing roams, thin as a mantis, eating squirrels and cackling, calling out to unnamed gods.

Finn Groomer had dragged Rob Chappell to explore the Weird House on a simmering mid-summer day. They'd searched basement to attic, rat-torn couch to stinking refrigerator to bowed and cobwebbed bed frame, encountering no one and nothing, and emerging decidedly non-cannibalized. Finn knew for a fact that Mr. Gauthier turned up his nose every time Miss Knell passed; he didn't like her enough to even say hello in the morning, never mind to dance naked with her by the moonlit swimming pool. And out in those desolate hills? Finn on an overcast Sunday afternoon hiked for the better part of an hour to the place where the brook trickles down a broad, steep incline into the shadowed hollow, and nothing lived there among the towering black oaks but birds and squirrels and worms. And mosquitos. Lots and lots of mosquitos. For Finn Groomer, the myths of Leeds High were just another string of disappointments in an adolescence teeming with them.

Finn still held out hope, though, that he might one day finally hear the radio broadcasts he'd heard some seniors talking about one day in the cafeteria. Emanating from somewhere down in the lower numbers of the FM dial, the opposite end from where the classic rock stations blared *Two-Fer Tuesdays* and *Rock-Block Weekends*, the transmissions were rumored to be connected in some mysterious way with the kids who'd go missing from time to time. As to what could be heard, reports differed depending upon who was telling the tale. Some said they heard odd music, jaunty and discordant, backed by the cries of the tortured or the weeping of lost children. Some heard a man talking, or a woman, of unspeakable things. Others claimed to have heard thousands chanting, black masses, twisted blasphemies and perversions, the cries of the damned in the furnace of Hell.

You couldn't just stumble on the station or find it at any old time you went searching. Circumstances had to be right. And the exact nature of those "circumstances" differed as well. You had to be vulnerable, in pain. You had to be susceptible to hypnosis and open to the possibilities of the supernatural. You needed a special radio, or a regular radio touched by the hand of a warlock.

***

Three weeks into Finn's freshman year, Bentley Langschultz, a sophomore, drove to school, walked to the edge of the football field with his father's shotgun, sat among the varicose roots at the base of a dying old oak tree, and blew his head apart. On an oppressively hot summer afternoon back when Bentley was nine years old, his mother had absent-mindedly walked into the sliding-glass porch door, causing it to shatter. A shard of glass tore into her throat as she fell. Harriett Langschultz bled to death on the ugly green-and-white linoleum floor in the kitchen of the Langschultz's raised ranch, alone. Bentley found her when he came home late from school, having lingered to talk about comic books with Garrett Kinder. She lay sprawled in blood, swollen and wide-eyed, ministered to by a cloud of flies.

The rumor born after Bentley's death, the subject of the conversation in the smoking area that chilly winter day, proffered by Heather Buffington, who claimed to have received a desperate phone call from Bentley the night before his death, was this: Bentley had happened upon the radio station on the way home from school, and heard the sounds of shattering glass, of his mother gasping, gurgling, trying in vain to draw in breath, and then, as clear as a voice right there in the car with him, crying out, "Bentley, oh, Benny-boy, where were you—you could have saved me. Oh, son, you let me die, you let me die." All of this, claimed Heather, was against a backdrop of comical music like you'd hear on the Saturday morning cartoons.

Since that winter day, Finn spent hours spinning the dial of his stereo between his fingers, searching for the signal in static-choked airwaves, listening for a voice, for music, for a wailing ghost, a chuckling demon. Maybe he would hear the voice of Bentley Langschultz. Or the voice of his own mother, who had leapt to her death from the French King Bridge before Finn was old enough to form a memory of what she sounded like. He never heard anything but static. Many times he fell asleep to that noise, so much like roaring rain, like the rush of traffic, like a fierce wind bothering the treetops.

And then one morning, at the muddy end of a long and wearying winter, the new kid showed up with the answer in his hand.

***

The kid climbed onto the bus at the corner where the shuttered factory slumbered among disarranged blankets of overgrown shrubbery. An oversized army jacket bounced around him as he climbed the steps and trod down the center aisle. Grey cargo pants with crumpled pockets, the hems rolled crooked, engineer boots. Jug-handle ears and a giraffe neck, a larynx like he'd tried to swallow a pear whole. His hair, the drab dark brown of an old penny, formed an ocean wave over his high forehead, a severe part over his right ear showing scalp like an alabaster path. Blue bug-eyes swam behind thick glasses with smoky grey frames. In one long-fingered hand he clutched a small portable transistor radio, scuffed silver with a tattered strap. He looked all of ten years old, except for his height: his hair nearly touched the curved ceiling of the school bus.

He sat down in an empty seat at the back, his knees up at his chest, and held the radio up to his ear. Rob and Finn swung around in their seats to check the kid out. He stared back at them, his eyes moving back and forth behind those massive lenses, studying their faces. An unintelligible radio announcer's voice declaimed breathlessly from between the small speaker and the kid's pimply temple.

Finn leaned in toward the radio. "What are you listening to?"

"Hey, I'll bet it's Tears for Queers!" Rob said.

The kid opened his lips to reveal a jumble of yellowed, chipped teeth. He hissed at Rob, bubbles of spittle forming at the corners of his mouth.

Rob burst out laughing, elbowing Finn. "Can I get the name of your orthodontist?"

Across the aisle, Becky Burns tittered a high-pitched arietta. Finn just stared at the radio as though hypnotized. The kid smiled widely, showcasing the mess in his mouth. His eyes were unfocused, the pupils dilated to pinpricks. His fist clenched and unclenched. He pushed the radio hard against his ear until the plastic casing cracked. Finn and Rob gawked.

"THAT WAS A MOLDY OLDIE FROM NIFTY, SHIFTY NINETEEN-FIFTY," the kid boomed in an unexpectedly sonorous voice. Becky Burns emitted a shrill shriek. "UP NEXT, THE THING THAT DWELLS WHERE THE BROOK TRICKLES DOWN THE EARTHEN MOUND, WHERE THE TREES BEND IN PRAYER TO THE STONE-STREWN GROUND. BUT FIRST, A WORD FROM OUR SPONSOR."

Then his voice jumped up a few octaves, became that of a chirpy commercial voice-over girl, "There was a girl on my road named Dirty Meg. A dark..."

Without warning, Rob popped the kid in the jaw. The thud of fist on flesh got everyone's attention, and they began to hoot and bang their fists on the seats. "FIGHT...FIGHT...FIGHT!"

"Whoa, whoa, whoa!" Finn said, grabbing Rob by the shoulders and putting him in a loose headlock. Rob struggled a little bit, half-heartedly, glowering at the kid, batting at Finn's arms. Tears gathered on the kid's lower eyelids. A splotch had blossomed bright red on his cheek.

"What the fuck was that, Robbie?" Finn said. "Really, what the fuck?"

The driver jerked the bus to the side of the road, threw it into park, and stormed down the aisle, belly bouncing under her blue sweater vest, face bright red under a sheath of dyed blonde hair. The other kids stopped chanting, but murmured excitedly, jostling each other, vying for a good view.

"Up," she said.

Rob and Finn got up.

"You're sitting up front the rest of the way. C'mon. Rob? Rob Chappell? I know your mother. Come on now, right now, and she won't hear a word about this."

Among cat-calls and jeers they followed her to the front. Finn spared a glance back at the kid. A trickle of blood ran down the side of his face from under the radio. When the bus stopped, Finn and Rob were among the first to exit. Rob hustled off to class, but Finn waited. He wanted to look at the kid's radio, to see if that dial sat down in the low numbers, to brace the kid and steal his damned radio and listen for himself. But the kid must have slipped by him somehow. Finn never saw him get off the bus.

***

That evening, Finn and his father sat across from each other in the dimly lit dining room, eating dinner in silence. Tom Groomer demanded that Finn have dinner with him every weeknight, though Finn could not fathom why, as the television was always on, and they barely spoke to one another. Finn was volatile, agitated. He had searched for the kid all day, looked for him in the halls between classes, in the cafeteria. He was nowhere to be found. He didn't even show up for the bus home.

"Miss O'Connell says Leeds has more missing kids than any Massachusetts city of this size and population count," Finn said, trying to force eye contact.

Tom Groomer looked at a spot about a foot over Finn's head. He tore off a piece of garlic bread and his brow furrowed as he dabbed the bread in sauce. "She doesn't know what she's talking about. I've been ten years on the force, I know cops in every city in Christendom. Miss O'Connell should stick to Physics."

"Do you know three kids were pulled out of school last year so their parents could home-school them? And they were never heard from again."

His father burst into derisive laughter. "Never heard from again!"

"It's true. Kelly Kitter."

"Finny, I know the Kitters. Do you want me to call Carol right now? Kelly left school, what, junior year? Carol home-schooled her, and she got accepted at Oberlin College. Full ride, housing and all. As far as I know, that's where she is right now. Now, that's the last I want to hear of it."

Finn nodded, jabbed his fork at a piece of ravioli, shoving it around the plate. Kelly's best friend Margot hadn't seen nor heard from Kelly since the day her mom pulled her out of school. When she called, Mrs. Kitter said Kelly had gone out. Or was studying. Or asleep. Asleep at seven in the evening! Kelly hadn't just moved to Ohio without calling Margot, without saying goodbye. Tom Groomer stared blankly at the television, where the long smoke trail from the space shuttle explosion billowed across the screen for the umpteenth time. He was lying, Finn decided. His father was lying to his face.

***

Finn dreamed that night, nightmares strung together like grotesque garland, an anthology of abominations. He would remember only one, the last, ultimately interrupted by the insistent screech of the clock radio alarm. He stood in the midst of a vast, noisy carnival under a sky of dirt. Rocks tumbled above, in defiance of gravity, making a noise like thunder. Lightning spiked down from the dirt, lightning made of long, wriggling glowworms. A mad barker bellowed inanities into a megaphone from a warped seat at the apex of the rusted-out Ferris wheel, the voice echoing throughout the fairgrounds. The air smelled of popcorn, charred meat, wet animal fur. Finn walked over to a metal gate, beyond which a colorful Chair-O-Plane spun, its angled column lined with lights, cadavers lolling in the basket chairs as they swung sidelong through the fragrant fry-o-later air. A ragged skull tumbled to the hard-packed earth and bounced along toward Finn, coming to rest at the base of the gate. It bore patches of skin, wisps of hair. Maggots orgied in its eye sockets and feasted on its putrefying tongue. Finn backed up, circled the ride, headed toward the Ferris wheel. The voice of the barker sounded familiar.

He walked alongside a row of trailers, between which laundry sagged from greasy clotheslines: massive brassieres, a gape-mouthed bear costume, long johns, garters and frills and feather boas. One of the trailer doors hung open, and a face popped out, all bushy eyebrows and matted hair. The man's face loomed swollen, squirrel-cheeked. "Kid," the man whispered. Finn turned to look. The man's belly lolled over the belt of his bathrobe. At his feet a slack-haired woman slithered, her eyes dead, her tongue tasting the mud-caked floor. Her body was that of a snake, diamond-patterned, scaled, draped in a feces-stained slip. "Come in! Test your strength!"

Finn gave the door a wide berth, just catching the edge of a miasma of shit and rum and body odor. As he reached the end of the line of trailers and approached the Ferris wheel, the barker, silhouetted, leapt from his seat. Black wings bloomed behind him, curving upward, forming a parachute. He sailed to the ground, turned, and walked into the mist. For just a moment, in the light of a fried dough stand, Finn had recognized the destroyed features of Bentley Langschultz, his blond head split eight ways and smoking like a spent firecracker, face peeled down in flaps, long shredded tongue dangling obscenely. Finn followed Bentley. Beyond the borders of the fairgrounds sprawled a moldering marsh, swarming will-o'-the-wisps illuminating the brackish, moss-strewn water. Bentley walked in, was wading away. The sound of sloshing water overtook the carnival music until it was the only sound. By now, only the ruined back of Bentley's blond head could be seen. Then he turned, and he wore the face of an antique radio: large, mesh-covered eyes, a knob for a nose, and a wide, rectangular mouth that glowed yellow. At its left-most end a withered red tongue slid back and forth, as though searching for that elusive signal.

***

Finn saw the kid the next day after lunch when he stepped outside to get a gulp or two of fresh air, as if saving it up to last him two more interminable hours in the stuffy classroom. The kid stood at the edge of the woods beyond the football field, not far from where Bentley Langschultz had blown his brains out. He held the radio down by his side, his head tilted as though listening to something in the sky. Finn walked toward the kid. As he approached, the wind kicked up and the image of the kid shimmied, briefly blurring, separating into a boy-shaped stack of horizontal lines. Finn felt dizzy, off-kilter. It seemed as though it was taking a very long time to cover a short distance, as though the kid and the edge of the wood retreated imperceptibly with each step Finn took. The afternoon stretched, tinted blue with overtones of dusk. Had the bell rung to signal the resumption of classes? If so, he hadn't heard it.

At length, after picking up his pace, almost jogging, he began to close the distance. He cleared his throat to alert the kid to his presence. The kid turned.

"What's your name?" Finn asked.

"Eric."

"Eric, I'm Finn." He spoke quickly, fearing that Eric would dismiss him, or walk away. "Listen, I'm sorry about the bus. Rob can be a wicked asshole sometimes. Can you tell me what you were listening to on the radio? I've been thinking about it non-stop."

Eric shrugged. Then he lifted the radio and extended his arm so that the speaker hovered a few inches from Finn's face. A tinny voice spoke: *Through gore-clotted conduits He makes His way, slithering, flattening himself like a cat, going liquid, slender snake, wriggling worm. He comes to summon His herd. Join me on the riverbank. We'll pull down the sky. We'll pull down the sun and we'll pull down the trees. We'll pull down the shade of—* a rising wave of static overtook the voice. Eric pulled back the radio, frowned down at its face, fiddling with the dial and extending the antenna between two pinched fingers, pointing it this way and that. The voice went on somewhere back there, straining to be heard, calling out, but the static won. For just a moment, his face distorted, Eric looked considerably older than a high school kid. Older...or harder. Finn couldn't decide. Maybe both.

"You can get way better reception out at my place in the woods. Will you come to the woods with me?"

Finn grimaced. "I don't know. I have English, like right now. I'm probably already late."

"If you're already late, what's the harm? Follow me."

He walked into the woods. Finn followed.

***

"Is this where you live?" Finn said. Yellow tents, ten or twelve of them, stood here and there among the clearing in the woods, a space ringed by tall oaks and red spruce, a space not that much larger than the Groomers' modest back yard. Along the easternmost border stood a row of thin trees, evenly spaced like the rungs of a crib, beyond which the forest devolved into a jungle-like tangle of deadfalls and vines and profusely thorned thicket, dotted with virgin's bower and jack-in-the-pulpit. At the sound of Finn's voice, the wind kicked up, rustling the trees and the tents, which shivered as though cold.

"They're down at the river, praying," Eric said, answering a question Finn hadn't asked.

"Who?"

"Let's listen a while. Close your eyes."

"How come?"

"Close them."

Eric turned on the radio and cranked the volume as high as it would go.

The notes of a flute meander, climbing, faltering, climbing again. A male voice mutters and chuckles, sniffs. *Please don't*, says a small voice, a toddler's voice, trembling with fear. Flames crackle and far off voices rise and fall in an insistent cadence, no stopping for breath. A cheering crowd, now ecstatic, now raging. A female voice, husky and insinuating, emanates from the center of the clearing. "Masks and mirrors, gentlemen," the voice says. "Mirrors and masks. Flesh on marble. Fountains of blood, carriages of carrion. Mister Ben will eat your worries, slurp them up like stew. Mister Ben's boarding house has beds to spare, clean linens, perfumed halls, nurses on call with hands softer than silk."

Mom?

"Oh, darling, I'm talking to the boys, the sweet boys. See them? Such handsome young men."

Mom? I'm hungry.

"Darling, shush."

I want tongues. Tongues and lips. Sweat in my cup. Piss mug, dog's water, gristle to chew.

"Soon, sweetie, soon."

Dog mug, piss water, blood under my tongue. Sweetbreads and sputum. A savage giggle, deepening in pitch, bending and warping.

Again the flute, fleeing, shrieking as something pounds the low keys of a piano with violent force. A tuneless whistle, and then a stomp, a shriek. More stomps, splatter and crunch. A bow moves across the strings of a violin, is yanked away. The howl of space. Whimpers and pleadings, zippers unzipping, rustling clothes. A child gags and retches. A bird says CHUR chattle CHUR chattle CHUR. A pipe organ, brazen and fierce, spedupsuperfastchipmunkfast. Calliope and callithump, wheeze and whine, high-pitched, a crying dog, bereft and disconsolate. Night falls like a shade, with it that familiar roar of static. Finn drops away...

***

...and Finn awoke. He lay face up, staring at the ceiling of a tent, which glowed an alien green. He was clothed, save his shoes, which sat at his side in a chaste *soixante-neuf.* He wanted to know what time it was, and he wanted to drift back into blackness. Something shifted, a rustle of clothing, a sniffle. He pushed himself up onto his elbows and saw Eric sitting Indian-style at his feet, the transistor in his lap, its dial glowing green. From the speaker a voice whispered a phrase in some unknown language. A chorus of young voices sounded just outside the tent in surround-sound, repeated the phrase, and the voice resumed.

Finn opened his mouth to speak and Eric leapt from his crouching position, his legs trailing behind him like those of a frog. He landed on Finn's stomach. Finn bellowed out all the air in his lungs, and then Eric pushed the radio into his chest. Finn punched at Eric, landing blows on his shoulders and neck and chin, but Eric pulled back his head to avoid the blows. His arms elongated, snaking out from his sleeves. Finn heard cracking that he first mistook for thunder, or a tree breaking open. As pain radiated from his chest into his arms and neck and nausea grew in his stomach, he realized that he was hearing the cracking of his ribs.

Eric began to sing in a high, clear voice.

Mary sit with me by the river

Cymbals hissed and whispered from the speaker.

We'll pull down the stars from the sky

The kids outside the tent ooohed and snapped their fingers.

We'll pull down the moon and we'll pull down the sun

Their shadows slithered like serpents on the green glowing walls of the tent.

We'll pull down the shade of the eye.

Eric bore down on the radio as Finn's chest caved in like a sinkhole. Finn could not gather enough air to scream.

***

He awoke again, hours later, this time in muted daylight. The shadows of leaves cavorted on the tent walls. It was hard to breathe. His chest and arms ached as though he'd been in a fight, but he hadn't been, not that he could remember. He'd been listening to the radio with Eric, and then...and then he'd awakened. He'd never lost time like that before...and he didn't remember having had anything to drink. He ran his hands through his hair, wincing, and ducked out of the tent. The worshippers had returned, apparently. A bunch of them—all teenagers—stood here and there, looking up at the sky. A few tended to a makeshift grill where flames danced up among a grid of soaked sticks suspended over a circle of rocks. A battered frying pan sang a song of spattering bacon; another bore eggs, the yolks orange as the ascending sun. "Good morning," said a girl with big eyes and purple hair, dressed in cartoon character pajamas. "How do you want your eggs?"

The other kids looked at him. There was something about them...something he didn't see in any of the kids at school. It was as though his classmates were a cable television station to which he didn't subscribe: he only saw glimpses of them swimming through wavering distortion. The kids in the woods were a local station, beamed in from a close-by antenna, clear and unbroken. Their eyes hummed with life. He felt impatient to befriend them. But he detected a note of caution in their eyes, or suspicion. Maybe just a wariness. Except for the purple-haired girl, whose face bore a vague resemblance to that of his mother; narrow, aquiline nose, small eyes, dimples—a face he'd seen only in old photographs, trapped under transparent photo album plastic. The girl's eyes were bright and welcoming, interested even.

"Scrambled?" he said.

"Was that a question or a statement?" She pulled a large, rusted metal spoon from a wire basket near the fire pit.

"Scrambled."

She stirred the eggs, keeping her eyes fixed on Finn's. She salted and peppered the eggs and slid them from the pan onto a Styrofoam plate.

Finn sat cross-legged, eating with his hands, watching the denizens of the makeshift city as they dressed themselves, sat reading, or gathered soap and towels to wash at the brook just over the hillock. Just as he was scraping the last bit of egg from the plate, Eric emerged from a tent at the far end of the clearing. He threw down his backpack—stuffed to the point of straining at the seams—and began dismantling the tent from which he'd just emerged. "You're really going," said the purple-haired girl.

"It won't be just me in the end." Eric folded the tent, his voice a reassuring purr. "I'll tell them all about you guys, I promise. I'm good with words. I know I can get them to accept you. Maybe not all of you, but some of you."

The purple-haired girl bounced on her heels, while a greasy-haired kid in a jean jacket shook his head. "They won't take me. I have anxiety."

"Danny, I'll tell them about how good you are with, like, sleight of hand," Eric said. "I'm sure they'll find a use for you."

Danny scoffed. He spit in the dirt and muttered.

"Where are you going?" Finn said. "Who's 'them'?"

The kids tittered. A secret flitted among them like static electricity. "The people in the deep woods," Danny said, hooking his thumb toward the dark tangle of thicket-choked trees. "They're...they're kind of like church leaders, or priests, but not all strict, not worried about morals and shit. Finn...is this life enough for you? Do you feel like you're part of anything? Like there's any real purpose? With them, it's different. All we have is questions. They have answers. And a mission."

Eric frowned, spoke up. "Have you ever seen the real Leeds? In dreams, or in your thoughts? It's a place between here and...it's where they came in through. It's like where we live, but better...there are skyscrapers, and these sort of...community centers, let's call them...and a fair that runs year-round.

(Test your strength.)

"It's always October, Finn, always. And what they can give you..."

He paused. The kids all looked at him. Their eyes blazed a warning. A beatific look passed over his face.

"Ecstasy. Exaltation. Transformation."

"In exchange for what?" Finn said.

Eric shrugged. "Nothing big, I don't think. Nothing important. Nothing you'll miss."

Without further ceremony, Eric hauled up his pack, nodded to the group, and walked through the line of trees into the tangled wood. Everyone stood, watching him go, until they couldn't see nor hear him. No one spoke.

Finn tended to blather when nervous, just to break the tension, to dispel silence. He said, a little too loudly, "Guys, can I, like...can I get some stuff and come back and stay with you? In Eric's tent, maybe, or, or I could bring my own?"

He'd tried to modulate his voice, to avoid using a pleading tone, but it crept in nonetheless. They stayed silent, still staring into the woods as though transfixed by the last glimpse they'd seen of Eric.

The purple-haired girl spoke up. "Yes, please. Please. Why don't you stick around? You don't need to go back there, maybe not ever again. We have everything you need here. Everything." She put her hand to her chest and smiled an enigmatic smile.

Finn's heart sped up, but he held his resolve. "I'll come back tonight. Promise."

She put on an exaggerated pout. "You better."

"I will."

He headed back down the path that led to the school. He walked until he guessed he'd gotten far enough from the encampment, then circled back, jogging, giving the clearing a wide berth. After a time, he found the brook and followed it through the thickening trees.

***

He was nearing the hollow when he caught sight of Eric's yellow pack. He hung back, treading carefully, avoiding twigs and pinecones as best he could so as not to be detected. Eric crested a small hillock and descended into the hollow. Finn followed, moving very slowly.

When he attained the hillock and looked over, he saw that Eric had put down his pack about a yard from the edge of the hollow, where trees tall and crowded guarded the way to the deeper, darker woods that comprised the state forest. Finn crouched down behind a deadfall that lay at the base of a tall, ungainly oak. Eric stood, stretched, and removed his jacket and shirt, folding them neatly and piling them to his left. He looked thin and vulnerable, his shoulder blades jutting like nascent wings, bracketing a serrated spine. He pulled the transistor from his pack—a different one, Finn noticed, with green plastic casing and slightly bigger than the one he'd had on the bus—and held it high above his head, aiming it into the woods. The leaves stopped rustling. The birds stopped twittering. Finn dared not breathe.

A hum, low and long, and the world shivered. The scene in front of Eric shimmied as though painted on a thin tapestry behind which unknown things slithered and twitched. Eric's body again separated into horizontal lines. The lines moved back and forth, independent of one another, righted themselves, and it was just Eric again, thin and pale and alone, that one arm holding aloft the small transistor, red elbow jutting. And then the man stepped out from the dense wood.

He was tall, frighteningly so, at least a head taller than Eric. And broad of chest and hip. Finn thought of the time he saw a moose tromping along a quiet road in New Salem, slow, lumbering, but dangerous in its very bulk. The man was clad in cuffed and creased trousers, an immaculate white shirt held fast to his torso with suspenders the color of storm clouds. His hair gleamed black, oiled and slicked back. His eyes blazed from over an impudent nose. His thin lips, set under a neat mustache, were set in a frown, and he carried himself as though very bored, but menace lurked in the taut muscles of his neck, in the set of his jaw. He was thick-footed, claw-like nails long-neglected, clotted with mud or dried blood. He stopped just a few feet from Eric, appeared to size him up.

Eric stood very still. Finn could not see his features, but he appeared to be staring into the man's eyes. Then the man spread out his arms and a fervent, hungry look spread across his face. A cracking sound, like a tree split by heavy wind, and the man's skull broke vertically under his skin, widening and swelling until his face sloughed off his skull and fur sprouted from his cheeks and forehead. His eyes slid apart to the sides of his narrowing head as his nose elongated into a snout. His pupils flattened. The tip of his nose popped, cartilage flying like shrapnel, laying bare a flat, brown nose with slits for nostrils. His teeth grew like ancient gravestones rising from earth, gingiva crumpling, cheeks splitting open all the way to the ears. His clothes fell away, and the walls of his human form followed, great shards landing in piles, blood showering over them. He pulled a gnarled branch from a tree and rubbed his furred hands along its length until it smoothed out into an elegant black cane.

Eric thrust the transistor radio up toward the man. It began to sing a trilling tune in a high-pitched, child-like voice.

The man, now a hunched goat, bellowed a wordless reply, tongue wavering in the air.

The radio responded with tinny ragtime music, bouncing piano, whispering cymbals, a cavorting clarinet.

A sheet of skin separated from Eric's back, fluttered into the air, nearly translucent. Then another, thicker, white. He screamed out as his body went pink, and then red, as sheets of skin hovered around him in the air. Masks of his face followed, rising into the sky like the gape-mouthed heads of ghosts. His hair stood on end and began to fall like rain from his head.

And then the goat lunged forward, jabbed his cane into the tender flesh under Eric's chin, lifted him into the air and swung the cane in an outward arc so that Eric faced Finn. For a terrifying moment, Finn thought he might impale Eric, thrust him to the ground and devour him like a ravenous dog. But instead he held the boy aloft like a gator on a catch-pole. Eric's arms and legs swam in the air. His eyes showed only whites. Drool swung in a bobbing pendulum from his lower lip.

"Phineas? Dear, earnest Finn," called the goat in an unblemished baritone that echoed through the trees. Finn crouched lower, his mouth hanging open, staring. "How you've grown. Your mother brought you to me, you know? You were just a boy. A sapling, a whelp. I remember it well. Jessica carried you into the wood and stood right where Eric did. She flung you to the forest floor, offered you up like a prize. She begged, begged like a wretch, cried like a brat. She was very demanding." He shook his head sadly, condescendingly. "And I tell you now even as I told her then, sorry, boy, but you are simply not worthy.

"She never hit the water, by the way. She landed on the rocky shore, broke into pieces on the sharp and mossy stones. They needed more than one tarp to hide her sad, broken body from all the rubberneckers. Not that they didn't get an eyeful though."

Finn fell to the ground, grabbing handfuls of earth, crushing it in his fists, and sobbed. His mother had betrayed him. She didn't love him. And then she had taken her life, left him alone with an obstinate liar of a father. Why did she do it? Out of sorrow and remorse? Or because her offering had been refused? He sobbed himself hoarse, beating the muddy ground with his fists.

They had to take him. They had to. He stood. The goat and Eric were gone. The forest stood still and silent.

"If you won't take me, kill me," he shouted into the thick wood. "Kill me!"

The only response was his echoing voice.

Snuffling and panting, Finn searched out the piles of skin that had pulled away from Eric and fluttered to the forest floor. As he gathered them, he heard music from somewhere, he couldn't tell where, the insistent beat of a thousand drums, overlapping, rising in volume and intensity. He piled the skin in his arms and headed back toward the clearing where the kids waited among their tents. He prayed that they would take him in for keeps. He prayed to see his mother again, that he might forgive her and once again fold himself into her betraying arms and offer her his forgiveness. And he prayed that one day he might find that signal hiding in the static at the low end of the dial, and it might tell him how to become worthy.

LEEDS 2600

W HEN THE FAMILIAR raspy call of the bicycle bell rang out, I rose from among the pile of unwrapped gifts and ran to the kitchen window, to see my cousin Kendrick's old green Schwinn leaning against the side of the garage. My first thought was that something was wrong. Why else would he show up alone at our house on Christmas morning? He lived three towns away, and it was cold out, bitterly cold, and the wind was kicking up great clouds of snow from the rooftops.

Kendrick practically burst through the kitchen door, shivering and sighing, a crust of ice gilding the edge of his knit cap. Mom and Dad greeted him with surprise and possibly feigned exclamations of joy.

"Just visiting," he said, "just coming by to say Merry Christmas!" Dad offered him a cup of cocoa, then pulled out a chair at the kitchen table. He followed Mom as she went to call her sister to see if everything was okay at home.

Kendrick looked up at me, his hands gripping the mug, knuckles flecked with dry skin like ash, cheeks red with cloud-like splotches. Little tawny rocks of sleep crowded the corners of his eyes. I wanted more than anything to pick at them. Kendrick looked left and then right, as if checking the kitchen for spies, then he pulled from the inside pocket of his coat a small grey cartridge.

"For your Atari," he said, and handed it to me. It wasn't wrapped, and it had no label, just the remnants of the one he'd torn off—traces of adhesive like clumps of snow left after a cold winter. Scrawled in thick black lines—I caught a whiff of that pungent permanent marker smell—was LEEDS 2600.

"I made this," he said, eyes serious. "Now that the protection spell can't hold you anymore, it should be of some efficacy. It's important, Loretta, that you know about Leeds before Leeds knows about you."

I already knew a little from my classmates about the myths surrounding the town. Ghosts of long-dead occultists and grave robbers. Disappearances, dangerous derelicts and their tent cities in the trees, all of it somehow connected to some creepy radio station down at the low end of the dial. It was just rumors, I thought then, just the stuff conjured up by the bored residents of a town on the wrong end of the state, so far from Boston, to try to make the city seem more interesting. Besides, I never spun the dial any further down than 96 WTIC FM, whose signal carried the Top 40 hits all the way up from Hartford.

Kendrick lowered his voice and leaned in. "And while I'm at it, look, I'm a little high, so maybe I shouldn't be saying all this, but... Loretta, when you get your first car, I want you to have the dealership take the radio out, okay? And never go into the woods, not past the point you can still see the road, or a house. No matter who tries to get you to."

Somehow, coming from him, it bore more weight than the babble from the other kids. He looked so serious when he said it, so worried. I would do as he said.

I always had a little crush on Kendrick. He was tall—gawky, even—with long dirty-blond hair that fell around his shoulders in curls. His thick glasses sat atop a bent beak of a nose, framing lively, alert blue eyes. He had a receding double chin, cheeks ravaged by acne, and full, puffy lips occasionally bisected by the yellowed edges of his buck teeth. His flannel shirts were always too big for him, his jeans frayed and stringy at the seams. He called me *Kid* and *Sweet Girl* and *Lovely Loretta*, and was the only one of the adults—hardly, he was sixteen or so, but he was the most mature of all the cousins—who would indulge a twelve-year-old girl with pimples and braces and a book always at hand.

***

It's been a long time since Kendrick disappeared. I never thought he had come to harm and I refuse to believe that he's dead. His was simply too restless a mind to stay in any one place for too long, and I think his family did the worst thing they could do to him short of neglect or abuse: they bored him.

I didn't bore him. That has always been a point of pride for me.

He was the kind of kid to take everything apart to see how it worked. I think it was only a very basic sense of right and wrong that prevented him becoming a serial killer. I remember him holding a stray cat in his lap, prying open its mouth gently but firmly with his fingers and looking down its throat. The cat protested and Kendrick released it, but there was a deep disappointment in his eyes, and a fervent, obsessed look. It worried me. Maybe electronics and computers were a distraction. Maybe they saved him.

But maybe—and I don't like to consider this—maybe he disappeared in order to fulfill that forbidden desire: to separate people into their component parts and study them.

I know he'll come back to me one day and tell me all about where he's been and what he's been doing. I can't wait. I hope they let me see him—they're very cautious about my having visitors.

***

Nurse Angel sails into the room, tapping with the tips of her fingernails on the open door as she passes, not to request entrance, but to avoid startling me. I admit, I do startle easily. Still, I dislike rudeness, and entering without asking permission is terribly rude. Only Kendrick could get away with it. Kendrick and, I suppose, Nurse Angel.

-Good morning, Loretta. What are you writing today?

-Another diary entry, Nurse Angel.

-Can I see?

-No.

-Come on now, Loretta. It's part of your therapy. We have a Full Disclosure policy, my dear, and you know this.

-Zero Tolerance. Full Disclosure. Open Door. All your policies are two words, Nurse Angel. Did you ever notice that?

-I never did, Loretta. Thank you for enlightening me.

-Don't condescend.

I chuckle.

-That's my two-word policy, Nurse Angel. Don't Condescend.

***

See, Kendrick was always very solicitous towards me. When I was little, maybe eight, our family was over to his house for a barbecue.

After we ate, his Dungeons & Dragons buddies came by. While the parents drank and told stories and roared with laughter outside on the patio, the kids all hung out in the basement. I was sitting cross-legged in the blue beanbag chair, my teddy bear Rochester curled up in my lap, listening to the strange and unfamiliar language of the big kids, when all went silent. I looked up, and everyone was staring at me.

Kendrick laughed and said, "I was talking to you, Loretta." He asked if they could do a "protection ritual" on me. At the time I had a very limited understanding of what the ritual was supposed to protect me from...but it sounded good on general principles. I had to be unclothed, but my cousin let me change on my own behind the water boiler and wrap myself many times over in a king-sized bedsheet, and when Jimmy Goodrich looked at me funny, Kendrick smacked the glasses off his face, and then confiscated them. No pervert stuff happened, by the way, no matter the accusations of my parents and the innuendo of the staff here, lurid garbage that says more about their own twisted imaginations than it says about Kendrick and his friends.

The ritual consisted mostly of the boys chanting, and me repeating strange syllables they were throwing at me. At one point Kendrick rubbed some kind of brown dust behind my ears—the aromas of charcoal and clover and something vaguely flowery. Then he gave me a necklace with a small purple-blue stone.

"That will hold you," my cousin had said, "until puberty." I had no idea what puberty was, but it sounded like something far away.

Whatever the aromatic dust had consisted of, whatever the chanting had meant, I really did feel protected. The bullies at school retreated from me—some still taunted me, but from a safe distance. They never shoved me anymore, never kicked me in the butt or swung me into the lockers by my backpack. I imagined a force field around me, a kind of agreeably fragrant aura shimmering in the air. I could reach out, I imagined, and feel its outer edge. I never slept better than I did in the four years before I turned 12.

That necklace is long gone, but I still have the stone. I kept it with me wherever I went. I have it with me still. Kendrick gave me a lot of gifts through the years: books, musical instruments, puzzles and brain-teaser games. I kept all his gifts in a trunk at the foot of my bed, and all but ignored everything given to me by Mom and Dad. LEEDS 2600 was the best thing he ever got me, not least because he designed and built it himself, but because it probably saved my life, just as it probably put me in this gentle prison with its seasonally decorated corkboards and its two-word policies and its sweet but no-nonsense nurses with long needles in syringes full of liquids in primary colors.

***

Mid-mornings are quiet in the ward. The morning medications have all been dispensed, the patients mollified, sedated, or else knocked out cold. Televisions mutter in the other rooms. The Quiet Television policy, one policy with which I happen to agree, dictates that the volume must never go up above a 3. So the overlapping of voices and music is not altogether unpleasant. Birds twitter outside. Faux fingernails tap at computer keyboards. The phones purr.

I've become quite adept at detecting unfamiliar footfalls. The nurses walk with an officious gait, they go *clunk-clunk-clunk*. The doctors too, but the sound is softer, somehow more self-important. The patients shuffle, of course, or step lively, recovering some semblance of youth in their demented thralls.

But the steps I hear now quicken my heart, for they are noticeably different: they are measured, patient. They slow—it's barely perceptible, but they do—as they pass open doorways. Somebody is searching for someone. Searching, possibly, for me.

I wish for that protection spell to reassert itself. I wish for those searching steps to come from Kendrick's always-untied sneakers, not the hooves of some horrible, ghoulish goat-man. Wishes are like dishes, they never get done, Mom used to say. She was constantly inventing little phrases like that, phrases that crumbled under the merest scrutiny. Honoring Mom's words, I stop wishing and ring for a nurse.

***

The night after Christmas, Sunday, a school night. Mom and Dad had gone to bed. I waited until I heard Dad's rasping snores and I crept from my bed, retrieved the cartridge from my trunk, and inserted it into the Atari. I turned on the television. The screen went black. I don't think I'd ever seen such a deep, untainted black on that old Samsung. It looked like you could reach in and pull back a hand soaked in ink.

COHARK PRODUCTIONS LTD appeared in white on the screen in a blocky font. Against all that blackness the words were a ray of light beamed into the dark of my bedroom.

The music began. You know that old *bleep-bloop* Atari music. Something like a simplified, synthesized mix of "Tubular Bells." The words disappeared, leaving a ghostly afterimage that ultimately faded. Then a small white square, not much bigger than a deer tick, appeared in the middle of the screen. More dots clustered around the center like rapidly metastasizing cancer cells as the music sped up...and then the colors filled in, turning the cluster of squares into the pixelated image of a girl, maybe the heroine of the game.

I hopped up and clasped my hands over my mouth. Though it was just a stack of pixels atop a couple of outward-facing Ls for legs, I recognized myself right away. Red hair in a ponytail. My favorite blue-and-white checkered dress. A little line of brown dots that somehow expertly mimicked my eyes, which always looked a little squinty. My little legs rotated and my avatar strode purposefully to the right, off-screen. The black deepened and the music segued into something more like Brahms.

A row of trees, evenly spaced, grew up from the bottom of the screen, then a dense grey line bisected by yellow lines lifted them up to the middle. A road. Under the road, that thick and inky black. Above, a dark blue sky in which little square stars twinkled. My little avatar came in from the left side of the screen and stopped. It turned to face me and a little red explosion of pixels appeared on its face. It expanded and contracted, that little mouth. *Bleep, bloopbloop*, it said. *Bleeleeeleeloooleeloop.* I laughed out loud, because it sounded like a robot talking underwater. I felt just on the edge of being able to make out words. The other me stopped and stared. I ejected the game and popped it back in, watched the opening sequence again.

Bleep, bloopbloop. Bleeleeeleeloooleeloop.
Bleep, bloopbloop. Bleeleeeleeloooleeloop.

I woke up when Dad turned on the light. I was sitting Indian-style, leaning forward, face almost touching the screen. The night had gone by as I sat there. I was so late for school that he didn't have time to yell at me.

I didn't concentrate that day. I just wanted to get back to the game, to that strange and inky street, to hear my avatar speak her impenetrable patois, and to start the girl's journey. When I closed my eyes, the colors behind them took on the shapes and aspects of the game, clustering themselves into pixilated shapes that formed and re-formed as buildings, trees, people, blinking as they changed color and shape.

I closed my eyes a lot that day. My teachers didn't seem to notice.

***

Nurse Carol pokes her head into the room.

"What is it, dearie?" she says.

"Nurse, can we go outside?"

She helps me from the bed, slides slippers onto my feet. Walking down the hall, past the nurse's station, past vacant gurneys and medical waste repositories and doctors in blue conferring in intimate clusters, I listen for the footfalls. The searching steps... I hear them...we're approaching them. My grip on Nurse Carol's arm tightens.

I'll steer her down the long hall by the courtyard, I think. And then I see him. It's just a flash as he traverses the corridor left to right, beyond the doorway at the far wall. He is hunched, covered mostly by a tattered, fly-blown black blanket gone charcoal-grey with age and time. His shoulders skim the ceiling tiles. His neck protrudes from his chest, his horrible horn-topped head covered up by the blanket, only his raw, scraped, blood-matted snout visible. His hooves discolor the floor tiles. One buckles like wet cardboard. The lights flicker above him. People pass him, consulting clipboards or staring at the floor. I am the only one who can see him, it seems. That doesn't make me feel any less unsafe.

When we reach the end of the corridor, we turn left toward the exit. I don't dare look behind us. My heart is beating so fast and so hard I fear my ribs might crack. I hunch, draw inward. Nurse Carol strokes my back, whispers words I cannot make out. We step out into sunlight. I tug her arm and we head for the far end of the lot. I want to feel safe, but I fear that even in the birdsong-filled brightness of a late spring afternoon, that abomination might burst from the building, stride across the lot, sweep Nurse Carol aside and bring me into the woods where terrible things dwell, things that can take you apart and put you back together...wrong somehow...things that make you into a monster.

I close my eyes and listen to the birds and the whispering treetops. Somewhere in the sky a plane groans its long and weary groan. I think of Kendrick, and again I start to wish—to wish he was at my side, holding my arm, watching for trouble. I know, I know. Wish in one hand, put a joystick in the other.

***

I went right to my room when I got home. I spread out my homework on the bed and switched on the TV. I laid down on my stomach and pushed in the cartridge, then turned on the Atari.

My avatar, who I had decided to name Lottie, did not try to talk to me this time. Instead she danced on the screen to the electronic music, her little stick-legs pumping. I tilted the joystick and she began to walk. The trees moved behind her, as on a platform. Ones and zeroes, wires and circuits and signals, console and cartridge interlocking invisible fingers somewhere behind their molded plastic facades. Processors, chips. Colors: green trunks, green treetops, black background. Thin black vertical lines to counterfeit the texture of bark. Zig-zag lines to indicate leaves. Somewhere in the machine all the little parts were doing calculations, responding to the movements of the joystick, the pressure of my thumb on the circular red button. The impulses of her brain moving her hand. Calculations in the neurons, thrumming with echoes of Kendrick's work—he is in the machine, in a way, his will and his thoughts enmeshed in the circuitry.

The noise of her feet, little baritone squelches. There were more trees now, or little Lottie was moving past them faster. Another noise, something new. I stopped Lottie in her tracks, leaned forward, and turned my head so that my right ear was nearer the television's speaker. A quiet squelching, growing steadily louder. Something approaching.

My heart started to beat faster, and the faraway squelching did too. I grabbed for the joystick, fumbled with it, and then sent little Lottie running, the stick pushed all the way to the right. The trees slid by. Faint colors flashed between them, suggesting eyes, as though there was someone...or a lot of someones...watching in the middle distance.

Little Lottie ran and ran. Then it appeared before her...a hole in the ground, underneath it a ladder. The squelching sound of footsteps shook the walls of my room. I sent her down the ladder.

She walked now below ground. Above, the footsteps faded. The roof rose until the surface of the ground disappeared beyond the upper boundary of the screen. Carnival music now. And onto the screen rolled an enormous Ferris wheel, little carts dotting its circumference. Behind it rolled a cart with a podium at which stood some sort of pale grey figure. He must be running the controls, I thought. At the center of the wheel where the spokes met was an image of the visage of what looked like Jesus—a bearded face with swollen eyes, a drooping mouth, and a crown of thorns. It stayed right-side up even as the Ferris wheel turned. I tried to pilot Lottie past the wheel, but one of the carts scooped her up and she rose into the black sky.

Then the crown of thorns began to separate, break off. Each piece became a brown spider with black eyes on the end of wriggling antennae. They crawled up the spokes toward my cart. The one in the lead, the largest, reached the cart just as it reached the apex. I hit the button and Lottie leapt to the next cart, all the spiders changing direction to follow her. She jumped to the next, and to the next, and then to the ground. I sent her running.

From the right now came a bouncing skull. I hit the button and Lottie jumped it. Then something I couldn't identify, something rolled up and grey, like a fetus, bounced toward her. I jumped that. Then a torrent of them, skulls and fetuses, heads and curled-up spiders. I couldn't save her from them all. Some hit her head on, flattening her. She'd rise and re-form with a little popping sound, then a skull would bounce off her head and she'd fall to the ground again. My head started to sweat. I wanted to scream. I wrestled with the joystick, moving her forward, sending her jumping.

Then it was over. Lottie was harder to move now, bent a little at the waist. I felt exhaustion too, and the beginning of a terrific headache. A ladder appeared on the screen and I sent her up. The below-ground part sank and Lottie was on the surface again. Before her stood an angled wall of simple brick, bisected by a black gate. She approached. The gate opened for her and she disappeared as she passed through.

The woods, the wall, and the gate were replaced, from top to bottom, by the number ONE. The music was low, bouncing, foreboding...

The door to my room slammed open, and I heard my father's voice calling my name. He sounded distressed, full of fear. I didn't like hearing him like that. It made me feel unsafe. I tried to speak, to calm him. I'm fine, I just fell asleep. But nothing came out. I pushed myself up into consciousness.

"Oh, Loretta," my dad said. I felt warmth down below and realized I'd wet myself. The television roared static. Mom appeared and shut it off. They hustled me out of my room and out of my clothes, to the tub. Dad ran the water and Mom asked me if I felt sick, if I needed to go to the hospital. "I'm fine," I told her.

I feel very much alive, energized. All I want to do is get back to the game. I didn't tell her that.

I missed school that day, no great loss. They took me to Doctor Moyer, who couldn't account for my having passed out. In his little room that smelled like tongue depressors and rubbing alcohol, he had me follow his finger with my eyes. He peered inside my ears with his little light. He pressed his cold little stethoscope onto my back, had me breathe, listened to my heart, pressed down on my stomach with his surprisingly warm hands, asking if I felt any pain. I felt no pain.

"She's fine," he said. "Nothing to worry about."

***

We sit, Nurse Carol and I, on the curved cement bench facing the fountain, a big-bellied angel vomiting dirty water from between pursed lips, sinking in it, up to her knees now, her eyes, without pupils, begging the sky to call her home. I keep a careful eye on the doors and windows of the institution. The nurse drones on and on about her life, her grown children, their jobs, their struggles, their kids. I'm not listening, not really, but the sound of her voice is so soothing. I consider the idea that she might be my protector, that Kendrick's spirit, or soul, or whatever, is in there somewhere, calling out to me from behind the wall of Nurse Carol's monologue. I can almost make myself believe it. Such is the nature of faith: it is merely a pretty mask made of wishes, swathed in finery, bejeweled in baubles, covering a face contorted, made ugly, by fear.

"Let's go in—it's getting chilly," says Nurse Carol.

Button up, buttercup. I'm not sure it's safe yet.

"Let's stay a little longer. It's not that cold."

"Piss and ginger," Nurse Carol says, shaking her head. "Ginger and piss. What are we going to do with you?"

***

Friday night I dreamed about little electronic Lottie striding down real sidewalks, past denuded trees and ramshackle houses, past boarded up schools and churches with ruptured, sunken steeples, past overgrown lawns and parking lots bracketed by slumping chain-link fences. I'd wake and she would be behind my eyes, trying to talk to me, making little electronic sounds of frustration.

Then I'd slide back into dreams. In one, Lottie approached the surface of the television, becoming more and more blurred the closer she got. When her body filled the screen, it split down the middle, and a sickly looking avatar emerged. He wore a tall hat and his skin was as grey as his clothing. His face pushed from the screen and his mouth opened to blackness...until a pile of squirming pink neon worms poured out into the room. Quickly they covered the surface of the floor and began to pile up toward the ceiling. Dream-me tried to swim up through them. I could feel them slithering into my nostrils, my ears, and my mouth, the nauseating rot-smell making me gag.

One of the worms wore the face of Mother. "Too many worms devalue the currency," she said. "Ain't got no hogs no more, remember?"

At some point everything faded and I plummeted into a deep and dreamless void.

***

I opened my eyes to a bright and cloudless Saturday morning, the whole day before me. My parents headed to Boston for lunch. They asked me if I wanted to go, I said no. I'm old enough to stay home.

"I guess," Dad said. "But I don't want you in front of that television all day. Get your homework done early so you're not scrambling tomorrow night. Or read a book, kid. We've got shelves chock full of them."

"I will."

"Sure."

I pushed the curtain aside and watched their car back out into the road and speed off.

Back to the game.

I closed the curtains, like I was concealing a forthcoming misdeed.

I switched on the television and the Atari.

Little Lottie danced, she called to me, and then, again, she walked.

In the road before her glowed a set of blue headphones. She touched them and they went to the top of the screen. The words YOUR WEAPONS AND DEFENSE CACHE appeared above the headphone icon.

We walked on.

The trees changed color, brown to grey, and the leaves fell to the ground and vanished. The stripped branches flickered and disappeared, the treetops narrowing and bending at right angles, a yellow cluster of pixels forming at their terminus. They had become streetlights, and featureless buildings grew up behind them from the horizon. Lottie continued through this new cityscape, passing streetlight after streetlight, greys and yellows. The music faded out and the only sound was the squelching of her feet. Okay, I thought, time to stop the game. There's nothing happening here, and I have homework to do, and reading.

But...

Just a little further.

An hour, two, then three. Nothing but streetlights and a cityscape in grey. The blue background deepened, went to dusk, then to dark, then to black. The yellow from the streetlight bulbs colored the room.

I slept, my thumb pressing the joystick, while Lottie walked. I don't know for how long. Void, again. Blackness, deep and inky and all-encompassing. What woke me up was static, insistent and fierce, pouring from the little speaker like smoke. Cold rode the wings of the static, pulled up the bumps on my skin, numbed my toes and my fingers. When I looked up at the screen, fear shot through my body in spasms and shudders.

Lottie was surrounded by tall trees—green, squared-off treetops along the slightly curved top edge of the screen. Grey faces with Xs for eyes shot around the treetops and something large and tattered moved behind the thick bars of the trunks. Lottie had gained another weapon while I slept in that trance-like state. Next to the headphones floated a sharp wooden spear.

I summoned them down to her without even touching the controller.

The headphones shot down over Lottie's ears and the spear flew into her hand. One of the grey faces zig-zagged down with alarming rapidity. I pressed the red button and Lottie caught the thing on the tip of her spear. It slid down the shaft slowly, leaking red pixels. The other faces screamed, their eyes tearing open, black mouths elongating their faces into distended ovals. They sprouted wings and became fat leeches. Another flew down and Lottie caught it on the spear. Red pixels shot out in all directions from the thing, filled the screen until it was all red. I backed away from the screen, which was giving off an intense heat. The door and windows of my room shuddered in their frames. The ceiling glowed red and bubbled. I reached out and shut off the television, pulling back a singed finger.

When Mom and Dad got home, I was sitting in the corner of the couch downstairs in the living room, swaddled in blankets, an ice pack in my hand.

"I burnt myself," I said, holding up the ice pack. "On the stove." They came around cooing and inspecting my reddened hand and ruffling my hair. They ordered a pepperoni pizza, my favorite, and we sat down for dinner as a family for the last time.

***

I'd kept Nurse Carol occupied with pointless anecdotes and meandering stories until I felt it was safe to go back into the building. When we get back to the room, I am still shaken, anxious. I don't want to be alone. I ask her to stay, and so she grabs her book and sits in the cushiony chair next to my bed. She reads to me, some bit of fluff, a historical romance with a conflicted soldier who has fallen for a cute little maid with a rebellious streak and a facility with weaponry. It is not a compelling story, and she drifts off amusingly quickly. Now she snores, head thrown back, her thumb bookmarking the page.

The phone rings, a jarring trill, very loud in the room. All the other sounds fade into the background. Nurse Carol snores no more, but a glance tells me she hasn't awakened; in fact, she's very still. The phone's call is insistent, shrill, it seems to grow in volume and resonance with each ring. No one is coming to pick it up. I rise from the bed and approach the phone, lift it from its cradle, hold it up to my ear, then pull it away with a hiss. The speaker is crowded with the cries of desperation, thousands of people clamoring to be heard. Somewhere in there is my cousin's voice. My hand goes to my mouth. I strain to hear. I catch only fragments.

I'm so sorry... Lottie... got into... goddamned circuitry... never would have... Anne... Inter... my fault... never wanted...

The other voices begin to crowd his out, to grow in volume, shrieking, babbling, howling. I call to him.

Are you alive? Are you alive? Please, tell me if you're alive!

Somewhere in the cacophony, another voice begins to rise to the surface, a goatish, grotesque sound, full of wormy, blood-saturated mud and desecration and dripping caverns far under the graveyard earth. I slam the phone down. I'm still calling out to Kendrick. The room echoes with the shrieks and screams. I cover my ears.

Nurse Carol wakes up. Her eyes are rolled to the whites. Her mouth opens.

***

Snow day. That jolt of joy when LEEDS appears in bold, unequivocal letters under the face of the geeky meteorologist (to whom Dad referred as the region's most accurate virgin, to Mom's endless delight). The happy confirmation that comes with looking out the window at the snow pouring from the sky, the pristine dunes and drifts and dips that result from a wind-swept Nor'easter.

Mom and Dad have an earnest discussion; they're both going to brave the weather because they are working on Important Projects. Mom cooks up some eggs and pumpernickel toast, an extra treat, for weekdays usually mean the unimaginative pairing of cereal and milk. I eat to the sound of Dad shoveling and grunting as he brushes off the cars. At 8, they head out, calling to one another... *be safe... love you...* I wave at them, blow kisses.

I'm afraid for them, I want to call them back, to spend the day among them as they sip cocoa in their pajamas and read the paper and joke around.

But the game beckons.

I wrap myself in blankets and sit before the TV, plug in the cartridge.

Where was Lottie? The screen was crowded with little figures on a field of black, milling about, little heads turning left, then right, little legs moving under them, the soundtrack a cacophony of blips and bleats. I moved my joystick around, but none of them followed the movement. I put it down, finally, and watched as the little people swarmed over the screen.

Then the sound cut out. The people stopped moving. Their little heads tilted upward. All was still. A beat. Two beats. I started to rise to shake the console, and then all the lights shut off in the house. The refrigerator's hum wound down until it was silent. Somehow the television stayed on though, the game still on the screen. The digital people, looking up. Even made up of pixels, their faces projected tension, tension quickly giving way to terror.

It came from the top of the screen, the goat man, huge, filling the television. The avatars crowded to the sides to give it room. Its hooves brown and blood-tipped. Its legs knobby like old walking sticks. Its torso draped in a brown tattered shawl. Its white horns curled back to its shoulders. Its eyes took in the scene below, horizontal eyeballs sweeping left, then right, then back again.

Then it shrunk down until it was only twice the size of the others. They began to crowd back in, tentatively, like they wanted to inspect this new creature, to sniff at it. It occurred to me then, somewhere back in my brain, that night had fallen. The only light in my room was that of the game. Had the whole day gone by? Or... and I remember thinking this was a real possibility... had the sun cut out along with the electricity? Was the light from the television the only light left in the world?

A frantic, overlapping bleating tugged my attention back to the game. The goat man's arms had elongated, snaking out like segmented centipedes across the screen. Its pincer hands snipped off the head of one figure, then another, then another. Their heads floated up and off-screen, turning grey as they went, their eyes changing to Xs. Then the goat man whipped off its shawl. Whatever it was between the goat man's legs, there were two things of which I was absolutely certain: the first was that it was not—could not have been— the work of Kendrick. The second was that this was something that I was not meant to see.

The goat man's long arms pulled in three characters, little round black mouths, electronic screaming and babbling, and deposited them into his shawl. He dragged them off-screen to the right. Headless bodies lay strewn everywhere.

WHERE IS LOTTIE flashed on the screen, blinking rapidly. Where, indeed. I felt my eyelids fluttering. I moved my hand in front of my face in the illusion of slo-mo. Faster and faster it blinked. In my peripheral vision, something very large moved through my room, something that gave off a great, damp heat, an odor of clover and decay. I froze. The blinking stopped and the screen went blinding white.

I stared at that white screen until my eyes hurt. When the screen went red, it felt like dagger tips piercing my corneas. I think I may have screamed. The screen went black quickly, and trees grew up from the ground, filled the left and right of the screen, leaving the center open. The goat man appeared in the center, a half circle of robed, hooded figures behind him. Slate grey chins jutted from the hoods, red lines for mouths, little pink tongues moving back and forth along those red lines. The goat man undid his shawl and the figures he had stolen rolled out, limp-limbed, their little faces somehow registering shock. Then the hooded men came from around the great goat and set upon them.

Lottie appeared at the edge of the screen. I gasped. She was in profile, watching the proceedings.

Then she turned to face me.

She stuck out her arm, extended a tiny finger, pointing at the scene, where a puddle of red had begun to form under the huddled, hooded men.

Bleep, bloopbloop. Bleeleeeleelooleeloop, she said. *Bleep, bloopbloop. Bleeleeeleelooleeloop.*

What are you saying, Lottie? And where did you go?

Help me understand! Kendrick! What is she saying?

Up from the violent scrum of hooded men rose one x-eyed character, its mouth curved into a jagged grin. Its legs, longer than before, dangled and danced like the legs of a hanged man still alive. Its arms undulated. Its face was elongated, its hair grey, its mouth in a grimace. It sang a low, mournful note. Another rose behind it, deformed and hunched. The third rolled out into the blood puddle, dead, dappled with green, its head bent at the jaw.

The goat man's centipede-arm shot out and grabbled Lottie and the hooded men descended. She screamed a single, piercing, buzzing note. As I raised my hands to cover my ears, a great, gnarled hand encircled my body and lifted me right up off the floor. My room was crowded with people. Outside my windows was a deep blackness, deeper than the screen the first time I turned on the game. On the screen, and in my room, the hooded men doffed their hoods. I swore I saw Dad's face among them, and Mom's. Their hands grabbed at my clothes and I couldn't find the border between what was real and what was not. Finally, somewhere within my body, my mind became unmoored. It sailed off, a crushed, unsalvageable ship launched into dark and dangerous waters whose expanse knew no boundaries.

***

Lottie!

The voice that comes from Nurse Carol's mouth is not hers. It's small and scared, shouted from somewhere back in that long red corridor. *I'm coming! I'm coming to get you!*

Kendrick! Ken! What were you trying to tell me?

Now a terrible groan, not Kendrick, but Nurse Carol. All the air flees from her lungs. She stiffens and then lets go. I peace-sign my fingers and close her eyelids, like they do in the movies.

Was that Kendrick calling from Nurse Carol's dying throat? His voice sounded too much like it did in my childhood for me to trust it fully.

Footsteps now, loud. Floor tiles crack and buckle, ceiling tiles go to dust. I hear framed pictures pushed from the walls, glass shattering. I run to the door and lock it. It shakes in its frame.

Lottie, my cousin's voice calls, cracked and mud-caked and foul. *Lottie!*

I pull from my pocket the small, purple-blue stone. The doorknob rattles. Something smashes into it, hard. I close my eyes and wish I was Lottie. I wish for a spear. I wish I could fight. I wish I could have heard what she said.

It could be Kendrick on the other side of the door. It could.

Couldn't it?

The Long-Lost Parent

By Matthew M. Bartlett and Tom Breen

From the Orford Parish Vituperator, June 5, 2016:

BENEDICT, Conn.—State police have urged residents to be vigilant about their pets after a third attack on a homeowner's dog by what is to believed to be a coyote or pack of coyotes.

The most recent incident occurred Saturday morning along the stretch of the Orford-Willimantic Walking Trail Greenway near Stumble Brook, leaving a 3-year-old pit bull mauled so badly it had to be put down, according to Resident State Trooper Glenn Barbeau.

"The dog's owner didn't actually see the attack; he was down by the brook, collecting lucky water," Barbeau said. "This is one of the reasons we're urging folks to keep their dogs on a leash, and to keep their cats indoors if possible."

Sarah Franken, a state animal biologist at the University of Connecticut, said coyote attacks, while unusual, have happened in the area before.

"What's different about these attacks is the damage inflicted isn't consistent with what we know about coyotes," she said.

***

A man in damp flannel, red, white, and grey, stands with his back to the door of a brown, leaning shed. He coughs, a raucous volley of sharp, dog-like barks, wet and raspy. He lifts a ruddy hand to his chin, wipes away a smear of snot, rubs it between finger and thumb until, as if by magic, it's gone. The shed door is held shut top-to-bottom with all kinds of locks, combination locks, key locks, padlocks, and deadbolts. Scattered at the base of the door are old, rusted locks, like blood-flecked bodies of legless, gape-mouthed rodents.

A jaunty, electronic ditty sounds, muffled. The man's hand flies to his pocket, digs out a flip phone. The electronic bleeping notes are garish interlopers, clowns at a funeral, pajamas at an opera. He flicks open the phone with his thumbnail, holds the display an inch from his red, tear-bleared eyes. "Yah?" he says into the mouthpiece.

***

Text of an anonymous flyer posted on the community bulletin board at Wilbur's General Store and Dry Goods in Benedict, Conn., June 2016:

THESE ARE NOT COYOTES

The police and the University are LYING to us. They are trying to prevent us from knowing THE TRUTH.

Secret government experiments in the 1970s at the University are the cause of this. They created a laboratory called the Wolf Enclosure and brought in a doctor from Germany and a musician from Leeds to thwart God's plan for nature. All of this is contained in a book called The Long-Lost Father *which contains plans to convert the natural world into a Bioprison.*

The CIA and the Free and Accepted Masons published the book in 1861 to foment civil war and overthrow God's authority.

NOTHING NATURAL committed those attacks. Bill Hartwell's pit bull couldn't have been killed by a coyote. The truth they don't want to tell you is the dog was eaten from the inside.

But not just that—Bill swears on his wife's grave that dog is still alive, and returning to him.

KEEP YOUR GUNS * DON'T LISTEN TO THE RADIO

(Reports that the flyer was removed by a state trooper shortly after it was posted could not be immediately verified.)

***

Winnie stuck her head through the pass-through, the frizzed red crown of her bouffant jostling the order tickets that dangled above.

"Oooh, don't—he'll see you!" squeaked Chrissy, covering her mouth and bouncing on her heels.

"He IS hot," confirmed Winnie. "You want to take this one?"

"Really? You've got counter."

"Are you gonna argue with me, girl?"

Chrissy jostled her blonde hair with her hand, pulled a strand from the bun to hang by her eye. She adjusted her top and exited the kitchen. She grabbed a couple of silverware setups for no reason, started to walk by, then turned to face him, opened her mouth to speak.

The man, slender, silver-haired, in a grey suit and conservative blue and red tie, lowered his sunglasses with a long finger. "Yes?" he said.

This was unexpected, and Chrissy stammered. She could feel her ears warming up, turning bright red. "Do...do you need a..."

"Coffee," the man confirmed. "Black. Room temperature."

She looked into his eyes and a grimace, despite her best efforts, distorted her features. "Yes, sir," she said, and practically fled back to the confines of the kitchen. She stood by the sizzling fry-o-lators, put her small hands over her eyes, and burst into tears.

Winnie hustled over, fat hips swiveling, little fists pumping. This was the kind of thing she lived for. "Honey, what's the matter?" she said. "Did he say something to you?"

Chrissy couldn't summon words. She dissolved into sobs. The saggy-eyed chef gawked and the dishwasher muttered something about needing a smoke before skedaddling away. *Those eyes*, Chrissy tried to say but could not. *Those terrible, empty eyes.* They were the eyes of the demolished deer, the flattened squirrel. There was nothing in them. Nothing at all.

Winnie detached herself from the sobbing girl, poured out a cup of coffee, and rushed it over to the man, and was surprised to see that he had been joined by Eric Katter, the middle-aged, low-bellied, broken recluse who barely left his cabin except to pick up a pile of Healthy Choice microwaveable dinners at the Y Market by the highway exit. Katter's flannel hung damply from his shoulders and he looked weary and worn and out-of-place, especially in contrast to the neat, slender, long-fingered man.

"It's over," she heard the grey suited man say to Katter as she placed the mug before him and turned to fiddle with the orange-juice machine. "No more."

"You owe me a hunnert," rasped Katter. "And you're gonna give me a hunnert."

The grey-suited man picked up his mug and sloshed the liquid around, held it up to his nose. He turned on his stool and looked Katter directly in the eyes as he slurped it up. "Follow me," he said.

***

Transcription of discussion on BiblioNot.com, "The Internet Home For Books That May Not Exist," accessed on 6-15-16:

TOPIC: The Long-Lost Parent

RADOWICZ: So, gentlemen, a curious tome of lore this one, referred to both in Octalan's catalog and the Spanish government's report on the Beringos Brothers. Not much encrusted by Internet-borne fakelore, either. Any guesses on whether this is a real one?

DENTON: Obvious reference to the "Long-Lost Friend" in the title. I'm inclined to say hoax. Discordians or someone like that. Isn't there supposed to be some kind of government connection?

RADOWICZ: Depends on who you listen to. My hesitation in branding this a fake is that pedigree I referred to above; Octalan may be a mischief-maker at times, but why would the Spanish government perpetuate a Discordian prank?

ASHMONT: What did the Spanish government report say? Forgive me, I've been up to my neck in a priori languages. Haven't followed the latest cryptobook news.

RADOWICZ: Spanish government just listed it as one of the titles sold by Beringos. No worries about missing the start of this, Ashmont; it just came up recently. Something in Connecticut, perhaps.

ASHMONT: Someone find a copy?

DENTON: Coyote attacks that the easily frightened are attributing to bad spooks, old juju, goat-men from Leeds, that kind of thing. Somehow *The Long-Lost Parent* came up in all this. Swamp Yankee jitters.

ASHMONT: Ah.

RADOWICZ: I know you live nearby, Denton, but I'm not sure it's as easily dismissed as that. I could be wrong, but some of this tallies with what Octalan says.

DENTON: Which is what, precisely?

RADOWICZ: Octalan says the book isn't so much a collection of spells or anything that simple; in fact, he says the content is pretty unremarkable, all told. But he says the presence of the book almost always means catastrophic misfortune for wherever it happens to pop up—like there's an aura independent of the text itself, attached to the book, that means the worst.

ASHMONT: Sounds like my last girlfriend.

DENTON: Sounds like all your girlfriends. I still think the book is a red herring. There may be something weird happening in some little town, but I don't think it has to do with a volume we're reasonably confident may not be anything special.

GREAVES: Hello, lads, sorry to butt in, but I was just looking up the reference in Octalan's catalog, and wanted to make a clarification. He doesn't say the *presence* of the book is what brings misfortune exactly.

RADOWICZ: Ah, good of you to drop in! What does he say? I don't have it in front of me at the moment.

GREAVES: Octalan says that the *name* of the book is what causes calamities to befall people. Specifically, writing the name.

RADOWICZ: ...

DENTON: Oh, come on.

ASHMONT: Been nice knowing you gents.

***

The Cadillac bounced along on the moonscape of ruts and hillocks and potholes, all mud, still mostly frozen from the previous winter with its record lows and intermittent blizzards and ice storms and sleet squalls. The grey-suited driver and the cadaver in the passenger seat bounced in synchrony, dancers in a blasphemy of a ballet. The driver's sunglasses bounced on his nose and his teeth clacked. His expression remained neutral. The cadaver's chin bounced off its chest, its lank hair rising and falling, rising and falling.

The car passed a dilapidated barn, a line of moping trees, the scattered remains of a wooden fence, now termite-chewed and strewn with blood-colored graffiti, a rusted-out jeep somewhere in the middle of the glacial process of being sucked into the earth and subsumed. Here the road dwindled to a path, then tire tracks, then nothing but matted grass and sunken stones, tattered brown leaves. The driver hit the brake hard and the cadaver's head hit the windshield, leaving a splotch of cold perspiration.

The driver exited the car, went around to the trunk. When he had retrieved what he needed, he went around to the passenger side, opened the door, and stripped the flannel from the cadaver, flinging it into the back seat. Then he went to work on the body. He worked slowly, conserving energy, keeping a watchful eye on the distant tree line. Whenever something moved, or he heard a rustling, he stopped, tensed. Each time, nothing came of it, and he resumed his grim task.

***

Transcript of "Nightjar Radio with Jon Denton," WICX (Orford Parish Community College Public Radio), June 19, 2016:

CALLER: Jon, what's your take on what's happening in Benedict?

DENTON: The coyote attacks.

CALLER: It's more than that though, right? Noises, strange lights, police roadblocks, I mean...

DENTON: You've got something in mind?

CALLER: Doesn't it sound like classic UFO behavior to you?

DENTON: Hmm. Maybe a false flag to get people thinking it's UFOs? This is more or less SOP for the Deep State. Remember the time in '98 when people in Quaker Heights left their homes because of mysterious lights that turned out to be a promotion for the outlet mall? Tell me that wasn't the MIC at work.

CALLER: Yeah, Jon, maybe you're right. Maybe it's not UFOs. You know about the Wolf Enclosure?

DENTON: That a biker bar out in Chaplin?

CALLER: In the Seventies, up at the university, the CIA and the Bilderbergers created this lab to test their theories on how to subjugate nature.

DENTON: Huh. Okay. Go on.

CALLER: Couldn't this be something from that? Like something went wrong—or something went right? They were—there's shortwave transmissions where people say they see bodies coming out of the river—and there's, you know, it's all in this book they had. All according to plan.

DENTON: Book? A book at the lab, or a book the government was using?

CALLER: Yeah, it's called *The Long Lost-*

DENTON: Caller, I'm sorry, you're breaking up.

***

Two polished shoes, placed neatly alongside one another, in the mouth of each a black sock folded into a square. Laces dangling like slack arms. A shadow moves from the tree line, low to the ground, a scout, maybe, or an emissary. It slides under the car, nostrils dilate and expand, taking in the odors from the shoes, sniffing, snuffling. More shadows emerge from the tree line, upright, human, it seems, but with long arms that swim behind them like streamers, fingers that trace inscrutable designs in the shadows' wakes, writing words or symbols or something on the page of the air. The trees warp behind these figures, the air sours and crumples, goes a nauseous yellow. The scout, still sniffing the ground with a brute avidity, follows the footprints into the mosquito-dotted marsh. The shadows follow, the ground sinking behind them. The moon, an obese lolling blur, breaks out in black splotches, begins to bleed brown. Birds break apart like blood-bloated ticks. Clouds stretch out and go thin, gasping. A yellow fog covers them like a pox-infected blanket.

***

Message posted on the Facebook page operated by the town government of Benedict, Conn., on July 2, 2016:

ATTENTION BENEDICT RESIDENTS AND VISITORS

Due to the recent air condition quality warnings issued by the National Weather Service, the annual Fourth of July Community Parade will be rescheduled from Monday, July 4 to Saturday, July 23.

After further consultation with the National Weather Service and state Department of Environmental Protection, it has been determined that the "yellow haze" many residents have identified is NOT a significant source of harm, but may cause respiratory difficulty in senior citizens and young children, as well as those with compromised immune systems. For this reason, and out of an abundance of caution, we have decided to move the date of our Fourth of July parade.

Thank you for your patience. Please limit the amount of time you spend outdoors until after the warning is lifted.

Comments (1):

B. Orton: WAS IT COYOTES THAT TOOK BILL HARTWELL

***

The door hangs open, revealing a darkness somehow darker than the night. The moon has crumpled and been digested by the fog in preparation for the clouds to feed. The only light comes from the occasional firefly, revealing degraded tree bark, a section of corrugated wall, something that might be a slack, chinless face, the light blinks away too quickly to tell for certain.

For once, the man in the grey suit seems unsure. He stands before the open door. The leaves rustle behind him. He doesn't turn. If they have come, as the radio said they would, turning will not help. There is not a fight to be had. He must decide quickly. He enters the darkness of the barn, becomes darkness himself.

His fingers, stretched out before him, encounter a curtain. It feels like velvet, maybe, unpleasant somehow on his fingers, like touching the wings of some foul, otherworldly moth. He pulls the offering from the inner pocket of his jacket with his left hand. With his right, he pushes, and the fabric gives. He finds a division, shoves his way through. He steps into a bright, terrible light. His eyes dilate to needle holes and he falls to his knees, drops the offering to the floor. All he can see are shapes, coming together, separating, fluid, coagulating.

Though hardly louder than a whisper, the voice that crashes through the silence is like a finger pushing into his head just above the nose, pushing through his grey matter, wiping out memory, scrambling speech, and scraping the back of his skull. For once, his composure breaks and he cries out.

***

Talking points for State Rep. Eric Atkins, R-Coventry, guest of honor at the Benedict July Fourth Community Parade:

DRAFT/NOT FOR PUBLIC DISTRIBUTION:

- Welcome ladies and gentlemen, etc.
- 78th annual Fourth of July Parade
- Congratulations to the winner of the float decorating contest [winner's name will be given to you before remarks]
- This really shows the best of what our rural towns have to offer. The true spirit of our state and our country.
- If our Founders were here in Benedict today, they would be very proud to see how well we've carried on their legacy and honored their sacrifices.
- As your representative in Hartford, I'm working hard for Benedict. Your priorities are my priorities, which is why I'm fighting hard for full funding of the expansion of the Orford-Willimantic Walking Trail Greenway and the restoration of the Route 32 bridge at Monroe Street.

- (In case of public questions: State assures me the yellow fog was a brief atmospheric condition that was a result of increased pollen, thanks to the mild winter. A similar phenomenon was recorded in 1861.)
- (The restricted-access coyote hunt was a tremendous success. Twelve pelts were harvested, state biologists expect this will put an end to the attacks.)
- (Reported disappearances in town recently are a matter of concern to all our citizens, and state police are working diligently. My office is demanding regular updates on the investigations.)
- Today is a wonderful day, a day for celebration!

***

Tanya Johns lit her third cigarette off what remained of her second. This year's parade sucked, and it wasn't even on the fucking Fourth. What WAS that? Totally not right. Like moving Halloween into November, or cancelling Christmas, but this was worse! An affront to *America*! She dug into her purse, retrieved her iPhone. Doug hadn't called back yet, hadn't returned her texts. She scrolled up. Eight texts, all her own, without one reply from him. She'd gone out of her way to go by his place before the parade, and it was shut up tight, blinds drawn. With the unkempt lawn and the stripped trees—shouldn't green leaves have returned by now?—the place looked all but abandoned.

The parade floated by unnoticed as she checked Facebook to see if he'd posted a picture of a goddamned fish or a duck-faced selfie or a picture of his finger sticking out through his fly, one of his personal favorites. Nothing.

In fact, the only people who'd posted in the last four hours were Cassie out in San Diego (a picture of her dog grinning brainlessly at the end of its leash in blinding sunlight) and Rick in Utah (some gibberish about the governor being a Nazi). It was weird, because everyone from the store and from school posted stuff, like, all the time. Couldn't go five seconds without shouting into the screen. A scream sounded from down the road, from whence the parade came, sauntering along, flatbed trucks with waving cheerleaders, a bunch of teenagers in yellow and black uniforms, blaring trumpets sticking out from their mouths, screeching into the yellow-blue firmament, a Prius bearing an ugly bank logo, pony-tailed tellers in green polo shirts flashing white teeth at the crowd. Then another scream, and in her periphery a telephone pole fell to the ground as though in slow motion, wires snapping, sparks whipping in the air. Another scream, a duet, and then a chorus of them. She held her phone up as far as her arm could reach and snapped a picture. She pulled it back down and saw only black and red blurs.

She thumbed the phone back over to messages. Nothing. To Facebook. Just blank now, with grey lines and empty boxes. All the posts gone. No service, no icons along the top. The screen went yellow and she heard a terrible shout and the revving of an engine. She looked up. The bank car squealed its tires and sped ahead, causing the trumpet kids to drop their instruments and scatter. Two went down under the front wheels. She heard their heads hit the pavement. Then behind it, speeding forward, she saw the float, the contest-winning float, and what was on it, and what hung off it, and what trailed behind it, and she added her own scream to the terrible chorus.

***

Letter to the Editor, Orford Parish *Vituperator*, Wednesday, Sept. 14, 2016:

To the editor,

As our country reflects this week, 15 years since the terrible tragedy in New York, I want to take a moment and thank the many people in our hometown who have stepped up so wonderfully to respond to a more recent tragedy close to home.

I realize there is little I can say to ease the terrible trauma experienced by the people of Benedict, both those who suffered directly and the grief-stricken people left behind. This is perhaps the most profound mystery of human life: the mystery of suffering.

However, there is a bright side to all this: the way in which so many people have rallied to open their homes and their wallets, to roll up their sleeves, and to simply lend a shoulder to cry on. It's an old saw that you never know a person better than when adversity strikes, but it is true, and today I can say I know my fellow Orfordians better than ever before.

Everyone—from the police to the nursing staff at Orford Parish General Memorial, to the Orford Parish High students who created the #BenedictStrong hashtag—had something to offer to people when they most needed it, and their kindness will be, as the Bible says, a house raised in justice to them.

I wish I could say the same of everyone. While I realize that graffiti is a lesser annoyance for Benedict right now, after all those people have been through, it is shocking to me that someone would bring what must have been many gallons of gray paint to splash around those grand old buildings in the little village center. And while it isn't obscene, it is utterly nonsensical—what are we to make of the phrase "Long-Lost," with a third word scrawled over so as to be illegible, over and over again?

The people who did this are sick, and the only proper response is to pray for them, as we pray for the people of Benedict, who will rise from this tragedy, strong as never before.

Yours sincerely,
The Rev. Curtis Smyke
Third Congregational Church of Orford Parish
#BenedictStrong

We Pass From View

" C LOSED UNTIL FURTHER notice—family emergency," read the words, scrawled in red marker on a sheet of notebook paper taped to the shop's door. I cupped my hands to the window and peered in. Bookcases and their shadows tilted away from one another in the faint luminescence of the security lights. The red EXIT sign glowered over the poster-plastered back door, illuminating the register, giving it the aspect of a hunched, frog-like thing with green zeroes for eyes. There was no sign of Purcell, no sign of anyone, not even the shop's congenial, one-eyed black cat, who typically sat at the large window, squinting in the warmth of the sun's light. He, Purcell, had discontinued his email and social media accounts since his last vague yet frantic message appeared in my inbox; a call to the store returned only the irritated bleat of a busy signal.

The shop, Bookworks, occupied the central space in a quiet commercial block, along with a laundromat, a package store, an optometrist's office, and its by-far eldest tenant, Boyd's Grocery, which sat a few doors down at the street corner. I walked over to Boyd's, my footsteps accompanied by the pleasing sound of birdsong and the distant whisper of interstate traffic. Spring had commenced, and the air swam with aromas shaken free from the frosts of March, of rain-awakened soil, of fresh cut grass.

The bell sounded a faint, desultory clank as I pushed open the door, scattering dust motes into beams of sunlight diffused by grime-streaked windows. It felt as though I'd pushed myself back through time into some old tintype, jolting awake the slumbering past. I often had that reaction when I entered Boyd's—the place reeked of age; it had existed in that same spot, in some form or another, since colonial times. Half tobacconist, half convenience store, inhabited mainly by old men and dowagers, the place seemed suspended in sepia, a preserved relic, an atmosphere that not even garish modern packaging could dispel.

A cadre of insects cavorted over a crate of browning bananas. Stacks of newspapers leaned this way and that, garroted with yellow plastic strips. Behind the counter, under perforated banners of lottery tickets, loomed an ancient, stout clerk with a liquor-swollen nose and hands like crumpled paper bags. I asked when Bookworks had shuttered its doors, and received in reply a shrug and a grunt. The effort seemed to take a lot out of the clerk, and he leaned heavily on the counter, elbows locked, arms taut, and closed his eyes.

***

A few months before, I had self-published a collection of stories, most of which were set locally, several scenes taking place in a fictional version of Bookworks. Anne Gare's Used and Rare Book Emporium, the name I gave the shop in my stories, served as the dark locus of occult activity in Leeds, Massachusetts, a small city that seethed with shadows and dark history. In reality, Leeds is a small, unassuming village in the western region of Northampton whose main attractions are a golfing range fronted by a milkshake and burger stand, and a small (but smartly stocked) liquor outlet attached to a convenience store.

Purcell had first contacted me through a Facebook message. He had seen an article about me in the local paper, and through an Internet search he learned of my book's connection to his shop. He asked whether he might stock the book on consignment, and I promised to drop off a few copies that weekend.

In the tale "The Sleuth" (which Purcell later admitted was his least favorite in the collection: its opening "perfunctory," its supernatural elements "trite" and "not scary"), I made mention of Anne Gare's shop's prodigious occult section. Bookworks's selection was somewhat more modest, the bulk of its one shelf taken up with New Age titles and dog-eared books on Wicca and Earth Magick. Otherwise, the shelf, slightly bowed like a splintery wooden grin, bore a few yellowed, crinkle-spined Whitley Streiber mass markets; Colin Wilson's ubiquitous Occult compendium; and several books on black magic with lurid covers that belied the drab clichés within. I offered to supplement that section with some duplicate occult titles I'd accumulated over the years, and he agreed.

***

I came by the following Saturday with a box of occult books and four copies of my own title in an old shopping bag. I had seen Purcell before in the shop during my infrequent visits, but had never spoken to him. I get a little foggy in used bookstores—the smell of the books, slightly musty, but not displeasingly so, drops me into a delirium as I scan titles, flip through ancient pages, try to remember books I need to complete this or that collection, study unfamiliar covers from different editions of titles I own. It's rare that I acknowledge other customers, and an inclination toward shyness prevents my entering into any kind of substantial dialogue with the clerk when it's time to settle up.

Purcell greeted me warmly, and accepted the books with gratitude. He stood about a half a foot taller than my six-foot height, slender but not over-thin, save his scrawny arms, which reminded me of stripped tree limbs. He had dark hair, with a neat beard and glasses, a nose and Adam's apple that jutted like knife points. I followed him around as he shelved the new titles and, attempting to overcome my introverted tendencies, I confessed disappointment that the horror books sat intermingled with fantasy and science fiction. He told me that he'd just received a quantity of new horror mass markets in decent shape, and planned to give horror its own set of shelves. "Are you a Lovecraft guy?" he asked, and so we whiled away the afternoon discussing the usual suspects: Machen, Blackwood, and the like.

And so it was that I found myself bringing a couple of steaming coffee cups into the shop most Saturday afternoons after that, leaning on the counter, talking with Purcell of this or that, mostly, naturally, of books and writers. We both liked King, but we preferred different books of his, and found amusingly little overlap. We shared a distaste for Richard Laymon, and neither of us had delved too far into Clive Barker since the *Books of Blood*. From time to time the old black cat would venture up from the downstairs and sit on the stool between us, black as a shadow, green eye glinting companionably. He'd curl his tail around the front of his paws and look back and forth at us as though he was following the conversation.

This new acquaintanceship came at the right time, at just the right time. I had become increasingly aware that I'd been steadily and inexorably retreating from the outside world. Lights shone too brightly in shops and malls. Sounds crowded my ears—music everywhere, even at gas station pumps; the inane, faux-cheerful jabbering from the speaker at the self-checkout supermarket lane; advertisements—causing me to stay home more and more. While in one sense I was content to be at home, I knew that it must be psychologically bad for me. I worried about becoming some kind of morose hermit.

But the lights of the bookstore shone low, and no music disrupted the lush, library-like silence. Purcell spoke softly—so much so that at times I had to lean in to hear. He was easy to talk to, laid back, not uncomfortable with lapses in conversation, with companionable silences. My Saturday outings kept me back from the red, burnt-edged precipice overlooking what I feared would be a serious and profound psychological withdrawal.

***

On a freezing late February Saturday, I entered to find Purcell hobbling around on his knees surrounded by boxes and towering stacks of freshly unpacked books, a nerdy Godzilla in a city of paper and cardboard. He was lifting out a dust-darkened stack of videotapes bearing titles like *Scared Stiff* and *Confidential Report* when he registered my presence. "These boxes were out on the stoop when I got here," he said by way of explanation. "Check this out..." He tilted one of the boxes back. BANTAM was written in neat, fat letters on the side.

"From the Bantam house!" I said.

"I assume so."

"Weird thing with that family," I said. "I haven't picked up the Gazette in a while—have there been any updates?"

"None," said Purcell. "Maybe I'll find some clues in these boxes." He looked up at me, and I knew exactly what he was going to say. "What happened with that family...you should totally use that in your next book."

"Definitely," I said, without much enthusiasm. "I really should."

Then Purcell gasped, started digging down into the box. "Shit," he said. "Oh, oh, oh, well, look at this. The holy fucking grail, the grail, the grail."

He lifted out a slender book bound in faded blue cloth, held it up to the light as though it were some kind of stone idol. "*We Pass From View*," he said. "Heard of it?"

I hadn't.

"It was written by this notorious British occultist named Roland Franklyn, the guy disappeared a long, long time ago. Not too long after, all the copies of this book disappeared too. So to call this a rarity is a massive understatement." He shook his head. "An absolute treasure. I wouldn't even know how to put a price on it."

I couldn't help but smile at his enthusiasm. I held out my hand and he paused, and then handed over the book. "Gently," he said, and I scoffed.

"I know how it sounds. But gently." His look was as serious as I'd ever seen it. I abandoned my plan of pretending to drop the book. The title sprawled across the cover in gold leaf, a font approximating a frenetic cursive scribble tugged from both ends until it sat squat like a hilly horizon. I opened to the first pages and a fly shot out as though it had been hiding in the spine. I suppressed the instinct to swat at the thing with the book, as Purcell would probably have had a heart attack. The little thing rose up to the ceiling, where it buzzed madly about the top edge of the window. Purcell stared up at it.

I looked back to the book, turned a few pages. The third page bore a blue stamp reading BRICHESTER CENTRAL LIBRARY (all of the Rs were raised a touch) and a card with ancient stamps in varying shades of faded red, like lipstick from long-forgotten kisses, only four, indicating the instances that the book had been checked out. True Light Press, read the next page in gothic lettering. The accompanying logo depicted an amateurishly drawn lightbulb in the palm of a seven-fingered hand.

"So," said Purcell, his grin crooked. "Haven't you always wanted to discover your infinite self?"

"Hardly," I said. "I can barely be bothered with the finite one." I skimmed the book, flipping pages, reading a paragraph here, an aphorism there. "It seems to be mostly drivel," I said. "Reincarnation stuff, lucid dreams, astral projection. Pretty run of the mill for something so sought after." I handed it back to him, pinching the corner between thumb and forefinger, letting it dangle, a look of exaggerated disgust on my face, as though I was handing him a dried turd.

He snatched it back, shaking his head. "From what I've heard, it goes a little deeper than that. It's not about past lives as much as it is about, I guess, concurrent lives."

"Well," I said, pretending offense. "Keep your precious book. See if you can talk to me in my dreams." That week, it occurs to me only now, I did not dream.

***

The next Saturday I arrived to find the store smelling odd, like burnt rope, but somehow peppery. "What happened in here?" I asked. "Batch of incense go bad?"

Purcell perched on the stool at the register, looking down into his lap. By the credit card machine sat a bowl brimming with a semi-transparent orange-brown liquid. On the surface floated six black moths, large, with bent legs like black pipe-cleaners. They looked like alien barges, spiked and barbed and intricately wrought. Purcell looked up. In the course of seven days, he had lost a significant amount of weight. The skin below his eyes puffed out pink, and a garish whitehead glowed like a barnacle on the side of his nose. He didn't address my question, nor the reek that permeated the store.

He lifted from his lap the copy of We Pass From View and marked his page with a receipt. It could have been the light in the shop, or that my memory had failed me, but the book seemed thicker, more substantial, than when I had first seen Purcell lift it from its box the week before. The blue cloth seemed brighter, newer, as well, the gold leaf on the cover fairly glowing.

"You're not getting caught up in that stuff, are you?" I said.

"Definitely not," Purcell said. "There's a lot in it, to be sure, some beautifully written passages, and some sections about existence and the universe that just..." He trailed off, his eyes going briefly unfocused. For a fearful moment I thought he might slide off the stool and onto the floor. But he regained himself and continued. "Look, I'm strictly atheist. There is no God, there are no gods, at least, nothing that sets our paths or feels one way or the other about what we do, how we act. It's just us, fending for ourselves in a brief flash of light in an eternity of darkest nothing. And demons?" He chuckled darkly. "Demons are just the worst versions of ourselves."

That's what he said, I'd swear to it in a courtroom. But in the small hours, when darkness creeps like water through the windows and into my head, I remember it differently. I remember him saying,

"Demons are just the best versions of ourselves." I swear that I remember taking a long sip of coffee, the burn on my tongue, the sugar spinning behind my teeth, and deciding that he'd misspoken, choosing to let it go.

***

The following Thursday, after dinner with my wife Kate, and after we'd watched some television, I sat at the computer to write but instead ended up browsing through Facebook posts like a man addicted to distraction and trivialities. An instant message popped onto the screen. It was from Purcell.

"There's one of me who is crazy," he'd written, apropos of nothing.

"What do you mean, 'one of me'?" I replied.

The pause after my question felt like it lasted minutes. I very nearly shut the browser window.

"There are many of us, Bartlett. Many of me, and many of you, out there in the world times ten or twenty, connected, but unaware."

"If there's one of you that's crazy, I think I'm talking to him right now," I typed. "Purcell, you're having a psychotic break."

"You have to listen to me. I need protection. He wants to bury me alive. I'm in terrible danger. Can you provide protection for me?"

Was he kidding? Having me on? Trying to provide fodder for a story?

"Who wants to bury you alive?"

No answer.

"I'm hardly a bodyguard type," I wrote, sparing a glance down at my considerable paunch. "And I have a full-time job."

"I can pay you from my savings."

A pause, three dots pulsing on the screen to indicate my correspondent was typing further.

"No, no, I can't. Ha! I don't have anything left of my savings."

"Tell me what's happening," I wrote. "Who wants to bury you alive? Why?"

He did not reply. I went to bed gripped by disquiet and worry. After a few hours of being unable to find a comfortable position, of running the conversation over and over in my mind, I dropped down into an anthology of flash-fiction dreams. Many were malformed, disjointed, lost to me now. I recall one segment wherein I threaded my way through a massive crowd, squeezed in tight, in some manner of ancient arena, trying to find an exit, seeing none. In another I sat at a desk in a too-bright office staring at computer screens, reports and spreadsheets and indecipherable strings of numbers and symbols, while outside oil derricks swung up and down in a lavender sky.

The last dream, the one that woke me, is the clearest in my memory. I lay face up in a shallow box that smelled of fresh-cut wood and ancient mud, of thousands of blind, pincer-faced beetles swarming under a stone after a rainstorm. The tip of my nose touched the splintery surface and I could not point my toes straight up. I fumbled in the darkness for my phone, pulled it from my pants pocket, raised it to my face. The screen filled the box with light, caused me to wince. My shadow, a distorted, haggard profile, loomed on the wood above me, demoniac and gape-jawed. When my eyes adjusted to the light, I saw that I had 106 unread emails—that number sticks in my mind for a reason I cannot fathom—and 12% remaining battery life. As I watched, that number leapt down to 7%.

I hadn't even begun to panic when I heard a thudding sound, repeating, first sporadic, slowly becoming rhythmic. I was to be saved, excavated! I called out, but my voice was muted, like I was calling from far away, down some fathoms-deep well. I could barely hear it. I tried again...and then something terrifying occurred to me. The knocking was coming not from above...but from below. I reached my hand down to my side and felt something next to me. A doorknob.

Then two things happened simultaneously: the phone went dark, plunging the box into utter blackness, and the doorknob turned under my hand.

***

I woke to rain tapping the window with a thousand fingernails. I slipped from the bed, not wanting to disturb Kate's sleep. I grabbed my robe and pulled it on, walked over to the window to look out upon the roiling river. Morning light traced the horizon in a blue-white glow. Off in the far distance bobbed a cloister of boats in snowy shrouds. Beyond that loomed the shadow of the shuttered marina. A moaning train whistle, raspy and prolonged, underscored the rain's patter. I shuffled into the kitchen and started a pot of coffee. Presently Kate joined me. Her curly hair was unkempt, billowing around her head. "Good morning, Louis the Fourteenth," I said.

She affected a scowl, flipped me the bird, and poured herself a cup. As she went about the task of measuring the perfect amount of cream and sugar, I told her about my dream. "Well, that's your Sunday cemetery walks. You should spend a little time among the living."

"Yes, but the living are so gauche," I said.

"For one thing, they won't ever shut up." She peered at me. "Are you worried about something?"

I'd never talked to her much about Purcell. There wasn't much to tell, at least not that she'd be interested in. I knew nothing of his life outside the store, nothing of his family. I didn't know if he was a native or a transplant, a college graduate or home-schooled. I didn't know where he lived, if he was married or otherwise attached, straight or gay. Though the town leans liberal, Purcell for all I knew might have been a right-of-Reagan conservative. We admittedly had a very superficial relationship, the kind that had been typical for me in middle-age. I had a few close friends, and a hundred acquaintances, those vague beasts that congregate in your life but never come close enough to touch it in any profound way.

I filled her in on the past weeks, the strange book, the stench in the shop, and, finally, the electronic conversation from the night before.

She considered everything, and looked at me with a raised eyebrow. "Well, he's clearly nuts," she said. "Next time you go in there, keep your distance. You may want to bring a box-cutter, or a gun. Don't accept food from him. It will most definitely be poisoned."

I laughed, and she shook her head, took a long pull from her mug. "He sounds harmless," she said. "Maybe he should spend a little more time away from weird books."

***

A few days later, having stayed late at work to finish a complicated project, one I knew I'd feel better about when it was behind me, I drove a few miles out of my way to go by the shop on my way home. I don't recall whether I had a particular reason, or if I'd been driven by some kind of strange, keyed-in instinct. In any event, what I saw was so unexpected, so strange, that the memory of it still arouses shudders in me, still chills my scalp and raises the hair on my arms.

The shop had closed at ten, two hours earlier than when I drove by, but dim and flickering light as from a candle, or several candles, danced on the walls and the shelves and the spines of the books. Restless, billowing shadows milled about like will o' the wisps. I'd have thought it was some sort of after-hours store meeting for inventory or something, but Purcell employed a staff of but three, four at the most, and the crowd seemed substantially larger than that. Nor could I imagine his having opened the store for some kind of midnight sale: I had never seen more than two or three shoppers in the place at any one time. Who were these people milling about after hours? I pulled over across the road, rolled down the car window, and peered out.

A group of at least twenty, all wearing hooded robes, swayed in clusters among the shelves, long, gossamer sleeves bunched around their slender, raised arms. Purcell loomed behind the counter—he must have been standing on a chair, or a pile of books, as he towered above the others, addressing the group. Behind the proliferation of swaying arms, he looked like a displeased demon-god in a storm-savaged wood. The candlelight cast dark, angled shadows onto his features, rendering his expression cruel and humorless. It looked almost as though wedges of his face had been cut away.

Then two of the hooded figures nearest the window turned and looked right at me. What I saw momentarily paralyzed me, as it was impossible, its implications, especially in light of Purcell's recent messages, hideous. I gasped, fumbled the gearshift into Drive, and sped off. Tears welled under my eyes. The streetlights reached out to each other, yellow light smeared like toxic garland from bulb to bulb. The moon's face sagged, its empty sockets black as pitch, ragged holes at the bottom of which unthinkable things wriggled and writhed. The dashboard glowed alien green. The sound of my gasping filled the car. I wrenched the wheel, pulling up onto the curb, grabbed my asthma inhaler from the glove box. I hadn't had an attack in six years. I puffed, exhaled, drew in another dose. I looked in the rearview mirror, saw, or imagined I saw, shadows sinking behind parked cars, ducking into alcoves, threading through the trees that lined the west side of the road. I pulled away and sped home, gripping the wheel like a drowning man.

***

I dreamed again that night, and this time the nightmares started right in and held me in their sway for what felt like the full stretch of the night. I was back in that dreaded box, now facing downward. The knob turned in my hand and the floor fell away, spinning into darkness tinged red at the edges. A thousand slender-fingered hands took hold of me, tugged at my clothes. Ghastly creatures with eyes like bulging radio speakers dragged me down through root-strewn, worm-threaded mud and muck. They buzzed at me in some unknown language. They were naked, sinewy, slimy, and their touch burned like acid. We dropped through a ceiling, tiles turning to powder as we hit, and the creatures swept off into the shadows. I landed on a great pewter platter on a dinner table that stretched into darkness on all sides. Other men crawled around the table, some of them covered in skin translucent or else tattered like junkyard couches, revealing strata of muscle and organs. From far off came the warbling of a hellfire-warped bell that set the other men whispering to one another in frenzied, wheezing fear.

And then it materialized from the darkness on a thousand white tapered legs like a cluster of spermatozoa. Eyes of various sizes covered its ovoid body, some bloodshot, all rolling wildly in their sockets. From between the eyes sprouted long, wispy grey hairs. On the thing's side gaped a cluster of empty sockets, like a bite from a corncob, but clotted with dried blood and black putrefaction. Something, I thought, had been at it. Then, hideously, a mouth opened up at the front, bisecting the demented creature, causing all of the eyes to roll wildly toward the aperture. In that cancerous mouth, surrounded by a cluster of purple-veined tongues, crouched Purcell, hair dampened with gelatinous saliva, skin melting away like when you hold a flame to a plastic bag, teeth elongated. He called to me.

The scene shifted to the street in front of Bookworks, the air a muted orange color that comes before a severe storm. Purcell stood on the yellow lines, a red can of kerosene at his feet, a cigarette lighter in his hand, his expression despondent. I stood in the shop, in the display window, among sun-faded paperbacks and cookbooks. I called to Purcell through the glass. As in my earlier dream, my voice was muted. Things slithered at my feet, but I was too afraid to look down to see what they were. Somewhere in the shop's basement the cat hissed and warbled, screamed and hissed again. I kicked the things away as I banged on the glass, calling out to Purcell, telling him he could come live with us, with me and Kate, that we'd get him help. He looked at me and shook his head. He mouthed the words, "There's only one way."

He poured the kerosene over his body. He wept, the tears merging with the fuel. He lit the lighter and there was a *fwoomph*. The world warped around him, blurring and then blackening at the thousand edges, creeping inward to devour, to destroy, to turn everything to smoke. Somewhere in the conflagration I saw the darkness of his body go to its knees. His arms flailed at his head. He pitched forward.

I woke. My phone was aglow, the room blue. I picked it up and squinted at the message that filled my screen. It was from Purcell. Out of respect for the missing, for the presumed dead, I can't in good conscience repeat exactly what he said.

***

Outside of Boyd's now, on the cement stoop, lottery tickets with silver abrasions lay scattered like suicide notes. Cardboard covers the windows of the laundromat, and the street—the whole intersection, in fact—gives the discomfiting air of having been deserted. An expansive black stain mars the pavement in front of Bookworks. It makes me nervous to see it, as though somehow my dream broke through into reality and left a physical mark, a psychic bruise that firemen's hoses couldn't wash away, nor could a hundred rainy days and nights, nor the ice and snow of the three winters since gone. The shop's still shuttered, the interiors of the windows and the doors obscured by old newspapers, their garish advertisements and outdated horrors faded and muted.

When I'd left Boyd's on that April morning, the shop cat had sauntered out of the Bookworks alcove. He regarded me with his one green eye, walked up to me and fell onto his side, showing me his belly. I scratched his chest and he purred madly.

"Where's your dad, buddy?" I asked, and his eye rolled around to look at me. Somewhere in its kaleidoscopic shapes and angles, in its many green windows, secrets lived. I knew this at once, and he knew I knew it. That green eye had seen things that I might only guess at. I scooped him up, held him at my shoulder like an infant, and he reached out and gently took the tip of my ear between his teeth.

The cat lives with us now. He is mostly distant, but he seems largely content to sit and stare, or to nap. He occasionally perches on my lap while I read or watch television. He purrs mightily when I pet him, but usually after a few minutes he lifts his head as though he's heard something awful, and bolts from the room.

Last Saturday I went around to Boyd's to pick up some groceries. It's not the nearest grocer to my house, but I do go around there from time to time. As I was exiting from Boyd's, someone mirroring my own movements exited from the shuttered bookshop. I turned, and gasped. From the brown hood of the sweatshirt stared a face that looked just like my own. I remembered what I'd seen in Bookworks that terrible night—the hooded figures who'd turned to look at me. The men had both borne Purcell's features, distorted and warped by terrible knowing leers, but terrifyingly recognizable.

The man wearing my face grinned at me, and then walked in my direction, sliding his hands from the pockets of his jacket.

The Storefront Theater

I WAS SITTING up in my chair, sliding back and forth between musings and dreams, when a loud, insistent rapping on the door jolted me into panicked wakefulness. I do not like a knock on the door. My habitual response is to freeze in position, to feign absence until the interloper gives up and moves on. Fortunately, visitors are rare in my remote neighborhood, a bisected circle of streets just off a long, woody rural road that peels off from the Leeds city center and meanders for many miles through the forested land that covers the western quadrant of the state.

The motion detector light had come on, lending the gossamer curtains a nauseous glow that colored the room a greenish sepia. I climbed from the chair and was stricken by sudden vertigo. The curtains shimmied and the floor tilted at disconcerting angles. The walls swam like disturbed surfaces of coffee-milk. The echo of the knock seemed to linger in the room, an intruder in itself. I put my hand on the wall to steady myself until it passed.

Never had anyone knocked this late. It occurred to me that the phone company had discontinued my service three days earlier. I thought with a mixture of hope and dread that my long-estranged wife, thwarted upon trying to call, had driven back out to the house in order to renege on the separation upon which she'd insisted despite my desperate protests. Whatever the reason, going against my instinct, I rose and clicked the indoor switch to illuminate the enclosed porch. I pushed back the curtain.

In the yellow light sat a pile of white balloons like a cluster of blisters. From the darkness of the far end of the walk emerged a grinning white face with inverted black triangles under the eyes and lower lip. I found myself unable to move. The face began to sway back and forth like a pendulum bob on a grandfather clock. As the face approached, I saw that it belonged to a man in a black leotard and cape, some sort of clown or mime. He performed a travesty of a curtsy and signaled with a half-revolution of his hand for me to open the porch door. I did, moving like a man in the thrall of hypnosis, and the man proffered a small white card. I plucked it from his gloved hand and he retreated, walking backward, into darkness.

The front of the card read THE STOREFRONT THEATER and provided an address in the unfamiliar-to-me eastern part of town. On the back was scrawled a date, three days hence, and a time, 9:12 p.m. I looked up from the card to the darkness of the road and the wood into which the silent clown had disappeared. I watched and listened for a long time. I heard no car engine, saw no lights. The night was silent as a tomb. Then in rapid succession the balloons popped like a fusillade of fireworks. The cacophony, accompanied by my wavering shriek, echoed for a long time out in the trees.

I slept poorly that night, owing to my premature dozing in my chair, and to the shock of meeting my mute late-night caller. From time to time the motion detector light went on, and I would brace myself for another knock. None came, but I had to fight the temptation to pull open the blinds and look outside each time. I feared I might see the man doing some horrible capering dance on the green of the lit-up lawn or, worse, his face right at my window, leering, grinning. My heart thrummed in the darkness. Somewhere in there I must have slept.

***

I had nearly reached the end of my savings. My rent was two months in arrears. I spent many hours in a fog of tobacco, drunk and despairing, missing my wife, replaying her callous goodbye in my head like a situation comedy repeat played over and over as some sort of outré television station gimmick. Having gone through a period of abject homelessness in my twenties, I could not countenance doing so again, not at my age and not in my condition. I had been dispatching my résumé in bursts to anyone advertising openings, more as a distraction than anything else. There was little use these days for a man with grave anxiety and no computer acumen. I didn't remember having contacted the Storefront Theater, but I might well have done so.

On the day of the appointment I refrained from drinking, losing myself in television and paroxysms of frantic tidying. I bicycled into town in the evening when the sun was singeing the treetops, the light from the headlamp wavering before me on the tree-lined road like a fleeing ghost. When I reached the eastern part of the city, I chained my bicycle to an iron fence that bordered a dank, brackish reservoir and proceeded by foot to the theater, which sat between a kitchen fixture showroom and an electronics repair shop. Above the tattered black awning, a mud-spattered marquee advertised something called a night circus at 2:33 a.m. on Friday, and a Saturday evening "kitchen psychodrama" featuring a traveling troupe called The Orford Parish Players.

I approached the darkened double doors, my blurred reflection mirroring my movements. Then my reflection made a move I did not. Its hand reached up and tousled its own hair. I stopped, but it continued, reaching out, opening the door. For a moment the door showed two reflections of me, one shocked, drawing back, the other leaning forward, arm outstretched. Then there was only the latter, emerging, coming out onto the carpeted walk. From behind him the open door exhaled a miasma of mildew and buttered popcorn. And the man, who looked exactly like me, down to the blue shirt and tan khakis, fell to his knees just past the threshold, slapping at the walk, helpless with laughter. His laugh was high pitched and bubbly, nothing like my own. "The look on your face..." he said, smacking his thighs with his long-fingered hands. Finally, he stood, his laughter subsiding into mirthful sighs and squeals. He raised his hands to his face and pressed his fingers into the skin, reddening it. His manipulations made a sound like crackling bubble wrap punctuated with the occasional *crack* like the snapping in two of a pencil.

He pulled his hands away to reveal the anonymous, plain-featured face of a man just approaching middle age. It looked nothing like my own. "Theatrics," the man said, grinning. "I used to be known as the man with a thousand faces." He reached out with two ruddy fingers to touch my cheek and I flinched and ducked back. "A thousand and one," he amended, his voice wistful.

Then he reached out rattlesnake fast, took my hand in both of his and shook it with great vigor. "Come," he said. "Come." He led me past a dust-glazed, empty concession counter and down a carpeted hall whose floor was lit on each side with a row of tiny white bulbs.

Through a set of open doors I glimpsed a leaf-carpeted stage crowded with very realistic looking trees; somewhere in the middle hung three pink, flickering faces, as though in their center there danced a flame shielded by the curve of a hand. A monotone voice droned unintelligibly. We continued past and then turned off into a small, cluttered office. Papers sat in askew piles atop rusted out file cabinets. The desk was a jumble of office supplies, some still in their boxes; more papers; unopened mail; and framed photographs of actors in leotards gesturing and mugging wildly. One picture depicted my interviewer himself, grinning madly under red stage lights, dressed in an elaborate costume of a many-legged spider with a blossom of sharp blades emerging from under its black mandibles. On the floor sat a variety of computer monitors ranging from the current to the antique.

The man kicked aside a monitor or two and pulled a wooden folding chair from the wall. He set it in front of the desk and went around the back to his swivel chair. "Well," he said. "Here we are."

"I have to ask," I said. "Why did you contact me, in particular?"

His eyebrows flew up his forehead one after the other, like startled centipedes. "Did I?" he said. "Did we? I had no idea you were coming. In fact..."—he plucked a tobacco-stained calendar from his desk and flapped it around—"I was supposed to be traveling today. It's only by happenstance that I'm here." He flung the calendar to the floor. It was from 1988.

"Is there a job opening?"

He laughed. "I guess that that depends on you."

Then he leaned back in his chair and closed his eyes. The only sound was that of the voice from the stage, far off, unintelligible, unceasing. When my interviewer's silence became uncomfortable, I launched into a description of my work history, from farm work in my early teens, to dishwasher to bookseller to file clerk. When my monologue came to an end, my interviewer did not respond. He sat still, eyes shut. He was very still. For a moment I thought maybe he'd died, or gone to sleep.

To rouse him, I said in a loud voice, "What brought you to the Storefront Theater?"

"Oh," he said, his eyes fluttering, "the interviewee has become the interviewer. How novel." His voice went wistful, dreamy. "What brought me here? Oh, conduits. Conduits and way stations, avenues and thoroughfares and waterways. Alluvial tunnels. Clandestine channels. Have I told you about my work as a personal assistant?"

"You've barely spoken a word since we started," I said. I was at this point eager to leave this madman and resume a serious search for employment.

"Ooh," he said, sitting up, his eyes widening. "I don't think you're supposed to raise your voice to your interviewer. A transgression. A spot of drama. I like that. I like the *gumption*. Moreover, it speaks to my anecdote regarding my work as a personal assistant.

"I was a young man, fuller in the face, full of piss and Windex. I worked for a man called Mortimer. I took his messages, arranged his meetings, booked his hotel stays and train travel. I fed and watered and walked Shard, his beloved Rottweiler. One day Mortimer, tired and worn from a night of drinking, failed to attend one of his own meetings, a meeting he had told me was 'terribly important.' He stormed to my desk, situated in a corner of his study, in a pique, berating me for failing to rouse him.

"I stood up," he said, "and came around the desk. I don't remember what I was saying. I just remember poking Mortimer repeatedly just below his collarbone. Shard began to bark wildly in his cage, butting his head against the door. Then everything went black. When I came to, I had locked Mortimer in Shard's cage. Shard himself was nowhere to be found. The man was a frightful mess. His eye was a swollen grotesquerie, his shirt undone. His face was a mask of blood. One of his fingernails had been torn off, along with some of his hair. Clumps of it sat about me on the Oriental carpet like silent watching animals."

As he told his story, a redness began in his neck and rose up to color his face. His hands climbed up and did their work, smoothing out his wrinkles and crow's feet, digging circles under his eyes, stretching out his cheeks. He tugged at the waves of hair above his ears, pulling out the dull grey color, leaving a more vibrant reddish-blond. He began to slam his fists on the desk, sending papers to the floor, causing his coffee mug to bounce and toddle, its contents splashing onto notebooks and papers, soaking into his desk blotter.

"For the better part of an hour I worked to convince him to simply fire me, to not engage the authorities. I begged. I cajoled. I promised to return to him my most recent paycheck and never darken his hall again. I must have worn him down. He let me go. I unlocked his cage and fled. Since that day, I've learned to show anger the door. I tamp it down, turn it away like the begging vagrant that it is."

"But I am angry now," he said. "At you."

"At me?" I said, incredulous and considerably annoyed.

He said, "You wake me at my house, my sanctuary, in the middle of the night..."

"Wait a minute," I said, holding up my hands. "It was someone from *your* Storefront Theater who woke *me*. At *my* house. I don't mind telling you, you people put a scare into me. If anything, I should be angry at you."

"Don't you *dare* try to turn this around on me," he said.

I stood, and swept my arm across his desk, knocking pens and paper to the floor. "You have wasted my time with this nonsense," I said. "You've called me here under false pretenses to...to *toy* with me. You have a place to go every day. You have a house, a sanctuary, a job to occupy your time and your thoughts. If I don't find work soon, I'll have nothing. Nothing. I will be on the street. I could have used this time to look for work."

"What about me?" he said. "My assistant died! Dead! Run down by Mr. White Noise's Mercury Sable, right in front of the theater, his body torn open like a sack of gore! I've had to do everything. Everything! The books! The booking! The stage direction and the cleaning! The phones! The search for his replacement has been a nightmare. Liars, deceivers, and the inept, the lazy, the dishonest, and the flippant! And you, insouciant and full of fictions and barely concealed insults."

He manipulated his face again, pulling outward, fattening his cheeks, tugging down jowls. He dragged his finger down along the side of his body, and his shirt and skin pulled apart, revealing a tangle of glistening pink and purple. Then he ran his finger back up, drawing closed the wound as though pulling up a zipper.

He smiled at me. "Theatrics," he said again. "All of it. Not to be believed." He tittered madly.

I wanted to knock him one in the jaw.

Instead I sat back down, exhausted. He put his hands up to his newly fattened face, worked his strange manipulations, and it was my face again. "Do you ever just get tired of it all?" he said. "Waking up every day, still you, always you? You wash your ridiculous body. You cover it with the same drab clothing. You think your tired, tepid thoughts, go about your routine, as everyone does. You ignore your proximity to oblivion. You eat joylessly, you mutter your pre-programmed inanities and get muttered at in return. Do you ever just get tired of it all?"

I stared at him, and his eyes softened. "Come work for me," he said. "I promise you only instability and fear, theatrics and distraction. Your duties will be to manage the day-to-day operations of the theater. You will pay the bills, negotiate contracts with the acts that I book. You will answer the phones, do all the maintenance and the cleaning. You may live in the unused projection room, which is equipped with a kitchenette and a toilet. There will be a modest stipend for your meals."

"Absolutely not," I said, and then from his mouth came the voice of my wife.

"Derek," she said. "Stop this." His hands went to his face. I closed my eyes. I could not bear to look. "When are you going to admit to yourself the truth?" my wife said. "When the doctor told us, your hand left my shoulder. You never touched me again, do you know that? You left me to be cared for by strangers. I needed your support the most then. I needed an ally and I got a ghost. What was it? Did I become ugly to you? Obsolete? A waste of your time?

"Look at me," she said, and I looked. Her face was gaunt, skeletal, grey, her eyes slack. Wisps were all that remained of her hair. Her lips were chapped and peeled, blistered. Green snot bubbled at the rubbed-raw edges of her nostrils. She smiled obscenely, and then raked her long fingernails along the top of her head, peeling away the skin. My interviewer's hair sat plastered underneath. She dragged her nails down her face then, the skin peeling away in curling ribbons. Underneath was white, greasepaint white, clown white. Black triangles hung below his eyes and his lower lip. I reached out to help him peel the skin away, and he reached for my hand in turn. When our fingertips met, I felt only a hard, flat surface, that of a mirror. I stood and rounded the desk, my hands out in front of me. My interviewer stood too, and came to meet me. The whole back of the office was a mirror. I pounded it with my fists and my interviewer mimicked my actions. Then I fled.

It was night, dark, dark, terribly dark. The bulb in my bicycle headlight popped and fizzled when I turned it on. I rode home. The house, which I had left dark, glowed brightly from every window. I heard a noise above me. Tied to the back of my bicycle seat was a string leading to a cloud of balloons that muttered and squeaked above me. I parked at the end of the road and untied the balloons. Carrying them, I ascended the porch and rapped on the door. The motion detector light came on. All inside was still and silent, though I did hear a brief rustle of clothing. I retreated down to the end of the walk and waited for the door to open. I wondered whose face would emerge from that silent house.

Deep into the Skin

T HE TOWN OF Hulse sits on a gnarled peninsula that juts from the face of Massachusetts like the chin of a Halloween witch. And me, I'm a Hulse beach rat, born and raised. I spent twenty-seven years breathing in the town's ocean air, absorbing its sand into the heels of my feet. Its name is inked into the skin over my heart. I never in a million years thought I'd leave. But I did, in the winter of 2007. I gathered whatever I could fit in my car and fled across the state to Springfield, and, brother, I'm never going back.

I ran my own shop back then. Mikey's Ink Chamber was the name, but I just called it The Chamber. We were at the far end of an unnamed strip mall on a long, desolate stretch of road between commercial districts. Most of the storefronts had long since been vacated; besides The Chamber, all that remained was a quiet electronics repair shop and The Wash Spot, a laundromat whose interior consisted largely of orange Out-of-Order signs.

It started on a February night, just before closing time. I was coming out of the scrub room when Susan, my cashier and bookkeeper, pushed her head through the black velvet curtains between my workstation and the sales floor. "The deposit slips are done and I've swept up," her disembodied head said. Then she stepped through the curtain, became a whole person again. "Do you want me to stay until you're done?"

"No need," I said. "I won't be long."

"Then...can you walk me to my car?"

Now, Susan may be small and slender, but she's a scrapper. A few years back a tough-looking girl had burst into the shop yelling something about getting one's own boyfriend and leaving other girls' boyfriends be. "Outside," Susan had said, and right there in the parking lot she climbed all over the girl like a spider with fists. Before the other girl knew it she was sitting on the curb with a black eye and a loose tooth, spitting blood into the snow.

So any other time this would have been an unusual request. But three nights earlier, Seasick Pete, my old mentor and the proprietor of Skull Kiss Body Art in nearby Deepwater, had been found murdered in his shop, sprawled and bloodied and broken in his chair. His t-shirt had been pulled up over his enormous belly, strange symbols carved deep into the skin around his navel. The killer had dragged Pete's machine all over his face and left it jammed into his mouth. They hadn't emptied the cash register. Instead they used it to stave in the side of poor Pete's head.

A local cop came by the night after the murder to question me. Did I know anyone mad at old Pete, someone maybe got a botch job, a misspelling, infection, whatever. I had no idea, I'd said. Pete had drifted out of my life some time back. Not that there was any animosity—he and I were just different. He was a mile a minute talker, one of those guys who tells you everything about himself within ten minutes of having met you. But he was a good guy, and had a good rep as an artist and a professional. When the cop was through with his questions, he gave me all the grisly details. It was like he was savoring them.

"It's one dead guy, Susan," I said. "I doubt someone's targeting medium-talent ink slingers. Maybe he got tangled up in dope, or townie bullshit. Think about the kind of customers he took on. Nothing to worry about."

"*Mikey*," she said, raising her painted-on eyebrows. "Would. You please. Walk me. To my car?"

I went to the back and grabbed my coat. We hurried across the lot through the frostbite cold, the wind lashing at our skin, stinging our eyes. The moon hung high up in the cloudless sky, thinner than an albino's eyebrow hair. The only significant source of light was the pollen-coated streetlight over Susan's rusted-out Corolla, flickering a bleary yellow, making the parking lot look like some old German movie. The other shops had closed. The road sat quiet, devoid of travelers, tourists long gone.

"Maybe they'll head over to BodyPunk and kill Dominant Gene," Susan said as she slid into the front seat and started the engine. "You never liked him."

She took off, engine revving. I jogged back across the lot and into the shop. I was in the back wiping down my workstation when I heard the bell jingle, which meant that Susan forgot her purse, as she always does. I went into the shop to give her shit about it and stopped cold.

Standing at the glass counter was a strange little assemblage of people, the most striking of the three a tall, curvilinear woman in a blinding white dress, with hair right out of a shampoo commercial. Next to her stood a squat, roundish man jammed into a black suit. He was bald but for a ring of longish white hair circling his head, tangled brown eyebrows like a toddler's scribbles. His papercut of a mouth was curled into a tiny frown. In front of the two stooped a dazed looking girl who couldn't have been much older than 18. She was short, shock-blonde, clad in shredded jeans and a faded black t-shirt whose iron-on logo had long since flaked away, leaving an abstract impressionist painting of reds and yellows and blues.

"We're closed," I said, and the man walked over to the door and locked it.

Oh God, I thought, they are going to kill me.

***

From my sophomore year up until the time I left Hulse, I was the kid who'd decided to never remove his Halloween costume. I hid my face under a fearsome beard. My closet was black as coal. I was all boots and buckles, tattoos and piercings: canine bites and the Earl, and three others known only to me and to the middle-aged masseuses who populate the neon-lit parlors that line Hog Island Boulevard. I'm six-foot, fuck-you inches too, but I can't help that. I also can't do anything about the scar that runs from the side of my nose up to my temple.

You want a laugh? Have a look at my freshman yearbook picture. The requisite plaid shirt, buttoned at the collar. A helmet of wavy brown hair, buck teeth framed in a counterfeit grin. A weak chin that melted into a neck better suited to a swan. I was a mama's boy by default, as Pop had decamped for sunnier, childless climes before I was old enough to know his name. A mama's boy without a mama, in fact, because she was taken from me a year before that picture was taken, stolen away by a relentless cancer that spread through her midsection like a spray of buckshot.

I was every name the rough kids hurled at me and more. A nerd, a spaz, a book jockey. My unofficial first tattoos were bruises the size of fists. So I buried that lost, anxious kid under layers of leather. I inked him up and I covered his face. But he was still here under all that costumery. Shy, diffident. Repelled by confrontation. A coward in the costume of a badass.

The scar? I didn't win it in some bar fight or arcade brawl. I was eight. I'd been riding bikes with the neighborhood kids, when Frankie Moore turned onto Stafford Road and came after me. I sped out onto Nantasket Avenue, right into the path of an old Cadillac. Guy in the car hit his brakes just as I hit mine. I somersaulted over the handlebars and slid on my face for a few yards, ending up in a heap at the curb. The driver screamed at me as Frankie beat it. For eight weeks my face was a horror show. What remains, mostly under the beard, is a patch of mottled, gravel-pocked skin. And the scar.

***

The man cleared his throat theatrically, and then spoke. His voice was the croak of a frog—a chain-smoking frog. "I understand that it's after hours," he said, "but I have a job for you, and it needs to be done tonight. Consider your life to be the compensation."

"I just have to get set up," I said, and the girl bolted. She hit the door, fumbled with the latch, and stumbled off into the night.

"Be right back," said the man, and he walked calmly through the door after her.

I have principles. I do. I know right from wrong, and good from bad, and I knew the minute I saw the dazed—let's face it, drugged—look in the eyes of that girl that this whole situation was very wrong, and very, very bad. And the moment she fled, I knew, at least as far as the fundamentals, why Seasick Pete lost his life. He, too, had principles. And he'd made the fatal mistake of fighting for them.

The woman shrugged and came around the counter, hips swiveling. She walked right into my personal space. "You're tall," she said. Her swollen lips shone a startling red. She smelled like strawberries and cigarettes. She leaned in, her breast pushing up against my upper arm, the tip of her nose touching my neck, those terrifying lips closing in. "And you smell good."

"It's just soap," I said, and the door slammed open. The man and the girl came in, his hand gripping the back of her neck. The girl was smiling now, her lips pulled up over her teeth in a pained smile. Her pupil were pinpricks, her terror tucked somewhere back behind them.

"Well, I see we're getting cozy," the man said. "That's good. Why don't you be a good host and show us in?"

I led the trio back into the work area. As I prepped the table, the woman pulled the girl's t-shirt over her head and dropped it on the floor, yanked at her jeans so that the waist rested just above her pubic bone. She might as well have been tearing the clothing from a doll. Then she grabbed the girl's hair and led her over to the chair as the man pulled from inside his coat a snapshot. He handed it to me.

It was a picture of an antique, dusk-blue Ouija-type board laying on an Oriental carpet. Across the top it read SCÉANCE BOARD in a lightning bolt font. Below that sat the letters of the alphabet in two frowning rows, then the digits one through zero in a straight line. On one side the word YES sat in the grinning mouth of a pointy-horned goat. On the other side the word NO in the frowning maw of a curly-horned ram. Below it all the word GOODBYE, written like dripping blood.

"The whole thing?" I said, failing to keep my voice from trembling. "The full length of her torso?"

"Yes." He ran a finger along her left side. She flinched. "The top here," he said. "That's important."

The girl began to weep. The man and the woman stared at me, hard-faced.

People come in drunk to get tattoos, I thought, *and I do it without a blink. They come in high, go under the needle at the urging of snickering friends. I don't turn them away. I can do this. Get through it. If I try to stop it, if I refuse, I'll be as dead as Seasick Pete, and it could go worse for her, prolong this nightmare. After, I'll call the police. I'll get the license number and report it. The minute they're gone. The minute I'm safe.*

Resolved then. I started the prep, telling myself this was just another job, a willing client. I made direct eye contact and I explained the process as I went. I used the tender, neutral tone I use for first timers. After a short time, her tears ran dry. She just stared at me with those big eyes, like she was concentrating. I soaped up a towel and gently ran it over the contours of her body. Her nostrils flexed slightly when I uncapped the rubbing alcohol and wiped her chest and stomach.

"Relax," I told her. "Breathe. In your nose. Out your mouth."

She did as she was told. Her breath was grape-flavored gum and animal fear.

"Have you eaten?"

She nodded.

"Then here we go."

I started up the machine. At the buzzing sound, she closed her eyes tightly. When the needle first touched her trembling flesh, she hissed. Tears welled anew in her eyes. I looked over at the couple and jerked my head toward the box of tissues on the counter. "Would you mind wiping her eyes?"

It was hard to keep the anger from my voice, the disgust. The woman looked at me fiercely and with defiance, but she did it.

For the next several hours, the only noise was that of the needle doing its work. I surprised myself by falling into my usual sort of trance state, as I would under normal circumstances—the room softened and shimmered, the walls retreating until they were a faraway blur, taking the grim watching pair with them. There was only me and the canvas of skin, and the work. I added my own small flourishes to the symbols on the séance board, elongating the letters, adding flames and fangs to the eyes of the goat and the ram. I felt no fear, only a hazy, prolonged ecstasy. It may have been the last peaceful moment of my life.

A few hours later, I blinked, and the room was back in focus. The job was complete. I felt hung over and drained. I applied the bandages and recited the boilerplate instructions for cleaning and caring for the new tattoo, handed the man an aftercare guide. Fear rushed back into my system, bringing with it a discomfiting pairing of nausea and powerful hunger. *Now they'll kill me*, I thought. But they didn't. The girl stood, shivering despite the heat, and slowly dressed herself. The three walked out into the showroom and I followed.

"Now," the woman said to the man. "It has to be done now."

I braced myself as the man walked along the glass counter, looking at the stuff for sale in the cases: skull rings, dog collars, temporary tattoos, knives, pipes and hookahs. He stopped, placed his fingertip on the glass just over a scorpion hand-guard serrated-edge Bowie knife. "That."

I opened the case-back and removed the knife with a trembling hand. I handed it to him. I considered begging for my life as he opened up the knife, examined the blade. Then he nodded at the redhead, who grabbed the girl by her neck and the back of her pants, lifted her, and slammed her face down on the counter so hard that the glass cracked. The man jumped up, one knee on the counter, the other pressed against her shoulder blade, straddling her neck. The woman hopped up and sat on the girl's calves. I backed up until my ass hit the far wall. I didn't avert my eyes. I wish I had.

With his left hand the man grabbed her arm and stretched it out over her head, with his right he began to saw through the flesh of her wrist. The girl screamed. Blood spurted and flowed, dripping down through the crack, into the case, cascading over the countertop on both sides and onto the tiled floor. Then he pressed down hard with the blade, veins standing out in his neck, until the bones broke, and then sawed the rest of the way through. Curled upon the glass like a frightened bug, the hand looked terribly small. The man snatched it up and slid it into the inside pocket of his jacket as though it was a billfold. Then the couple climbed down. The man pulled a cloth from his pocket and tied it around the girl's bleeding stub. Then threw her over his shoulder and without a word the three left. The bell echoed and faded. The silence was awful. I slumped to the ground. I sat there for about a half hour in a haze. Finally, I got up, put on some music, and set about cleaning up the place.

The next morning the bell woke me up. I was curled up on one of the couches in the loft where we display corsets and boots, t-shirts and bondage gear. I remembered standing there in tears the night before, the phone in my hand, physically unable to dial. I remember sobbing, gagging, vowing to kill myself. I must have collapsed from exhaustion. I heard the *clomp-clomp-clomp* of Susan's Doc Martens on the stairs, and I pushed myself up to a seated position. She screamed when she saw me, went a foot up into the air. I was terrified for a second that she'd fall backwards down the stairs. "Holy mother of God," she said, fluttering her hand over her heart. "You scared the shit out of me."

She stopped, sniffed the air like a cat. "I don't think this place has ever been cleaner," she said. "What got into you?"

I swung my legs over the side of the couch and held out my hand. She walked over, fishing a cigarette from her purse as she did so. She slid it between my fingers and sat down next to me. I lit the smoke with shaking hands, and shuddered.

"Do you want to talk about it?" she said.

"You know...I don't think I do," I said. "I'm going home."

She said, "Hey, did you know the counter's cracked?"

***

Hulse is a town on the decline. It's plagued by the perpetual reek of low tide, its downtown tainted by a heritage of corruption as old as the town itself. The old-style political corruption, of course, graft, bid-rigging, nepotism. But a darker kind of corruption too. Witch-cults and covens, summoning of the drowned, moon-worship. Longtime residents know by instinct to avoid the sagging shacks along the shoreline. They know to avert their eyes from the dim-lit windows of the houses hugging the cliff-face up to the triumvirate of giant wind turbines that spin in slow-motion like the arms of alien clocks.

It had once been a lively and garish place that housed an amusement park, two arcades, countless shops and restaurants and nightclubs. In the mid-nineties the federal government raided the park and shut it down, and the town's reputation of corruption and dark doings, long known locally, hit the front pages of the national papers. Now there are more shuttered shops than open ones. The less well-to-do tourists still file in in the summertime, lounge on the beach in sagging canvas chairs, pick up six-packs at Chuck Tuna's. They ride the restored carousel, the one remaining trace of that old amusement park. They drop their hard-earned savings at the ice cream shop and the crab shack. They sit on the benches with their steaming cups of Dunkin' and watch the seagulls dive and squeal.

It's the townies who stay, who pay for the sins of the disgraced and dead. I counted myself among them, though I managed to hold onto the vain idea that I would remain untouched by the darkness of the town. I kept to the good streets, steered clear of the fire-lit beach parties, and even routinely turned away the stoic, intense men who brought in crude illustrations of ideograms they wanted tattooed on their faces and bodies, arcane, rune-like symbols that filled me with an atavistic revulsion.

In fact, I sent them Seasick Pete's way, telling them he was a better free-hand artist than I, and guaranteeing they'd be happy with his work. It wasn't technically a lie. Pete dealt solely in blackwork, was known for his painstaking detail, thin lines, shading and stippling, deceptively intricate. It was said he worked like the devil was guiding his hand.

Everything I did to avoid the darkness was for nothing. I knew it after the events of that winter night, knew that I'd stayed too long. I was lashed to the town, sewn into its fabric like a long black thread.

So when the invitation arrived, I was not at all surprised. It was sitting in my mailbox among the red-lettered missives from angry creditors, scrawled in purple pen on an otherwise blank white card. *Dear Michael,* (it read), *You comported yourself remarkably well during our recent visit. I want you to know that I exhausted all other ways before resorting to the vulgar display to which I forced you to bear witness, and to take part in.*

This, as ugly as it was, is a last resort, my last attempt at my own version of a ritual that has failed again and again. Cruelty is an essential component of this hopefully final iteration. It is my wish that you join us for the finale. I feel as though all the parties present for the first part of the ritual must be present for the second part—the important part—to work.

I'm sending this invitation with the hope that you understand that your presence is non-negotiable. I'd like to spare us both the effort and unpleasantness associated with bringing you here by force or by coercion. There has been enough unpleasantness.

The invitation concluded with an address, and a date and time. I stared at it for a long while.

***

The tenement stood out stark against a sky bruised and charred like a body someone didn't want identified. Shadows cavorted in the few lit windows, as though people were capering to the same arrhythmic music. A line of red lights above the double-door entrance shone upward, illuminating a trio of bas reliefs depicting medieval figures with their arms raised to the sky. Some dug into their ears with strange, tapered tools. Others clasped both hands over their mouths. I walked through the open wrought-iron gate and approached the double doors. I tried the handle, fully expecting it to be locked, but it gave instantly, with a shriek of rust tearing away as the door, loose on its hinge, swung away from me and slammed against the wall.

Windowed doors stood at either end of the grey checkered lobby. I chose the one on the right and made my way up the cement stairs under dim fluorescent lighting. When I reached the door emblazoned with a black, peeling-paint **9**, I exited the stairwell into a well-lit, red carpeted hallway lined with doors. I continued along until I reached Apartment 9998. The door was metal, painted red, though the paint was peeled away in large swaths, like peeling skin after a sunburn. A fogged-over peephole stared at me like a cataract-clouded eye. A splotch of pink chewing gum faded to the color of flesh stuck like a barnacle by the knob. I knocked, and the door opened.

It was as though I'd walked into some other world. High ceilings, chandeliers like octopi gripping flickering candles in their many tentacles. The walls were hidden behind vast tapestries depicting old woodcuts: blank-faced men swinging truncheons at a tusk-fanged wolf; a woman crouched like a gargoyle on a church rafter as gape-mouthed parishioners stared and pointed from the V-shaped rows of pews below; winged infants with rat kings clutched by the tails in their fat little fists. The room was unfurnished save a long wooden table on which pyramids of incense sent tendrils of smoke up to the Romanesque tin ceiling.

Behind the table stood the trio from the shop. They wore red tunics. The man was noticeably thinner. One of his eyelids was swollen and discolored. Black bruises stained his cheeks and his breath came in terrible howls. The woman looked much the same as she had in the shop, but she seemed to glow with anticipation. She grinned at me. "Watch," she said.

The one-handed girl dropped her tunic. She lifted her breasts and looked at me with fury in her eyes. I avoided her stare and let my eyes fall down to the tattoo. In the candlelit room it seemed to vibrate, the letters shimmying, the goat and the ram mouthing psalms silent but surely blasphemous. I was stunned by the pride I felt—this was surely my finest ink work, a faithful reproduction of the intent of the original, but the small flourishes made it my own.

Then the curved point of a blade appeared from the hollow of the girl's throat. Her eyes widened, then the life drained from them as the blade slid back in like a snake retreating into its black tunnel, and blood spurted out in great arcs. The girl crumpled.

The man dropped the knife to the floor. It was in reach. I looked down at it.

"Now," the man said, pointing at the woman. His voice was barely audible. "It has to be now. Quickly."

He grabbed the girl under the armpits, his face crumpling with the strain. The woman grabbed her feet. They lifted her onto the altar. From the folds of his robe the man pulled the girl's severed hand. It was purple, stiff with rigor. Someone had inexpertly sewn the tip of the thumb to that of the index finger. The stench of putrefaction filled the room, beating back the aromas of the incense. I gagged. The man held the hand up to his eye and peered at me through it. He winked, but his expression was humorless.

He placed the hand below the proscenium arch of the girl's rib cage.

The woman and the man stood together behind the altar. They let their tunics fall to the floor. The man's chest was caved in and bruised, nipples like tiny black pebbles. The woman's breasts hung over a pregnant stomach. They put their hands on the grisly planchette, gestured with their eyes for me to join them. I did. Their skin was cool—the cold of the dead hand imbued everything with a growing chill.

The man cleared his throat to speak, and instead his knees buckled. He grabbed the side of the table and a series of hoarse sobs wracked him, veins standing out on his neck. The woman stroked his head, leaned over, and whispered into his ear. He straightened.

"Are you here, Carolyn?" he said, his voice trembling, breaking. The streams of smoke from the incense curled into ribbons. They shimmied in the dim light of the chandeliers. The curled dead hand shook and shivered and slid over to YES. The man gasped. He looked at the woman, his eyes wide. "It's working. It's actually working."

"Focus, Nicholas," she said, her eyes wide. "I'm not sure how long she can stay on this side."

Nicholas nodded, blinked back tears. He cleared his throat. "Tell us," he said. "Please—tell me what you see?"

The dead hand grew warmer. It began to swell. A split appeared in the skin, revealing yellow fat with brown striations. The three of us yanked our hands away when it got too hot to touch. The hand twitched. The fingers rubbed against one another. It slid over to NO. Then it flew around the letters, but too quickly to read, the rapid-fire rant of a madwoman. A blue and powdery mist came off the body as the hand flew from letter to letter. It formed a twister and then dissipated into the air.

The tattoo began to fade, and in its place bulged the features of a large and screaming face.

"That is not Carolyn," screeched the old man.

A high-pitched scream tore across the room. It was the woman. Black splotches had begun to form on her forehead. They rolled down her face like tears of ink. New lines sprung from a beauty mark on her cheek, swirling like vines around the vertical lines. Acrid smoke poured out of the lines and swam to the ceiling as she fell to her knees. She looked up at me, her breath coming in terrible howls. Her eyes began to sizzle in their sockets, and then they burst, spraying like milk. I turned to run and the man stood before me. His eyelids blackened and withered as though eaten away by invisible fire, his eyes bursting just as the woman's had. He opened his mouth to speak, and his teeth exploded into powder, forming a cloud of white around his head. Wounds appeared on his tongue as though it was being strafed with fire from a miniature machine gun. Thin black lines burst across his forehead like a spider's web and ran down his face like tears, pinpricks of black spreading out from them like magnetic filings, pimpling his face. He made a terrible gurgling noise.

I ducked past him and hit the door running. It was only after I bounded down the hall and burst into the stairwell, after I took the stairs four at a time, my breath bursting in shouts from my lungs, only once I collapsed on the beach near the tidal pools and the concrete steps, that the revelation came to me...that of the details I had missed in that frenzy of blood and smoke—the face that bulged from the torso of the dead tattoo was a face I'd known. And I'd recognized the lines that had torn apart the faces of the man and the woman, the thin lines, the intricacy. It was not Carolyn—she was gone, her suffering done. No, it was Pete who had been summoned that night, Pete who took his bloody revenge.

***

It was that night, ten years ago today, that I fled Hulse. If you'd known me back then, you wouldn't recognize the man who addresses you now. The holes from my piercings have closed. I'm clean-shaven, gaunt but pot-bellied. I dress in whatever Walmart throws onto its discount racks at the end of each season. I live in a two-room apartment, no posters on the walls. I go to my temp job in a featureless high-rise. I come home. I eat take-out and watch television that numbs my mind until I fall asleep. Every morning I check the mirror. The black spot under my right eye, which I discovered in my rearview mirror on the road out of Hulse, has stayed the same size. Until this morning. It may have elongated, just slightly. The discovery sent a jolt coursing through my body. For the first time in a long time, I spoke to Pete. I talked to him all day. Remember hanging out at the shoreline, Pete? You bobbing out past the breakers, making fun of me for not daring to wade in past my ankles, me digging up mussel shells with my toes and looking out at the distant lights of Boston? Drinking on the rocks, flicking our cigarettes into the cove? What you must have thought, seeing me in that room. Please forgive me, Pete. Please spare me. I never had a choice.

Go to the Devil

ERIC SAINTE-DENIS HAD just settled into the warmth of the bath when the shrill ring of the telephone sounded in the sitting room and was cut off almost immediately. Sitting very still in order to quell the lapping of the water, he could just discern Marybeth's hushed and hurried tones, her voice perhaps louder than she would have wished in the wake of the jarring ring.

He looked around the room, at the décor he and Marybeth had chosen together in happier times: the deep blue tiles with specks of black; his-and-hers towels hanging side by side on the stainless-steel rack; the tilted mirror over the antique sink in which he could just make out his reflection through the steam, an oblong, featureless figure of pale white. He regarded the framed artwork on the wall, painted by Marybeth in her brief but piquant artistic phase: a dark cobblestone path between ancient, moss-mottled stone houses, a rose and charcoal sky above beetling cliffs topped with grasses dangling like hair.

He fought against the fury that threatened to overtake him. Surely the love that he and Marybeth had once had could be regained. But how could that happen if she kept secrets, spoke clandestinely over the phone, perhaps even spoke ill of him and his husbandly failings with her cackling friends or...or *suitors*. No. He could not ...*would not* quiet his wounded heart. He rose sopping wet from the pedestal tub, whipped his robe about him, and barged dripping into the sitting room, where she was just resting the receiver in its cradle.

The tableau was one he was certain would stay with him until his last day: Marybeth, seven months pregnant, in her night clothes, leaning forward from her high-backed chair, tendrils of hair hanging down to light on her bosom, the light from the crystal lamp casting shadows on her pale face, lending her the aspect of a jack o' lantern carved from a Lumina pumpkin, her fingers long and lovely, a dizzying length of unblemished alabaster leg revealed by her displaced gown, the backdrop of the lights of the city winking like a billion bright eyes behind the wall-to-ceiling windows.

"It's Rutherford," she said, breaking the spell with that loathsome name. "His mother has passed and he is just...*ill* with grief. He needs me to come to him. He really has no one, Eric."

"Of course she has," Eric replied. "And of course he is. And of course he does."

Something in his voice made her bring her hands to her round belly. He felt his face redden, his ears grow hot. That she would feel the compulsion to protect his own as-yet unborn scion, the seed of his proud loins—

The room went red, and then black. In a blink he was in the bath again, scrubbing furiously at his arms, baying like a werewolf at a harvest moon, and in another blink he was in the Stutz SV16, motoring through the saturnine streets of London to Rutherford's family compound. A light rain fell. Spectres teemed in the streets under umbrellas jostling like black motes. Far off sirens complained. The scenery flickered by, a sped-up film in black and white. The car purred like a great cat pursuing its prey.

The shock on Rutherford's face when he opened the door was, to Eric Sainte-Denis, worth a dozen Marybeths.

"Is she with you?" Rutherford said, his voice high and wavering. And then he fainted dead away.

Marybeth had caught Rutherford's eye at a lavish party hosted by Baron Thwackwaite in his Orfordshire manor. Or, rather, her bosom had caught his eye. Eric had spied him performing some kind of cruel pantomime on the balcony, gaunt and lank-haired, a thin man with the swollen, jowly face of a fat man, set in a wily and untrustworthy mien, as one afflicted with dwarfism. A round glass of Chardonnay sat precariously in his loosely cupped, swaying palm. Once his physical comedy was complete, he'd begun speaking unctuously (one need not have heard him to discern his tone) to the Baron and his daughter, who were facing him, backs to Eric and Marybeth, when he glanced past the pair and his mouth stopped moving and his eyes widened. With a dumbstruck expression he begged his host's pardon and bee-lined toward the couple, a wretched grin affecting bonhomie further warping his already disagreeable face.

"I do not believe," he said to Marybeth, sparing Eric the merest glance, "I have previously made your acquaintance, you lovely thing, and only now do I discover I've been very much the worse for it."

Eric suppressed a mighty groan and introduced her as his wife, attempting to maintain a neutral tone, and not succeeding. Rutherford glanced at him again, just long enough to dismiss him, and, undaunted, pressed on. "It is as though you are carved from soap. Might I ask you to dance?"

Aloysius Rittle, a physician friend whose counsel Eric often kept, had informed him on more than one occasion that anger is always a secondary humour, that it frequently masks something else, something deeper down in the psyche. The good doctor, a walrus-like man with prodigious jowls and runaway whiskers, often endeavoured to persuade Eric to examine himself carefully to locate whatever the mysterious primary humour might be. But when Eric was overtaken, he was scarcely inclined to introspection. His more immediate and practicable course of action was to tamp it down, stifle it, bury it under a façade of nonchalance. As Rutherford and Marybeth danced, this he did. As, over the course of weeks, a friendship developed between them, this he did. As he intercepted, read, and destroyed fervent and pleading letters Rutherford had dared send his wife through the post, this...he...*did*.

Eric dabbed the tips of his thumb and forefinger with spirit of hartshorn from a small phial he'd discovered in Rutherford's washroom and pinched the prone man lightly on the columella. Rutherford hissed and jerked away with a volley of curses, clawing at his nose, and tried to scramble backward, but was prevented from doing so by the back of the chaise lounge. He looked harassed and haunted in his garnet-coloured smoking jacket and robe, slippers hanging from his toes, hands still flailing about his face. Eric noted that the man's fingers, which he'd typically kept bare, were encircled with rings bearing insignias of dark and diabolical portent, symbols which Eric himself had encountered in the adventuring days of his youth; and whose power, in the hands of twisted, wicked men, had, in

Mönchengladbach, killed or driven insane seven of Eric's good friends and compatriots.

Looking now around Rutherford's study, among and atop the high shelves teeming with gorgeously bound books bearing names such as Huysmans, Catullus, and titles such as *Libellus Vox Larva* and *The Codex Gigas*, Eric's eyes swept across all manner of appurtenances of black magic: scrying bowls; wands of hazel; obscene statuary; jars occupied by unidentifiable biological masses suspended in gelatinous goo; cylindrical containers filled with powders, grains, and flakes of drab colouring; the skulls of animals; a slightly dented censer with a rusted chain; a withered, ensanguined human hand as brown as tree bark.

Rutherford cried out, giving him a start. "I am afraid," he said.

"Of what, exactly? Of me?"

The prone man laughed, but no mirth touched his features. Then he paused, as if distracted by a stray thought. His brow furrowed. He looked for all the world like a man on a stage who'd forgotten his next line. Then he blinked and seemed to recover his focus. "Of the darkness inside me."

When Eric scoffed, Rutherford shook his head fervently. As he said this next, his voice rose in volume and pitch until it reached a terrible level of frenetic, panic fear: "No, I do not speak in code nor subtext. The literal dark tunnels and crevasses and folds inside my physical body, past which blood flows and organs squelch and push up against one another. Sometimes I feel as though I reside in there too, not as my brain resides in my skull, but as my very spirit or soul is lost in that wet and fragile tangle. Lost and frightened, with no hope of ever finding my way out."

Eric slapped him hard across the right cheek and he gasped. He rubbed his reddened face and pouted, staring up at Eric like a scolded pup.

Eric crouched and laid his palm on Rutherford's forehead. It was hot as a furnace, and clammy. Grimacing, he wiped it on the pathetic man's smoking jacket. He glanced around the room again. "What have you been up to here?"

Rutherford snuffled and wiped again at his face, pulled his hair into unruly spikes. "I'm not like you. I never had a leg up. No wealthy parents to boost me. No good looks to coast on. Everything I've had, I've worked for. I was just tired. I'm just tired."

"What are you on about?"

"There is no shame," he said, "in asking for help."

"Help? Help from whom?"

Rutherford turned his face away, unable to look Eric in the eyes. "The Goat of Mendes," he said. "The very devil himself.

"He needs the weakest within these walls—the most vulnerable...in this case, a child, even unborn. He favours a younger vessel. Passing from one to another, or back into his own realm from a human vessel, is apparently gravely damaging."

"Blast! You were not after Marybeth at all!"

"Marybeth? I gave up on her long, long ago. What competition am I against the great Duke Sainte-Denis? Look at you. The perfectly shaped mustaches. The silver hair slicked back, not a strand out of place. What chance would I ever have had against those piercing, commanding eyes? No. Not Marybeth. Not with a wretch such as I. Try as I may, she was ever yours."

Eric felt as though he'd been socked straight in the solar plexus. His mind reeled. Marybeth—innocent! He would go to her immediately, he thought. Except...he could not anymore, could he? But why not? He closed his eyes and saw himself standing atop the cliff in Marybeth's painting. In this vision, Eric's hair was a blood-soaked tangle. A bloody handprint like a giant spider stained his face. His clothes were blood-sotted, his eyes wild. Fangs as white as marble protruded from his mouth. He blinked and shook the vision away. Confusion grabbed hold of him. He breathed, and then rage once again filled his heart. The enormity—the *profanity*—of Rutherford's abominable plan clouded everything.

"You were after my unborn child. You must stop the ritual at once!"

Rutherford laughed bitterly and his features crumpled like a November leaf. "The ritual began before you arrived, Eric. The saliva mixed with the evocation oils. The altar desecrated. Can't you feel it? The air is...electric. The summoned one has all but materialized. All that's left to do is utter the incantation. If I don't, the devil's rage will savage this house and both of us inside it."

"And which demon did you summon, you fool, you thick, feckless tyro?"

"I...I don't..."

"You don't know? You thought that any random demon would simply do your bidding, bend the world to your will? Did you put your finger at random on the page of a grimoire and begin reciting?" His face told Eric he'd likely done just that...or something similar.

"Rutherford, demonology and the occult have been my life's study. There are 7,405,926 demons, according to Talmudic calculations. There are more than that, I suspect. Who did you summon? Vepar, to vanquish an enemy with putrefying wounds? Abigor, to kindle lust and foment war? Morax, that you might know the secrets of the stars? I suppose you know of Grivvonus and Mastorcalum. No? They are *mazziquin*: mischievous spirits a botched or half-hearted summoning can call forth. And they in turn open the door to more demons of their cavalier and capricious choosing, demons who will bring only chaos, destruction, and pandemonium."

"I am certain I performed the invocation successfully," Rutherford replied, his darting eyes belying his insistent voice. "And when Ypos arrives, I shall enter with him into a *pactum expressum*. I will be handsome, Eric. I will gain courage, and wisdom. I shall finally take something from the world that has cursed me with this hideous face and bearing, the world that has taken everything from me."

"So what happens now? Will he be born from you? From me? If it's one or the other, I'm taking my leave. I'll gather my team—Mukasa Ononibaku, the blind Ugandan priest; Luciana Altamirano, the Segovian white witch; the estimable Bonifacius van der Westhuizen—and we shall surely take down whatever damnable thing—or things—you've unleashed, even if we have to call forth the great bearded Lahmu to dispel them!"

Rutherford climbed to his feet, laughing.

"Taking your leave? Ha! You may try to...I suspect... Oh, do try to leave, Eric. I want to see it."

Eric turned on his heel and flung open the door. The far-off lights of the city cast a penumbral luminescence over the treetops and the stars were profligate in the sky.

He turned and glared red daggers at Rutherford. "You brought this on yourself, you cunning monster," he said.

"Who is the monster? I see the blood under your fingernails, Eric, the wild look in your eyes. You've come unhinged." A light came on behind his eyes and he squinted. "Have you...done something?"

Eric flinched. *Had he...done something?*

Torn clothing. Bloody hair attached to patches of torn-away skin. Teeth flying in the air like shrapnel. Bone and muscle, chunks of fat. An impossibly small, breathing thing, its tiny, confused life ebbing away into Oriental carpeting.

"You did, didn't you?" Rutherford said, the accusation dripping from his voice. "You dare call me monster? Tell me you yourself don't deserve that epithet, and I will call you out as a liar!"

Eric stepped forward and swung with all his might, his hard fist connecting solidly with Rutherford's jaw. The latter stumbled backward and fell hard on his tailbone. His head hit the floor with a resounding thud that echoed through the house. He was still breathing, Eric noted.

Eric had much to do. He stepped through the doorway toward the car and was suddenly stopped by some invisible force. It felt as though he'd encountered a tough, tensile lattice made of unbreakable filaments, like the spinnerets of some alien species of spider. His face and chest burned from the contact. He tried to force his way through, ignoring the searing pain in his hands, until his skin began to sizzle and smoke.

He looked down. This unseen force field emanated upward from a line of spilt white crystals that curved off in both directions on the ground before him, entrapping the house in its impenetrable border—impenetrable, that is, from the inside only, for one could enter, as Eric had, but not leave. He would have to go back inside and telephone for reinforcements. Time was of the essence.

Stepping back over the threshold, he discovered Rutherford was gone from the front room. A staircase spiraled up to a balcony-ringed second storey. He ascended, listening for any noise, and inspected each room in turn. Nothing. He went back down to the first floor and found in the rear of the house a trap door under a runner of carpet on which dragons gamboled and leering monarchs and grimacing concubines cavorted in a succession of obscene, contorted embraces. Peeling back the runner, he kicked at the ancient, rusted padlock until it sprung.

The cellar of Rutherford's home had been converted into an occult dungeon of exquisite evil. Great brass sigils adorned one red-painted wall under punishing lights. On the other, horseshoe-shaped wall, here and there interrupted with doorways shielded by red curtains, a vast mural displayed legions of decrepit, elderly, liver-spotted men grappling erotically with voluptuous, callipygian succubi in a clearing in a sylvan wood. Among and between them infant devils pushed their swirling, curlicue tongues. Above, approaching the tin ceiling, the clouds in the painted sky suggested a time-savaged skull watching impassively over the obscene proceedings.

Chandeliers of bone, browned and desiccated flesh stuck to them like peeling decals, dangled from cobweb-strewn chains from the low ceiling above. A dark-stained oak prie-dieu bore a mighty tome open to the center pages, a red ribbon dangling from the spine like the hyper-extended tongue of a serpent. A rat the size of a small dog traversed the outer edge of the room and disappeared into a rupture in the floor by the red wall.

Eric stepped forward and his foot met a slight resistance. He angled his shoe away to reveal a small, curled-up thing like a snail out of its shell. Crouching to get a closer look, he recoiled. It was a human toe. Grasping it by either side of the nail, he picked it up and examined it, turning it between his thumb and forefinger. A tuft of black lint lay just under the quick of the nail and a whiff of dead skin and sock debris assailed his nostrils. He hissed and flicked away the offending digit, and then came the laughter—the laughter of what sounded like two different men: Rutherford's mad titter and a low, grim chuckle just beneath it.

Rutherford emerged from a rift in the curtains, bare-chested, in silk pyjama pants, black and yellow, the colors of death and quarantine, his stomach protruding, veins pulsing eel-like in his forearms. Sure enough, the middle toe on his right foot was missing.

Palas aron azinomas, he sang in a wavering baritone. *Tetragrammaton Elohim. Elohim Gibor. Eloah Va-Daath. Retragsammathon.*

"Cut!"

The actors stopped and turned. Rising from the director's chair, the man in the sweater, the ascot, and thick-framed glasses stormed onto the set, shoulders hunched dodging the boom mics, a look of confused consternation on his face.

"What the devil was that, Patrick? You're off script!"

Patrick shrugged. "You've given my chap Rutherford a line of gibberish here, Terence. I was simply aiming to inject a little...authenticity."

"But where..."

Christopher, shaking off the role of Eric like a robe, let his shoulders sloop.

"Gentlemen," he said. "I don't suppose anyone would mind terribly if I were to sit until you fellows sort all this out? I've contracted something of a virus recently, I'm afraid, and my muscles are quite sore."

"By all means," Terence said dismissively, as the actor pulled a chair in from off-set and reclined, lighting a cigarette and inhaling deeply, exhaling a cloud of blue smoke and sighing through the exchange that followed.

"Patrick," Terence said, his voice straining, trepidation showing in his glare. "From whence came that incantation?"

Patrick walked over to the wall of prop books, pulled one from the shelf.

"This," he said, holding forth a cobweb strewn tome with the title *Libellus Vox Larva*.

"Let me see that."

Terence snatched it from his hands and flipped through it. His face went white. "This was not on the prop list," he muttered to himself. "Who put this here?" Cast and crew shrugged as one.

Christopher coughed loudly, causing all present to turn their faces toward him. He winced, and then began to sputter and choke, his eyes reddening and filling with tears. Rising from his chair, he started to speak, then sniffled and snorted, his hands going to his throat, then to his face. As the cast and crew watched in horror, two long, black insects pushed themselves from his nostrils. Long as rack-stretched snakes, their whisker-thin legs pushed at his reddened nose, diamond-shaped heads bearing eyes like clusters of blisters tilting this way and that.

They broke free and launched from his face, gossamer wings peeling away from their sides and whirring in the air. They were humanoid, at least five feet long, with dangling legs, and horns like black thorns. Their buzz was as some foul, cancerous fart from the devil's very asshole. With tremulous, inhuman voices they began to chant indecipherably in a demoniac duet.

Christopher lurched forward, twin tendrils of pinkish-blue mucus swinging from his nostrils, and then stopped dead in his tracks. He raised his hands as though to clear his nose, but then stopped. His hands hung there in the air, paralyzed.

His eyes bulged from their sockets, causing his lids to withdraw, and pushed their way out with nearly simultaneous pops, spilling down his cheeks, along his lapels, and onto the floor. Festering black tendrils slithered from the newly vacated sockets, each tipped with a triad of sharp pincers that snapped blindly at the air. A large chunk of his forehead broke loose and tumbled away like termite-corrupted wood. A bit of skull popped as though from a small explosive charge,

MATTHEW M. BARTLETT

propelling a chalky cloud into the air where it floated like an indecisive ghost.

Christopher cried out in a deep and guttural voice not his own as he dug his fingertips into his chest. He tore his flesh away as though he was undoing a bathrobe, revealing a ribcage packed with organs. Two sets of char-black fingers poked out from between his ribs and pushed open the double-doors of bone with a sound like a board being split by a strongman. One of the ribs snapped, tearing into the organs underneath, which ruptured, spilling out great gluts of vermillion blood as red as fresh paint. As the crew fled, Terence and Patrick backed away from the stricken actor, mindful of the spreading red pool as he lifted the hood of his face to reveal the grinning skull beneath.

"We have to stop this," Terence cried. He turned to Patrick and seized him by the lapels. Patrick punched the director hard in the jaw, splitting his cheek, and then fled the soundstage, dodging hulking cameras and knocked-down chairs, spilled brandy, stepped-on cucumber sandwiches, and great large wires like black snakes; out through the studio door and into the hallway. Past offices and workshops, where for the moment hustle and bustle continued as normal, studio hands carrying props, trays of tea, nests of microphones. Finally he found an outer door and stumbled down the fan-shaped staircase.

Twenty panic-soaked minutes later, Patrick attained his luxury flat that spanned the entire top floor of Abseyworth Estates. Rushing about the room, he turned on all the lights, even opened the refrigerator to let its cold luminescence into the room.

What had he done? Why had he brought in that wretched book? Was it despair? The fear of slow deterioration and death in a life without drama, a terrible ironic fate to befall an actor? A sense that the world had gone mad and needed punishing?

The apartment trembled and a faraway rumble sounded. He went to the window and looked out over London. It lay spread before him in its decaying majesty and he watched, wide-eyed, as it was overtaken.

The ground shook as concussive blasts ruptured cobblestone streets. Windows shattered to knives, shards, and powder. Rubble filled the air, from microscopic fragments to great craggy shards and massive boulders, exploding out in all directions. Cathedral spires shot into the air like great grey missiles, coming down point-first into florists' shops, daycare centers, fields of sport. Fissures opened up in the earth; whole motorways tilted, spilling cars and lorries deep into earth-lined crevasses. Sirens called over one another and idiots shouted a babel of contradictory nonsense from loudspeakers. Dogs howled and people screamed.

And behind it all, a great rose and charcoal cloud climbed the beetling grass-wigged cliffs and launched into the stratosphere where it would surely stain the stars, swallow the moon, and taint the nearer precincts of outer space.

The Master of the House

*T*HE HOUSE STANDS *solid, stolid, and firmly anchored on the plot where it was built over two-hundred and fifty years ago by now long-dead workers, on Crescent Street in Leeds, Massachusetts, its foundations hemmed in by tall and impenetrable hedges, its cupola and hooded dormers brushed by treetops. Night falls quickly, its shadow sliding over the town like a soft sheet. The world seems to pause as though drawing in a breath. The house emits a loud and wavering creak, trying out its voice after decades of sleep. Then it sighs. It stirs. The house is newly possessed of a need, right down to its joists, its slats, its ancient nails. What happens next happens quickly, as the world exhales: the house splits in two, then into quarters, then into a thousand dusky fragments, then to powder. A revelation. Ecstasy and exultation. Glory in black dust. Surprised wires sputter sparks as they fall to the ground. A calico cat stares from a neighbor's second-story window, its pupils narrowing to slivers in its glowing green eyes as the edifice dismantles and disembarks. Bats swim in the new air of its absence, calling to one another with wordless questions.*

***

Christopher Conte lay face up in bed, mouth agape, lost in a dream. He was back in Leeds, all the way across the country, standing outside Serio's Family Market under a scarlet sky streaked with black clouds. The opaque glass doors parted to grant him passage to an aisle lined by floor-to-ceiling shelves of amber prescription bottles, like an avenue of window-walled skyscrapers reflecting a sickly orange sunset. It was cold in the market, and he buttoned his flannel shirt as he walked. From the loudspeakers a female voice slurred some old 'seventies song about people not staying in one place anymore. He reached the end of the aisle, turned left. Before him on either side sat frost-gilded bins piled with rotting vegetables: shrunken potatoes sprouting gnarled limbs; browned broccoli; bruised, blackened tomatoes collapsing into themselves. The buzz of flies underscored the singer, who now wept along to the music.

His father, dead nine years now, stood in the aisle, swishing a dried mop from side to side. It whispered on the cement floor. His knuckles were bloodied and his fly was down. He looked up at Christopher. A cluster of rusted nails filled each of his distended eye-sockets. His bald head was sunburned, but efflorescent white at the crown. Foul motes swarmed him like Sphaerocerid flies around a crumpled melon.

His father opened his mouth and his teeth and tongue were termite-torn hardwood. The wood began to expand, splitting his cheeks. His head burst open like a flower, the petals of his skull stretching into rippling curtains that now framed a door-lined hallway at the far end of which shone a sickly sepia light. Heat emanated from his father's exploded cranium, along with the aromas of a freshly stoked fire, burning wood, old newspaper going orange and black at the edges. The hallway expanded and grew, blotting out the walls of the market, until the doorway stood open before him. He stared down at the threshold where the market tile ended and the broad boards of the hallway floor began. He put his foot across, touching the toe of his shoe to the floor. Behind him, the singer began to sob from the loudspeakers as the music was overtaken and subsumed by the increasing volume of the buzz of the market flies, a radio stuck between stations, the outraged roar of some beast torn away from its kill. He passed over into the hallway.

***

The house moves at night: a seething mist of thwarted love and of rage. One might spy a thin, ropy cloud, longer than long, darker than black, snaking along the tree line, slipping past the moon, winding its way through the night sky—a mist of flies, black-cloaked maggots, corrupted motes, powdered coffin glass. It goes to ground when the horizon begins to glow red, and then it reassembles, staircases swirling up to meet newly formed floors, faded Oriental carpets stitching themselves across the boards, framed paintings—a bright flower garden under a sun-brightened canopy of leaves; men on horseback on a fog-enshrouded battlefield; ripe, robust fruit clustered in a wooden bowl —growing like moss on walls while wainscoting sprouts, panel after panel, under rafters reaching into an incrementally disappearing sky. Beams like arms intertwine, earth crushes into earth underground as the fieldstone-walled cellar pushes outward and fills up with rusted buckets, piles of wood, shrouded chairs, the propped-up cadavers of ancient floor lamps, as pipes

*unfurl along the ceiling and sprout cobwebs that hang in long tendrils.
Chairs and tables grow up from floors, chandeliers bloom like glass
flowers, windows like water spread into waiting frames. A furnace
uncrumples from shadows and grows arms. The* oeil-de-boeuf *opens
above the pediment, aims its baleful gaze at the street before it. The
house settles and sighs, waits again for dusk.*

*The first night it lands on a quiet street in Albany, New York, the
next on a patch of disused farmland in Locust, Pennsylvania. Gahanna,
Ohio. Hawkins, Indiana.* (That old house? It's always been there.
Unusual architecture for this town. Second Empire, I think that kind
of house is called. Or is it Georgian? Check out the mansard roof, the
arched windows. Imagine the view from that tower. I've never seen
anyone come or go, never seen the lights on. It's just one of those
little mysteries—every small town has one.) *Thusly it works its way
westward, carrying with it its history, physical and ectoplasmic. The
echoing moans of orgies, the thuds of fists on flesh, disconsolate weeping
and triumphant laughter. And human effluvia: thwarted spermatozoa,
night sweat, snot. Blood violently rerouted. Pus and piss, oils and hairs.*

***

Christopher opened his eyes in the darkness. Found the slender green
numbers of the alarm clock. 2:50 a.m. Kayla lay sprawled next to him,
snoring lightly. He reached out and put a hand on her upper arm to
feel her warmth, her solidity. He slid his hand down to her waist and
squeezed lightly. Then he slipped from the bed and out of the room.
The moon lit his path through the neatly ordered office, down the
silent white hall to the stainless-steel kitchen, where with a trembling
hand he poured himself a glass of milk and looked out the window at
the scattered array of stars over the saw tooth condominium roofs
across the parking lot.

It had been at least a year since he'd dreamed of his father, and he
was dismayed that the man had made a reappearance, especially one
so gruesome. Hank Conte had died of a cerebral hemorrhage three
years after Christopher had turned 18 and fled Massachusetts for
faraway Portland, Oregon. He did not return for the funeral; he had
called his mother and given empty condolences. Although she recited
words typical of a widow in a miasma of mourning, there was a
shimmer in her voice he'd never heard before: she sounded happy for
the first time since he'd known her. At least there was that.

He felt not the slightest sliver of shame when he found himself hoping his father had experienced fear at the moment of his death. Fear, and pain.

He lifted his hands, regarded them in the moonlight. He curled them into fists. As he'd filled out over the years, put on muscle and weight, his hands had begun to resemble those of old Hank, thick-fingered, full-palmed. He remembered Hank Conte's fists more readily than the man's face, which had receded into his memory until it was a blurred thing, puffy-eyed, weak-chinned, and stubble-scarred. Maybe a mustache, or just the shadow of his whiskey-swollen nose. The fists though, Christopher could call immediately to memory in high definition, crisp resolution, 3D, 1080P, hairy, thick fingers squeezed together, forming a stone, or maybe a club hammer, two of them, raining blows on Christopher's forehead, shoulders, collarbone with terrible thuds of fists on flesh. For the sin of kicking at Hank's legs while he was choking the life out of Christopher's mother.

Hank had chased him from the kitchen, where his mother lay striving desperately for air, out the front door, to the walk, where he grabbed Christopher by the hair and spun him around. This time it was like the man had twenty fists instead of just two. He fell to the ground, as much from the shock and the pain as from the sheer inability to comprehend what was happening. Hank leaned forward, grabbed a handful of Christopher's shirt—a shirt that he had bought Christopher at JC Penney, saying he would look like a man in it—and pulled back his fist for a blow that Christopher was certain would crush his skull like a hollow chocolate bunny. He pulled back, and to his—and Hank's—surprise, the shirt slipped free, and Christopher got his feet under him and ran.

Now, standing at the kitchen window, he felt his fingernails digging into his palms and unclenched his hands. He rubbed them over his face, through his hair. For weeks, maybe months, he had felt faded somehow, not entirely real, or not fully there, trapped behind gauze. He could not pick out a moment when it had started, no trigger, no event. He asked Kayla to repeat herself so often that she had joked—or half-joked—about his hearing going. He found himself getting up from his chair at the close of a work meeting in a dull panic, having no earthly idea of what the meeting had been about. He went from place to place as though by rote, and could not account for his days at the end of them. Sleep, even just the anticipation of the thrall of justifiable unconsciousness, was his sole source of relief. He thought of retreating into drink, but he'd never touched a drop, for fear it might ignite in him the violent rages that had taken over Hank Conte the first time whiskey had touched the old man's lips. Booze had killed whoever his father might have become before Christopher had had a chance to mourn the loss. The risk that he might raise a hand to Kayla—to anyone—was not worth whatever relief drinking might provide. He toyed with thoughts of suicide, but even that would require a series of willful acts, an unthinkable break from routine.

But now, at three a.m. on a Saturday morning, woken from a fathoms-deep sleep, he felt energized, felt the edge and dip of every pore, stood in the bright light of full awareness and the heightening of every sense. His feet against the linoleum. The low hum of the refrigerator. The lingering smell of last night's meal, of charred meat and paprika. His love for Kayla, curled up in sleep just two rooms away, the subtle but sweet change in his heartbeat when he thought of her, the cozy, intimate knowledge of her quirks, her weird humor, her secret grievances.

He had come back to himself. Because something had changed, something was different. He wished he could quantify it, put a name to it. It was like a word at the edge of his mind, something he couldn't get at, reach and claw though he may. All he knew was that something had arrived.

***

In the winter of 1952, when the last occupant of the house, a nondescript banker with an oily tower of hair and a perpetual half-smile, having returned from fetching his mail from the snow-hooded mailbox at the foot of the walk, was felled by a heart attack in the front hall, the house became the subject of a protracted and byzantine legal battle between the man's estranged and far-flung heirs. Since that time it had not known human habitation. Laughter no longer bounced off its walls. Voices did not call to one another from room to room. Its bedrooms no longer heard weeping and its enfiladed second story never again echoed with the slamming of doors nor the footfalls of man nor beast. Its mirrors beheld not one human face. For a time, the ghosts of conversations hung in the air, multitudinous, overlapping. Figures ducked from its mirrors before they could be seen. Laughter hurtled through its empty pipes, along its dead wires. But after a time, even its ghosts dissipated and dissolved. All went still. The house sat lonely, passed by, ignored, or scoffed at. Shunned. Teenagers and vagrants felt an instinctive, atavistic loathing at the idea of crossing over its thresholds and exploring its insides, and police barely spared it a glance on their patrols. Neighbors, mindful of appearances, tended to its modest lawn and its hedges, but hurriedly, and with great reluctance. Thus the 1920s furniture aged further into antiquity, the colors faded, a thin layer of dust settled over all, and cobwebs sagged at the ceiling. Like a restless sleeper, the house settled and creaked and groaned with no one to hear it. Until the late winter day in 1983 when Christopher Conte walked through its front door.

***

Kayla stirred awake. The dark room had brightened to an early morning blue. She reached over to find Christopher gone. It was just after 6 a.m., early for him to be up. She listened hard, heard his footsteps out in the kitchen. Her fears and insecurities rose from their own slumber. Was he depressed? Tired of her? It seemed like he no longer listened to her at all, no longer partook in the banter that for her was the underpinning of their relationship. His laughter had become almost comically fraudulent. When she talked to him, it seemed he was peering at the horizon over her shoulder, waiting for something to appear. She had begun to long for him in the way she had when they had known each other only as acquaintances. In those early days, he'd seemed unattainable. She'd admired his poise, his easy laugh, the way he told a story, in perfect beats as though rehearsed, but still coming out as naturally as you'd please. Maybe in the company of others he was his normal self. Maybe this was all somehow because of her. This new distance had resurrected insecurities in her she'd thought long gone, she thought, and she felt the heat of resentment redden her ears.

She hoped he was still in there somewhere, that this was to have been a strange and unaccountable phase, something she'd remember with slight discomfort years down the road. Maybe the worst part of it was the fact that she couldn't find the language to speak to him about it. When she lay awake in the early morning hours, unable to fall asleep, she tried it over and over in her head, phrasing and rephrasing, striking out this word and replacing it with that, fashioning a script. At times she came tantalizingly close. But in the daytime, always in the daytime, the words were gone, lost in the wonted clutter of the day-to-day.

It occurred to her that he might be out there worrying, or feeling lonely, so, in case he might need her (*please let him need her*), she pushed off the bedclothes and padded softly into the kitchen to find him at the window. He turned to her and smiled. It was an uneasy smile, but genuine. She nearly started—it was like running into an old love unexpectedly.

"You're up," she said.

"And about," he added. "Let's get breakfast out today."

"Right now?"

"Right now."

She raised her arms up to the ceiling. "Do I smell?" she said.

"Like a clogged sewer drain. Clean yourself up, woman."

And she went to get dressed. She felt like jumping up and down. Whatever had been distracting Christopher, maybe it was over now. It was just a moment, a quick smile, a mild witticism, a flash in his eyes, but goddammit, he was *there* again. *The lights are on*, she thought, *and he's home. Whatever it was, it's over and done with. It has to be.*

She grabbed a sweatshirt from where she'd draped it over the barrel chair, then tied back her hair, slid her feet into her sneakers. But when she went back into the kitchen, Christopher wasn't there. She called out to him, circled the condo. He wasn't in the bathroom, not in his office nor the living room. She looked out the kitchen window at the car to find it still and empty. A small, nameless fear crept up her spine as she went to the front door. She put her hand on the knob, and paused. She pressed her forehead to the cool surface of the door and whispered aloud a brief prayer, a holdover from a time before her Catholicism lapsed. She breathed in fully, and out. And again. She turned the knob, opened the door, and stepped out onto the porch.

***

It has arrived. Somewhere near, finally, finally, is the boy who played within its walls, hid in its cubby holes and secret places, who told the house his secrets and his confessions...and who dared disappear without a goodbye. The boy would lay flat on the cool floors in the summer and whisper into the floorboards, his hands splayed out. The house replied to him with creaks and clicks, groans and whispers, the whooping of the wind at its eaves, the hum and rumble of the furnace—its own strange and secret language. The boy learned that language quickly, if not its full meaning, then its import, and would reply with his own clicks, hums, and howls, stomping on its floors and running his fingernails along the walls, mimicking its low groans, its exasperated complaints.

He would go there right after school every day, and frighten himself running from room to room from the shadows the house sent to chase him. He'd hide, then leap into a doorway to catch the unseen creatures cold, but nothing was ever there. The house laughed at the boy. The boy laughed back. Sometimes, though, he sat and cried, and the house sent new shadows to cradle and comfort him. Now it waits, creaks with impatience. With love. With dejected rage. It crouches in the growing light, chattering like a cat on the hunt.

***

Christopher stood on the walk and stared. His heart thudded and he felt dizzy and sick.

This was impossible.

Impossible.

In a blink, he was a boy again, standing for the first time before the house, having fled his father's bruised and angry fists, having run along the tree-lined curlicue of streets until he saw the house, standing before him, abandoned, but somehow *alive*. Where others had balked, stopped, turned away, he'd gone right up the walk as though drawn there, passed between the silent columns and stood on the porch. The red door had opened at the merest touch of his forefinger. He'd stepped inside and the shadows had taken him by both shoulders and said, *Welcome.*

For a time, a long time, he thought of it as *his* house. That other house, the sagging bungalow with the carport, the darkened, low-ceilinged rooms, and the browned lawn? That was Hank's house, a place from which to flee, a place where he was always on guard, where he'd never felt safe.

He remembered the Crescent Street house with great clarity, in exacting detail, every hall, every room, every step of its steep staircases, every nook, every creeping shadow. The hours he would spend there, alone, blessedly alone...every minute, every second was a gift. Only with great reluctance would he leave the house and head to his father's in order to be in time for dinner. There was no being late—that was the unpardonable sin of unpardonable sins, and would surely result in an open-handed slap at best. There would be no questions as to where he'd been. He would eat, tend halfheartedly to his homework, and fold himself into the covers to read. At night he would dream of the old abandoned house growing into the sky, taller and taller, more floors forming, filling up with dens, libraries, and bedrooms; fireplaces and pillow-lined nooks and grand balconies. Up it would go until it disappeared into the ceiling of the sky, at its waist a corsage of clouds. He could climb forever and never reach the top, never reach its parapets and stare off at the curvature of the earth. He could not even dream himself there.

And now the house stood in front of him, real, as real as the cold concrete of the cement walk against his feet. His house, his secret place, stood just yards away, tall and solid and real in the parking lot, facing his condo, in the grass between two rows of parked cars. Its windows gaped at him. It was a relic though, a thing from childhood he'd left behind, like stuffed animals, like matchbox cars. It was a crusted and cobwebbed memory. As he stared at the familiar red front door, revulsion bubbled up acidic and burning in his gullet.

The house swelled slightly, then stretched and narrowed, creaking and groaning, like it was preparing to leap. Its windows opened in unison, all of them. Air rushed around Christopher and into the windows. The curtains fluttered. Christopher felt a strong wave of nausea. He swayed slightly, put his hands to his stomach. The front door swung open, revealing blackness. Something emerged from the blackness...something like a large, gloved hand made of dust. Christopher exhaled.

What happened next happened quickly.

The house broke apart, then went entirely to dust. It swirled upwards in a cloud, and shot across the street and into Christopher's mouth and nose just as he drew in breath. He backed up and his feet went out from under him. He landed hard on his back. Where the house had been now lay a patch of grass, all churned and disarrayed, black dirt bleeding from the fractures. He gasped for breath. He felt things moving inside him, like he'd been infused with a thousand restless tapeworms. He coughed, retched, rolled onto his side. He called out to Kayla.

***

The house saw the boy, saw the man he had become. He was unmistakable. The house called to him. But the boy's face twisted in confusion, then revulsion, loathing. Fury shook the house to its shingles, to its cells. And in its fury it went to dust and charged at the boy, all resentment and rage and roaring fury. The house went into the boy's mouth, into his nostrils, poured down his throat and into his trachea. It burst into his body like powdered glass, into his chest, into the crooks and creeks, into the cavities between organs. It shot down his spinal column, into his groin and legs, dug like grit into every curved wall of his insides, wove around every string, dug into every fold. It cavorted and frolicked and danced and called out. The boy's body sent soldiers to try to push the house away, to fight it at every gate, every stronghold, but too late, far too late. It was in his system now. It was home.

***

Just as Kayla opened the door, the condo walls shook and the lights dimmed, and the air pushed at her as though she was standing underwater in a storm-shaken ocean, insistent and powerful. The light bulbs burst and the windows cracked. As the door frame crumpled and fell away above her, she saw Christopher prone on the walk. She ran to him as he struggled to push himself up from the ground. His face was ashen, swollen—his whole body had swollen and gone a sickly grey—and he shook terribly. He took a few steps toward her, but the strain made it look like his legs were far too heavy to lift. His hair was wild, it and his lashes wadded up with some kind of grey gunk. His mouth opened and closed.

He began to sway, his eyes changing colors as though a thick ribbon was sliding by under the surface of his face: brown, grey, off-white, sickly green, mucous yellow. He hacked and gagged, a line of thick, brown drool swinging from his lower lip. He raked his nails down his neck, scoring the skin with garish red lines. With a trembling hand he reached up to his mouth, slid his middle- and forefinger under his tongue. He pulled out an ancient looking nail, tapered and rusted. He flung it to the ground. He sneezed, and more nails slid from his nose like rain turned to solid rust. He inhaled deeply and opened his mouth wide as if to cry out, but all that emanated from those cracked, bleeding, peeling lips was the sound of a creaking door, of wet, shifting wood.

She went to him then, against every instinct for self-preservation, reached out and gripped his arm at the wrist. It felt spongey, boneless. He reached out and grabbed her shoulder, and though his hand felt terribly cold against her arm, her skin reddened and burned. She screamed, but she was held fast in his grip. She put her hand to his face to push him back, and his skin flaked away like old paint. Underneath was woodgrain, streaked with blood and grease, veined with black wires. He grimaced, and his teeth crumpled and fell away like soaked cardboard. He staggered back, and then something terrible and ragged and coal-black shot up and out of his head and he exploded into a cloud of red and black, of purples and yellows, of shards of bone. Kayla stumbled backward against the hood of a car and slid to the pavement, her eyes unfocused, her mouth opening and closing. The cloud dissipated, and what was left was a thing she could not comprehend, would not comprehend. She fainted to the sound of people approaching.

***

The house was shot through with love, to the wires, to the grains, to the cells. It was warm inside the boy, and the house mimicked him, creaking and whimpering, babbling and laughing. It spun like a dervish. It roamed the caverns, spun through the passageways, cavorted in the dark alleys. When it had spread throughout the boy, toes to crown, it stopped. As before, the world inhaled.

It was time.

Time to reassemble.

Time to bring the boy home for good.

Like an atom splitting, like the insides of a grenade released, the house began to reform. It sprung open and upward, pushing out and splintering the boy's ribs, tearing muscle and dermis. It climbed out through the top of his head into the sky like a jagged, splintered spine of coal. But something was wrong. Its staircases were mere withered wires, its walls curled scraps. Its windows were sharp slivers, thin as human hair, its surfaces blackened and gnarled, all tilting ledges and steep crags. It strained with the effort to return to fullness, then crumpled to damp ash, the wind around it curling briefly into a twister, pulling up gravel and grue, and then parasite and host were gone, leaving only fused brick and metal, twisted wire, a pile of black particles that twitched and popped in the savaged grass.

***

A month later, in Leeds, Massachusetts, a few streets over from Crescent Street, Will Dinda stepped out onto his front porch, the kitchen garbage bag gripped in his hand. Clouds had swallowed the moon, and the darkness was almost total. Rain pattered down. He lugged the bag to the curb and dropped it in the barrel. When he turned to head back inside, he saw it: the thing about which he never told anyone, not his wife, not his therapist, not his parish priest.

The moon slipped from its envelope of clouds. A thin line of undulating dust snaked past. As Will watched, the line of dust expanded, its edges squaring off, forming corners and angles that pushed out from its borders. Wires like thin tentacles wriggled at its undersides. A tower slid up and dissolved. Glass formed into squares at its surface and shattered. Then the cloud cried out, a terrible, despondent keening that morphed into a terrible roar. It slid past the moon, creaking and crackling, and disappeared into the darkness.

Where Night Cowers

"YOU! COME FETCH ME!"

The voice, barely audible over the river's roar, emanated from a thicket too modest to hide a boy, never mind a man. The thicket nestled in a circle of smooth stones in a gap between two of the many large, flat rocks that separated the water from the land at the western curve of the riverbank. The boy walked a few paces to where a tree's roots stuck out from the ground in gnarled arches, and wedged under one of them the kerchief that cradled his nascent stick collection. His bundle safely moored, he went to the edge of the riverbank and peered across the rocks at the thicket.

"Fetch you what?" the boy shouted.

There was no reply. The boy was feeble, that's what everyone said, but he sensed—correctly—that the silence was not simply that: it conveyed frustration and maybe a touch of anger. He had encountered the same silence from Pa on many an occasion. The stones looked slippery, a sheen of water sliding over them like liquid glass. The boy pulled his hands into his sleeves, went to his knees, and crawled across the rock carefully, cold water soaking his forearms and shins, the river surging ahead of him.

He wedged his foot between the rocks and began extracting from the thicket handfuls of dried-out reeds and bent twigs, letting them fall, watching them slide along the rock, join with the river, and sail away. His brow furrowed when he saw what was nesting there in the circle of stones. It was a small, flat box, not much larger than the palm of his hand, silver in color, rectangular, with a circle of tiny holes on its face. A thin strap of leather was attached to the side. He lifted it from its nest by the strap and let it spin slowly as he stared at it. He ran his thumb over the holes, fascinated.

"Now bring me to shore," said the voice, and the boy yelped, startled, and let go of the strap.

The box landed on the broad face of the rock and slid toward the river. The boy lunged after it, crawling as quickly as caution would allow. It was just about to slide into the river when the strap hooked a branch that jutted from a jagged wedge of driftwood. The boy snatched up the box and crawled to shore, gripping the strap tightly in his hand.

Finally, he stood on the riverbank, regarded the box in the fading daylight. "How'd you get in there?"

"How'd you get out there?" The box spoke in a male voice, with a slight rasp, a hard-to-quantify suggestion of age or world-weariness.

"Hm," the boy said, very much at a loss.

The sky had begun to take on the curious orange hue that heralded the onset of dusk. Pa never said nothing about him being home by dark, but it seemed sensible to do so, as the dark could hide almost anything. The boy didn't like to think about the things that could hide in the dark, though he did think about them, thought about them quite a lot, sitting awake under the wool blanket, the candles snuffed for the night, the trees standing sentry outside, the moon illuminating not much more than the clouds that tried in vain to cover it, Pa snoring like a sleeping bear in the next room.

As clouds advanced, towing evening behind them, the boy took up his kerchief. He put the talking box into it with the sticks and headed through the tall trees toward home. From time to time, as he walked upon the dirt road that followed the river's path, he asked the box where it wanted to go. *Show me where you live*, said the voice, now that of a young girl. He asked it how it could see. Nothing. He asked it why summer was so blasted hot and winter so awfully cold. The box remained silent, but the boy could hear it breathing.

***

Here and there a man on a horse would clop by, kicking up dirt. Each time, the boy would edge farther to the side of the road, looking away from the road. When he had gotten about halfway home, one horse's hooves slowed to a trot until the rider was alongside the boy. The man smelled of tobacco and rum and unwashed armpits. "Boy, what ya got?"

"Sticks, sir. Just sticks."

"Now hold up." The man pulled back on the reins. "Ho," he said, and the horse stopped.

The boy stopped too, with great reluctance.

The man's pupils were as small as his mustache was large. The buttons of his shirt lay open at his neck, wide suspenders twisted. "S'pose you come with me? I gots rabbits, two of 'em, one fer you, one fer me, stripped and ready for the fire. I gots good stories too, fit to make you laugh 'til your sides hurt. It's cold, nights. I could warm y'up."

"Pa's expecting me."

Quick as a rattler the man's arm reached out and the ruddy fingers wrapped around the boy's wrist. As the boy hollered out, the box shrieked from the kerchief as though in duet, a high-pitched, searing note that rose in pitch and intensity and volume. The man let go of the boy's wrist and his hands jumped to his ears. The boy put his hands to his own ears, gritted his teeth.

The man slid from the horse, quick as you'd please, landing with a crack as his ankle broke on the hard-packed dirt, and the horse galloped off into the gathering dusk, fleeing that horrible screech. The man sat on the ground, eyes wide, foot bent wrong, hands still over his ears. Blood spurted in great arcs from between the man's fingers. Saliva pooled at the corners of his mouth and poured out, pooling in his lap. Finally, his eyes popped like milk and the sockets filled with curdled grey gunk like oatmeal veined with blood. He rocked back, exhaled a long and shaking breath, and was still. The noise abated.

The boy took his hands from his ears, gripped his bundle tightly to his chest, started again toward home. The cold drifted in from the river, dropped down from the sky, slid from the trees. He picked up his pace. He encountered no other men on horse nor on foot. The box sang some nonsense syllables, muttered to itself, chuckled darkly, and again went quiet.

***

A thin trail of smoke reached into the sky, almost obscured by night's black blanket. At its base an orange glow illuminated the cabin, the horse barn, and Pa, who was sprawled out in front of the fire on a kitchen chair he'd brought outside, a mostly empty whiskey bottle pointing up from his crotch. The boy approached, on tiptoe. Pa snorted and his foot jerked. The boy stopped cold as Pa's hand flew up and wiped wildly at his nose. His beard was caked with vomit. His eyes remained closed. He adjusted his weight and let loose a rattling snore.

"Whiskey!" shouted the box. "The elixir that snuffs out all pain!"

The boy flung the box into the hedge as Pa opened his eyes.

"Boy."

"Pa."

"You stay away from town?"

"I did."

"Where did you go?"

"I went down the river. I went to the base of the mountain. I walked on the road down by Hog's Bladder. I climbed a tree and saw what there was to see. I caught a frog and let it go."

"That's all?"

"That's all."

The box muttered something from the hedge, the crackling of the fire all but obscuring it. Pa's eyes went to slits.

"Who's with ye?"

"No one, Pa."

"Hm. You lie to me, you get a beating. Come 'ere, get your beating."

With that, Pa fell asleep. His mouth hung open. His snoring now came in light rasps. The boy fetched the box from the hedge and brought it inside, kicking aside the pamphlets that had accumulated on the porch, the ones that someone kept putting there though he couldn't read them and Pa didn't bother to. Once inside, the door shut after him, he snuffed the candles, lay on the floor in his clothes, pulled the wool blanket over him. The darkness above him rippled, as though invisible snakes were swimming in it. He thought that if he reached his hand up over his head, he might feel them passing over his skin like fingers. This he did not do. Instead, he whispered to the box, "Keep it quiet around Pa. Pa'll take you away from me. He'll throw you in the fire or crush you under his boot."

He put the box against his ear in case it might once again speak. Once he'd slid down into the gulf of deep sleep, it began to whisper.

***

The boy awoke in full daylight. He reached for the box, but it was nowhere to be found. He lifted the blanket, shook it. He scanned the corners of the modest room. He moved aside the chair, dropped to his knees and peered under the coat cabinet. Nothing. He scratched at his side and his fingernails lighted on an unfamiliar, rough surface. He bent his neck.

The box had pushed into the tender flesh just below his ribs, deep. He dug his nails between the puckered, reddened skin of his stomach and the edge of the box, but it stuck fast, and his attempts were met with shooting pains. Finally, he drew a bath for himself, stood in the water so as not to submerge the box, running a soaped-up cloth over his skinny body. He worked the suds in around the box and tried to pry it out, but still it stuck fast. Finally, he dried himself and then dressed in the clothes in which he'd slept. He went outside. Pa was gone. The bottle lay empty by the smoldering fire pit.

He lifted his shirt to inspect the box. It had taken on the contours of his side now, had darkened in color. It pulsed slightly, a counterpoint to the boy's breathing. He touched the tip of his index finger to it. It was warm, somewhat damp, certainly more pliable than before. He pulled his finger back, letting the shirt fall back in place, and inspected his fingertip. A liquid sat in the whorls, a muted pink, like blood diluted with saliva. He rubbed it on his pant leg.

From under his shirt, a chorus rose, female voices, some humming low, others soaring. It was glorious, the sound of angels, of tenderness itself. The sound gathered in front of him like smoke. He moved toward it and it moved away, fading just slightly. One more step forward. Two. A third and a fourth and it was as loud as you please. Then the sound began to fade. He made a noise of frustration, something between a whine and a growl. He cocked his head. He side-stepped to his left, and the voices rose just a touch in volume. Another step, even louder. The voices led the boy as surely as a leash or a harness. They went toward town, warping the air. The boy followed. His lips moved soundlessly. The word he mouthed repeatedly but did not dare speak aloud was: "Mother. Mother. Mother."

***

When Pa pulled the boy from schooling, he'd laid down some simple rules. Explore the woods. Collect sticks. Don't talk to people. Don't go to town. Now the boy found himself passing the white church with its modest dormer, the priest's voice rising and falling like storm winds within its walls, an odd, halting cadence. The cemetery, where men lamented with heads bowed over silent monuments. The general store, where old men rocked in chairs on the broad porch, solemnly engaged in discussing other people's personal business. The tavern, wherein younger men roared, bellowing over one another, women shrieking, raucous laughter, clanking and stomping. All drowned out by a chorus of angels as the boy walked, head tilted and hands grasping, along the forbidden territory of Main Row.

As he passed the cobbler's, a wave of exhaustion surged through his body, and he staggered, putting out a hand to the wall. Pains jolted his temples, zig-zagged behind his eyes, ran along the line of his jaw and under his tongue. His side throbbed where the box had burrowed. Then nausea caressed his innards and he retched, but produced nothing but rank and viscous saliva. He grabbed at it with his fingers, pulled it up from his throat, flung it to the ground. He rubbed his fingers together. He felt hot, in the grip of a powerful ague. His shirt had dampened where the box had worked its way in.

Then Pa was before him like a hallucination, tall and starkly removed from the context of home. He had stumbled from Crackerbarrel Alley, looking down, fastening his belt. Behind him in the darkness a twig-thin woman adjusted her skirts. Pa looked up, and his mouth fell open. The boy's mouth moved soundlessly. Pa's ruddy hand grabbed him by the throat, and the box started to chant, a chorus of voices, speaking in tongues like folks did at the church, overlapping, rhythmic. Pa swatted the air around him. His pupils dilated.

"No," said the boy. "Don't you dare kill my pa."

Shhhhhh, said the box.

Pa jammed his fingers into his ears. He pushed hard, the muscles in his forearms bulging, until his fingers broke through and pushed in deep, right to the knuckles. His eyes went dead and his jaw dropped. A long, rattling exhalation, a failed attempt to bring in air, and he was gone. He stayed standing though, feet pointed inward, elbows crooked. Something drummed in his chest and a dark stain blossomed at the crotch of his pants. The woman screeched and retreated into the darkness of the alley.

The boy stepped around Pa's propped remains, staring ahead, for now the singing had a source. Great translucent snakes swam over his head, overlapping, intertwining, taking on the color of the sky here, the clouds there, the treetops over there. He jumped up to grab one, and it shot right down like a lightning bolt, was slurped into one of the holes in the box, joining the chorus of voices that sang within.

The boy giggled. He left Pa, following the snakes from town, toward the forest.

A rider on a dappled horse gave him a wide berth, this mad boy, walking, leaping into the air, grabbing at nothing, twitching and chortling. The snakes took many shapes as the boy followed. A dog with a profusion of bulging, dangling breasts. A broad-chested man with a cane and an exaggerated swagger. A billy goat on hind legs, with horns curled toward the treetops. A sleek, long-limbed panther. Into the thick of the woods they went, the ever-changing squadron of snakes and the boy just behind. It seemed for a time that others walked beside him in the wood, long-legged, tall, with massive, sagging heads, all grinning mouths, teeth, and wild eyes, but he saw them only sidelong; when he turned, all he saw was saplings and ferns, reeds and vines.

The snakes led him farther into the wood than he'd ever gone before. Up great hills and down deadfall-strewn valleys, through gurgling brooks and over fallen branches. The trees were thicker out here, thick as houses. It was cold here too, and the boy's clattering teeth served as percussion, backing the breathless chorus. Up ahead, the deepest part of the forest loomed dark as coal, darker than under the wool blanket in his windowless, candle-snuffed room. This, the boy surmised, was the place that nighttime fled to when the sun tried to set it on fire.

The trees began to lean away from the boy, opening a v-shaped swath in the woods. He looked down and he was clad in the bejeweled clothing of a prince, a broad lace collar like a flattened flower, a patterned doublet in purples and reds. Breeches bunched at the knee, pristine white stockings, gemstone-spangled shoes whose bright buckles gleamed. Drums thumped in their thousands. Trumpets sounded a triumphant blare. On either side of him, great tapestries unrolled from the rafters formed by the high branches, depicting scenes of great revelries, long tables spilling over with food, lined by men in black hoods and sheep-headed men; a hunt wherein devils on the backs of muscular black mares drew arrows back in massive bows, shooting angels, mouths agape, from their perches in the cottony clouds; expansive beds upon which dozens of plump young maidens cavorted, wanton mouths agape, with six blank-faced elderly men sporting comically large, pink-tipped erections.

It all fell away in an instant, the trees snapping back, the tapestries lifting, as the forest opened up upon a grassy clearing, a hazy grey at the edge of the night's hiding place, where six men, tall, gaunt-faced, stood in a broad circle. The men were dressed formally, as Pa would dress when he used to go to church: cockel hats, coats, and capes. Their skin was as pale as a tree stripped clean of bark. The snakes took the form of a great bird, flew to the center of the circle, and disappeared. The boy followed until he stood in the center of the circle. The men's features were indistinct, blurred, secreted in shadow. The boy couldn't make them into faces no matter how hard he looked. The box whispered something, and the boy nodded.

And began to spin. His feet dancing a mad kuchipudi in the muddy earth, he spun and spun, the men whirling around him. A face began to take form as he spun, a face that formed from the six faces that surrounded him, a face that hovered over a rotating array of decrepit bodies. It was a leering face, a triumphant face, a face of a man—or something a shade different than a man—who had more than a passing familiarity with cruelty. The boy felt his side pucker and pull, and then a gaping absence as the box broke free. Cold rushed into his body through the ragged hole. The box, purple and swollen and gelatinous, fluttered through the air, a winged leech, and the man's tongue surged from his mouth and grabbed it, pulled it in. The man chewed, his eyes locked on the boy's eyes. Blood sprayed from the man's elongated mouth, trickled down from the corners.

The man's many hands took the boy around the neck and under the chin and under the armpits. They lifted him from the earth, his feet still dancing below him, like the feet of a man being hanged. The man inspected him carefully. The song of the snakes, of warped trumpet blare and thundering drums, stormed the woods, bouncing from leaf to leaf, leaping among the high limbs, rising into the sky, surrounding the man and the boy, and it devolved into whimpers and shrieks and forlorn lamentations as the man began the work of taking the boy apart in order to make from him something altogether new.

Mikeytown

SUNDAY IS YOUR day to get lost. No GPS, no smartphones, no relic of a bygone age called a *roadmap*. Just hop in the ruby red pearl Camry you've owned since you were sixteen, drive the known path for a while, and then, on a whim, turn onto a road you've never been down before and keep going. Undiscovered territory. New streets unfurling like scrolls before you, farms and houses and apartment buildings popping up over countless horizons along your path. Restaurants and mini-malls and general stores and antique shops and parks, to see and experience and leave behind forever, you casual tourist, you temporary drifter. Sometimes you bring your mountain bike. Often you bring Quint instead, because Quint is always game, and always available, especially now that he's no longer a kept man; big ups to Pamela for doing what Quint never would have had the guts to do.

You think maybe you're the only reason besides work that he ever gets outside.

This time, you've brought Quint along. He picked up the phone and said *Okay!* before you could even get the question out. He's waiting out in front of his dad's by the mailbox when you get there, a bulging plastic bag in his hand. The morning sun gleams on his newly shaved dome. A goofy, guileless grin bisects his big broad face, his eyes gleam, the expression of a schoolboy with an unexpected free day. Dropping like a boulder into the passenger seat, he pulls open the bag with great fanfare, revealing packets of junk food coated in radioactive-orange dust, mass-manufactured snack cakes, and tubes of leather-like beef jerky. "I got these," he says, unnecessarily, "for the trip."

And it's on.

You drive out of town, through the meadows. The radio preaches classic rock anthems, aggressive yet professional, mannered in their depredations. The on-ramp is a runway extending into the glare of the morning sun, past that, the unknown. You drive past all familiar exits, turn off onto another highway, then another. Over tributaries and train tracks, under bridges, alongside access roads, service roads, shunpikes. Other cars, transient companions, hang with you a while, then split, headed who knows where, who knows for what. You take a random exit, angle off onto Old Farm Road/Route 30; where 30 veers left to go to the downtown of a city called Anchorville, you keep going straight. Farmhouses and stands with racks and crates of vegetables. Old style gas pumps in front of one-story shacks with peeling paint and dirty windows. Barns like great freighters mired in oceans of reed grass. Quint crunches corn-based garbage food, his fingertips growing increasingly orange. The road splits; the sign to the left says

DARLTON
GAFFTON
LAKE CITY

The other says

MANSVILLE
BLACKWORT
REDGATE

REDGATE is in a slightly different font, smaller, like an afterthought. That's the route you take. More farmhouses, more barns; some stove in as by some great meteor, splintered, burnt planks sticking out like fingers with chewed-up nails. Tumble-down stone walls guard ancient New England houses set back from the road, backed right up to the tree line. Mansville is mom & pop grocers, raised ranches and clapboard houses with car ports, dilapidated paper mills, strip malls with video stores and laundromats and packies. Blackwort is residential, conspicuously affluent, with pillared mansions behind pristine brick walls and gates of polished black iron, lawns unnaturally green and perennially mowed, pastures and ponds and brooks meandering under small rustic bridges. A drone like a giant mechanical mosquito swoops by, then rockets up to the clouds, buzzing busily. Somewhere a dog lets loose a percussive, wet-sounding fusillade of barks.

Your stomach caterwauls and whimpers. Quint offers you a gnarled crunchy corn puff that looks like a mini-wizard's walking stick. You need real food, you say, warding off the gnarled abomination. Your stomach is eating itself. The lining is the tastiest part. Quint's wispy mustache is stained orange, and two spent bags litter the floor at his feet like cast-off cicada shells, but he says he could eat. Quint can always eat.

Especially post-Pamela. She once needlessly put Quint on a diet and, unthinkably, made him go on *runs* with her in the morning as she trained for yet another road race. He'd laugh when he told you how she'd berate him like a belligerent drill sergeant, but the distress was evident in his eyes. You'd kidnap him sometimes for Friendly's sundaes, Pamela standing in the doorway, lit dramatically with the departing headlight beams, arms crossed, knowing you were up to no good.

When she dumped him, he was miserable. Since he'd lost his mom to pancreatic cancer a few years back, he'd needed someone to baby him—not exactly a healthy thing to look for in a relationship. Newly freed, he was like some little lost boy, twice orphaned. Pamela had been—of course, of course—a mirror image of Quint's mom: demanding, unyielding, dominant. Your girlfriend Shawna, by contrast, is chill and funny; sure, disagreements happen, but they're reasoned and mutually respectful—you're equals. Shawna was pleasant with Pamela in person, but *oof*, when you were alone. "She's the reason women get a bad rap," she'd say. "Why can't Quint see it?"

Because Quint is Quint. He grins that little kid grin and rolls with things, even to his own conspicuous detriment. But that's over, gone, done; now he's looking a little more like his old self, cheeks filling out, a comfortable, homey paunch. He grins at you apropos of nothing, all gap teeth and red gums.

Now that Pamela's in the past? Hell yeah. Quint can eat.

After a few miles through ice-storm felled trees and wet leaves littering the road, the sign for the next town sits on a leaning post at the edge of an expanse of gravel. It's not the official state sign with the stately black lettering on a white background centered around the state seal. This looks handmade—black, with carefully hand-painted white letters reading MIKEYTOWN Est. 1986. Below the year is an italic inscription reading *INTERRED IN SHADOW*.

Below it a white sign reads DEAD END.

Below that, an orange sign: ROAD CLOSED—TRAVEL AT OWN RISK.

"What happened to Redgate?" Quint says.

Good question.

The post is festooned with pictures and fliers like those you'd see in a college town, but you're going too fast to see what they are. You think about going back to check it out, and then the car rattles and bounces noisily over a fallen metal gate camouflaged by dead leaves. Quint drops his snack bag and waggles his head dramatically, a twenty-something bobble-head doll.

He fishes the bag off the floor, then he says, "Mikeytown, huh? Where's Sheckyshire? How about Billysburg?"

"That's *William*sburg, you heathen."

"Is there a Freddiefort?"

"Tommyston?"

"Frankiesville?"

"Herbiesburgh?"

About a half-mile of forest-lined, pothole-laced rural road, and you've seen only one house, but it's abandoned, burned out, ripped up, crumpled roof, scorched beams, leaning dormer windows revealing swatches of blue sky. Dangling from the downspout, a tattered, singed banner reads LET MIKEY GO, must be some townie in-joke. A dusty skeleton clad in muddy flannel, clearly a left-behind Halloween prop, sprawls on a rocking chair on the crumbling porch. Quint cranes his neck to keep his eye on the house as you drive past.

Another half mile and you spy the restaurant sign atop a tall pair of poles at the roadside: MIKEY'S in comic-book style red letters tilting this way and that on a field of yellow adjacent to the Sunday comic-style face of a grinning, squinting boy with freckles and a mop of red hair. The lot teems with vehicles, mostly older cars, station wagons with peeling wood-grain decals on the doors; mud-streaked pickup trucks; dented minivans; a squadron of motorcycles paired up in half a row of parking spots. The structure consists of an old red diner car, a makeshift porch climbing up to double doors with oval windows, that smaller structure fronting a larger, featureless stucco building. Atop a slight incline to the right of the building, a flyspecked red canopy shades two rows of red picnic benches with wire baskets stocked with condiments and napkins.

"I'll bet they have Mikeyburgers and Mikeyfries," you say.

"I'll have the Mikeysausage, with extry Mikey," Quint cries in a comical Maine accent. "And a *daw*lop of Mikeysauce on the side."

A shrill bell heralds your entrance. It's not exactly like a movie where all conversation stops, the needle scratches the record, wary faces turn in your direction, a waitress drops a plate. But it's not *not* like that. The hum of conversation dips slightly and eyes swing your way, some furtive, some straight-out staring. But unlike the dozens of times you've stepped into small town bars and restaurants who serve regulars and *only* regulars, your arrival seems to have stirred a curious kind of excitement in the patrons. Their gazes are welcoming, if not adoring, some bordering on avid. "I know I'm good looking," Quint mutters low, "but I'm not *that* good looking."

"Must be me then," you say.

You grab a booth across from the diner counter. Behind the counter, above the juice and soda machines and cake cases, hangs a brightly colored clock with the same Mikey face as the sign outside; adjacent to that is a framed photograph of Mikey in overalls and orange and brown plaid, vintage 80s style, fist-shelf under the chin, a fake autumn foliage backdrop. Above that a grease-stained brass plaque reads "Dedicated to and Operated Humbly in the Memory of."

Your booth is equipped with a wall-mounted jukebox. Quint flips through the selections, reads them aloud: Beach Boys, Wham, The Monkees, R.E.M, Genesis, INXS.

"Hm," you say. "All Michaels."

"Huh?"

"All those bands have Mikes or Michaels in them."

"Wham, though?"

"George Michael."

"They really run with the concept in this place," Quint says, amazement in his eyes. He flips to the next page. "Wait, Nine Inch Nails, no Michael there, that's Trent Reznor."

"Real name Michael Trent Reznor."

"How do you *know* this shit?"

A waitress in a blue dress and white apron approaches, turns to face the table, and crouches, putting you in the strange position of looking down at her. She smiles solicitously, her eyes gleaming, her black pigtails swaying as she looks at you, then at Quint, then back at you again. "Boys," she chirps. "Welcome to Mikeytown. I'm Michaela, and I'll be taking care of you today! We sure are wicked glad to have you, Mikey and us!" She beams. "I'll give you some time to look at the menu. Drinks?"

You get a Moxie-and-Milk. Quint gets an is-Pepsi-okay. Michaela assures you that your drink orders are awesome. The menu is Mikey-themed as predicted, with Mikeycheeses and Mikeyshakes and the like. The kid's section ("Mikey's Favorites") has curiosities such as Peanut Butter N' Olive sandwiches, Toast with Ketchup, Chocolate Chip Grilled Cheese, and Roasted Weiner with Applesauce.

When she returns, you order a Mikey Melt (tuna). Quint orders the Mikeyburger (well done, the heathen, with grilled onions and dill pickle chips). "We'll need silverware too," Quint says, and the waitress plucks a couple napkin-wrapped bundles from the pocket of her apron. "The old silverware burrito," Quint says, and she laughs a little too loud and a little too long. Her smile resembles a reaction to extreme pain. She literally slaps her knees.

You see the devil in Quint's eyes and you think, *Hey, man, don't.*

He says, "Hey, so where's the Mikeyshitter?"

The flash of anger in Michaela's eyes is brief but piquant. Then it's all cheer ("Just head through the dining room to the bar, and it's behind the popcorn machine, *hon*") as she points the way and hustles off to fulfill a vociferous request for a warmup from a guy at the counter with bed-head and a popped-collar pink polo shirt. You say, "Well, this is going to be an uncomfortable lunch. Thanks for that, man. I really feel like eating now." He's laughing and shaking his head, not, you note, moving to get up.

"You don't even need the bathroom, do you?"

Quint is dying, holding his belly with both hands, face red. "Nope," he manages, through helpless giggles.

You don't either, but you might as well go anyway, if only to make Quint not look like a *total* asshole. The dining room walls are festooned with kindergarten and elementary school photos of Mikey in ornate frames and rustic shelves covered with matchbox cars, stuffed animals, bronzed baby shoes, unbronzed kid's shoes, and other detritus of childhood. The booths here are taller, wider. In one, a Norman Rockwell nuclear family prays over a plate of fried chicken and home fries. In another, a lone older woman sobs into her hands, large pink neon earrings jouncing, elbows denting the open menu. Across from her, a trio of teen boys in Oxford shirts under sweater vests dip wadded up napkins into their water glasses and fling them at one another, laughing like loons. Their haircuts are identical and make you think of those Hardy Boys book covers from when you were a kid.

The short passage between the restaurant and the bar is lined with framed report cards for diners' perusal, each lit subtly from below like a museum piece. At the bar, four or five drawn looking oldsters in dark jeans and pastel blazers stare up from their beer glasses at an incorrectly formatted widescreen television, where a distorted, wide Mikey stumbles along a winding path, Fourth of July sparklers in each chubby hand spitting bright white constellations. Sputters and streaks mar the video, obviously transferred from weathered Super-8 film.

You're relieved to note that the restroom doors aren't marked Mikeymen and Mikeywomen; just the usual neckless man-in-pants and woman-in-dress silhouettes. Standing at the urinal, you scan the graffiti on the wall. There's the usual John hearts Julies and the Pink Floyds and religious things like HE WILL RISE AGAIN and REJOICE! ANASTASIS! Near the ceiling in red pen there's a childlike scrawl that reads *if an idea can be born or reborn in the brain can't also a boy* and below that a heated exchange between a blue and a black pen.

Blue pen: *Fuck Mikey!!666*

Black pen: *WHO WROTE THIS*

Blue pen: *Mikey's fatass mom wrote this.*

Black pen: *You're dead.*

Blue pen: *I'm real scared!*

Black pen: *Jeremy? Jeremy Carter? I know your handwriting. Well, hello, Jeremy. Do you know how dead you are NOW?????*

There's a little mark of blue under that, as though Jeremy, or whoever, had started to write something else and thought better of it.

You open the door with your shoulder to avoid townie cooties and head back, arriving at the table at the same time as your meals.

"Enjoy...I mean, *really* enjoy," Michaela is saying as she slides the plates onto the table. She leans forward conspiratorially. You and Quint lean in. Quint's face is all suppressed laughter, so you focus on her. But her eyes are on him, and they're crystal cold. "I know you didn't mean what you said earlier," she says in a low, disappointed-sounding voice. "I know you wouldn't say something like that and mean it. Not here. Not in Mikeytown. Not at Mikey's.

"Say you didn't mean it."

All traces of humor are gone from Quint's eyes now. He looks chastened, embarrassed. You see sweat at his hairline. "I totally didn't mean it," he says, and this is the first time you've ever heard him sound sincere. It's strangely upsetting, like hearing a bird whinny or a cat bark. "I was just bein' a jerk. Mikey sounds like he was a pretty cool kid."

"He is a *very* cool kid." She straightens, puts her fists on her hips. "I just knew you didn't mean it," she says, sounding relieved, and she hustles off.

Before you can confer, a broad-faced twentysomething guy in faded jeans and a BEACH HAIR DON'T CARE t-shirt strides up to your booth. He puts his hands on the edge of the table and looks at the food. His wispy blonde mustache is speckled with marinara sauce. "Looks good, don't it?"

"Looks great," you say, thinking, *Please go away.*

He puts a big, scraped-up hand on Quint's shoulder and squeezes hard. "Chef Jeff is really a town treasure. You boys are about to find out why. He's Mikey's second cousin. And my best friend," he says, somehow making it sound like a threat. His face goes red, and he turns on his heel and walks quickly back to his table.

Quint affects a wide-eyed, smitten look and covers his mouth with his hands. You detect fear in his eyes. You're unnerved too. The both of you shoot each other a series of *what the fuck is this* and *damned if I know* looks, shrug, and tuck into your meals. The attention of the crowd hangs over the table like a pink fog, palpable and strange, accompanied by a hum of excited, hushed conversations. You catch people leaning out of their booths to check you out, including Chef Jeff's best friend.

You both have to admit, the food is good. Really good. When the meal is done, scraps and smears on the plate and melting ice at the bottom of the cups, you think you'd almost rather a little old-fashioned townie hostility. That, at least, is familiar, mundane in real life, exaggerated in horror flicks, but something you can deal with. You worry that someone will try to hug you on your way out the door. Wiping your mouth, you thank whatever gods lurk above the clouds that a twenty will cover the check and a better-than-decent tip, you tuck it under the tab of the plastic tray, and you and Quint get out of the place. The air outside is a relief; you feel like you didn't realize you'd been holding your breath for the last forty minutes.

Back on the road, Quint is quiet. You figure he's just full, but realize he's spooked when he says, "Do you want to head back?"

This means he wants to head back.

You do too, but something in you beats back the idea. "Let's explore a little. I'm intrigued. Aren't you?"

He shrugs and mumbles.

"Anyway, we have the whole afternoon. What are you gonna do if we go home now? Play video games?"

"Okay," Quint says in a small, peevish voice. He'd definitely rather play video games. And now he's working himself into a sulk. Knowing him, it should last three to six minutes, unless it's one of his rare, mighty three-day sulks. You hope that those mega-sulks have gone the way of Pamela. A ways down the road, he begins to thaw. He puts one foot up on the dash and executes a creaky fart, then gasps and grimaces and rolls down his window doublequick. *Hoooooo*, he exclaims. You glance at the dashboard clock. A four-minute sulk. "I need coffee," he says. "Let's find a Dunks."

"I don't know how you can drink that swill."

He shifts his ass in the seat. "You know...it has its own weird flavor. It's not Starbucks, but it's better than auto shop coffee or office coffee, see what I'm saying? I could pick it out if I was blindfolded, I swear."

"If you say so."

"I'm not going to say it's good. But it's *interesting*."

"Uh huh."

You pass silent gas stations, a brick firehouse, an elementary, middle, and high school evenly spaced, in order; you pass a strip mall with Mikeycuts and CineMikey and Mikey's Bar & Grill. No Dunks. No Burger King nor Wendy's. No McDonald's, which you figure would fit right in. "Yo, check out the street names," Quint says in a quiet voice.

You glance at the signs on the corners. They're clearly hand-painted, yet a perfect mimicry of the ubiquitous white-on-green street signs. His Little Toes Avenue. His Bright Blue Eyes Terrace. His Helpless Laughter Road. His Favorite Stuffed Bunny Lane. His Too Cute Dreams Road. The Way He Holds His Sippy Cup Way.

Way way, you think.

"His Enormous Horse Cock Boulevard," Quint says in a low, serious tone, and then he's flopping around in his seat, crying with laughter. You're thinking, your brain going a hundred miles an hour, wondering if those street signs show up on GPS, or if you'd only find their original names, whatever they were. What *is* this town?

"Hey, man, come on, that was funny."

A few more miles of residences, from clapboard houses to old colonials to Cape Cods, many of them with Mikey-face flags hanging over American flags, more of those fucked up street names, and finally ahead the road splits around a verdant town green dotted with tall shrubs and bisected by a winding sidewalk lined with benches; a few couples stroll laconically. You spy a conspicuously large blue-green statue of Mikey reaching for a butterfly, water pouring from its eyes, nostrils, and mouth. The effect is upsetting; it reminds you of footage you found online of some politician blowing his head open with a .357. Across the road that rings the green is a city center of old brick buildings that house banks, a pizza place, counter-service Chinese, a hardware store, thrift shops, boutiques, and quaint book/gift shops. Above, curtains billow from apartment windows, plants sit on windowsills, faint music plays.

You pull into a spot in front of a café with a large neon mug suction-cupped to a flyspecked window shadowed by a weather-beaten, faded awning. Quint goes in to get his coffee. Bored, curious, you get out of the car. You stroll a bit. The shops are quiet, mostly empty, bored looking cashiers leaning on the counters, running their fingers down smartphone screens. In a narrow alley between two of the brick buildings, a flagstone path lined with vine-strewn trellis tunnels leads back to a yellow Cape Cod-style house with a sign reading MIKEYTOWN HISTORICAL MUSEUM. A neon sign in the shaded window indicates they are OPEN.

You head back toward the car. Quint exits the café holding his cup in both hands like a treasure. You say, "Let me guess. You got the Mikey Blend."

He gapes at you. "On the fucking *money*," he says.

"What'd that run ya? Three Mikeybucks?"

"They didn't charge me."

"No?"

"Dude goes 'This one's on Mikey, my new friend.'"

You say, "Weird and weirder, this place. Check *this* out," and he follows you, sipping at his coffee.

"Ooh," he says. "History—my favorite subject."

"Sarcasm suits you."

"Shall we?" His disquiet has passed, thankfully.

"You first, my old friend."

When you step in, you see that this was at one time a family home, but the interior walls have been taken down. A carpeted anteroom opens into an expansive area with shining wooden floors. To the far left is a kitchen area with a fridge and a sink and pastries on trays under plastic covers. Opposite that is a replica of a living room, with an old-style 13-inch tube tv, a plaid couch and matching chairs, end tables, and a carpet teeming with stuffed animals and action figures. Beyond that, a wall-side staircase. Ahead at the far wall, curved rows of folding chairs face a narrow podium.

Behind the podium, balcony-to-floor banners of either photographs or hyper-real paintings depict Mikey at play. Vertical letters on each banner spell out MIKEYTOWN EST. 1986, though the pictures are tinged with that yellow-orange haze that screams 1970s. The boy is clad in plaid pants and turtlenecks in various shades of orange or maroon. Here he's kneeling by a pond holding up a fat frog for the camera, his mouth a joyful O. There he's hanging from the horizontal bars of a playground set, his belly exposed. There making a snow angel, his fingers and cheeks as red as cherries.

In the northwest corner stands a Stonehenge of museum-style displays. You walk over to check them out. In a lighted glass box atop a mahogany pillar, a crumpled pair of grass-stained overalls. At the base, a tricycle with colorful ribbons dangling from its handlebars, clear protective plastic covering the handles and the pedals. To its right a white wooden sign tinged with ash and char that reads REDWATER SURGICAL ASSOCIATES in Old English lettering. Beyond that, recessed wall cases display a clay mold of a small hand on a rectangular teak base; a soiled diaper; a slightly kinked red plastic slinky; a ragged, eyeless teddy bear with a tiny felt tongue and dots for nostrils; a folded dollar bill that says FOR MIKEY FROM GRAMPA ALL THE LOVE!!!! in ball-point blue.

"Excuse me," a voice calls out, and you turn to see a young redheaded woman, hair in a ponytail, wearing a maroon blazer over a white sweater. She has smash-back lips and front teeth like great white double doors. Green eyeshadow and bright red lipstick decorate her face. She regards the two of you with a combination of surprise and delight. "Well, who do we have here?" she says, her lips curling up in something like a smile.

The absurd, forced friendliness sets something off in you. You're just about to snap back that you're potential paying visitors to this dump, when Quint says, "I'm Quint, this is Warren. We were traveling through." He has put on his charming voice and is smiling widely. Incredibly, he winks, and, also incredibly, her eyes soften just slightly.

Quint has a thing for redheads.

"Strangers," she says, tasting the word like it's an unfamiliar flavor in her mouth, new, but not entirely unpleasant. "Okay. Well, I'm Mickey." She tugs on the lapels of her jacket—it's going to be all business now, she seems to be saying. "It's a suggested five-dollar donation. This goes to the upkeep of the Mikey House, the preservation of artifacts, the destruction of pre-historical documents, security for the museum and the Shadow Spot, reparations for the families of Dr. Hartwell and his staff, and living expenses for Cary and Barb...um, Mikey's parents."

Pre-historical documents? Shadow Spot? Reparations?

You pull two fives from your front pocket and hand them over. She tucks them into an inside pocket of her jacket and clears her throat. "The History of Mikeytown," she announces in a somber voice. She looks at Quint, then over to you. "Do you want to have a seat?"

You take two chairs in the center of the third row, and she takes her place at the podium.

"First, a little bit of prehistory, from a town that exists only in the memory of the older citizens of Mikeytown, and will one day be lost to time...and the shredder. Michael Richard Beresford was born on July 8th, 1981, in Redwater, Massachusetts, an early birth, certainly because he could not wait to start his life with his loving family. His birth weight was 8.2 pounds, his hair a flaxen blond that soon turned to a gorgeous shade of deep red. His mother and father could not have been prouder. He was a very bright and alert infant, who did not fuss, who was a stranger to the screaming tantrum and the night-sobs. He cooed and gurgled, and his skill at communicating before the acquisition of language was remarked upon both by friends and by strangers, the latter of which there were fewer and fewer, as Mikey was a fixture with his mom on the town green, sitting up in his carriage like a little man."

1981 is prehistory? You were born in '76. You glance at Quint, who is sipping his coffee, a look on his face like that of a man trapped in an unexpected sales pitch. He shoots you the side-eye. *What have we gotten ourselves into here?* Your phone buzzes, and you slide it from your pants pocket, still watching Mickey, then glance down. It's from Quint, of course.

mikeyy would have given u the diaper off his back

Mickey doesn't seem to have caught this. She goes on and on about Mikey's childhood, in the tone of a proud parent, presenting the unremarkable traits of some random kid as though speaking about some king or earth-straddling deity. Your polite smile is giving you the traces of a headache behind your eyes. You tune her out, think about this and that, and then something in her tone has changed and you slide back into your ears.

"Mikey died on the town green at the age of seven years old." Her voice breaks. "That devil that you call *God* took him from us without a hint of warning. He was jumping after a ball—his favorite ball—when he collapsed. When he left us. Doctor Hartwell, Mikey's pediatrician, was on the green that day with his family. It's no coincidence that he was there that day, not in a town this small. It was a beautiful day." She stops, closes her eyes, puts a small hand to her chest. Then she blinks away tears and resumes. The gesture, the tears—it all seems to you rehearsed, part of a routine. "Mikey was gone as soon as he hit the ground. But we were upset—certain that Doc Hartwell had...*overlooked* something, or kept something to himself, not done his best, out of jealousy. His papers can be viewed on the second floor, where his office has been faithfully reproduced from promotional photographs taken before the fire. We hope the exhibition honors this great man, who cared for Mikey and truly cared about his wellness and who couldn't possibly have..." She sighed. "What happened to him and his staff is a source of great regret for the town, in retrospect."

As she goes on, it occurs to you that all of this is addressed directly to Quint, as though she's apologizing to him on behalf of the town. A lock of her hair has fallen across her face. She jabs at it with her tongue to move it away from her mouth. Quint is stirring in his seat. He raises his hand like a kindergartener. She laughs and points at him. "Quint?" she says.

"I'm so sorry to interrupt," Quint says, his voice low and excited, "but is there a bathroom I can use?"

"Oh, sure," Mickey says. "It's upstairs. Kind of a maze, this place." She's not quite Oscar material, but it's a hell of an acting job. "I'd better just show you. Follow me?" Quint slaps you on the knee and gets up to follow her, putting his half-full coffee cup on his chair. As she leads Quint up the stairs, she reaches back and takes his hand.

You can only shake your head. This is not the sort of thing that happens to Quint. Nor to you, for that matter. You find yourself amused, strangely aroused, maybe just a bit jealous. Rather than just sit there, you push yourself up and approach the podium. Mickey's script lays on the platform. Doodles fill the margins—fanciful doodles of Mikey as he might have been. Mikey as a teenager, hair long and combed back, one of him as a young man in a suit. A middle-aged

Mikey in an easy chair with a cat curled up in his lap. She's a talented artist...if completely out of her mind.

Finally, you head upstairs. At the top of the stairs, straight across, is a bathroom. The door is open. You walk in. The carpeted toilet seat is a Spiderman logo; the bathmat matches it. As does the open shower curtain. The tub is full of soapy water. Bath toys bob. The water is unsettled, as though someone just hopped out, but the floor and mat are dry. You step out into the hall. To the right is a closed door. You can hear the squeaking of bedsprings, low moaning. To your left are two more doors. The closed door has a wide window next to it, with drawn blinds. A plastic sign in a brass frame reads PEDIATRICS—Boyton A. Hartwell, M.D.

The other door sits slightly ajar, the room unlit. Affixed to the door, a small chalkboard with a metal shelf reads MIKEY'S ROOM—DO NOT ENTER in a childlike scrawl of fluorescent colors. You push the door open, releasing an overwhelming waft of lemon-scented cleaner, and feel for a light switch. It's not a surprise when the light reveals a typical child's room circa early 1980s, but not like some pristine exhibit—it's a mess. A mirror-topped dresser with a colorful lamp and an array of action figures, a yogurt container with the foil top pulled back, and an askew stack of children's movies on videocassette. A multicolored checkerboard carpet littered with kids' clothes, including underwear with a brown skid mark, spilling from a knocked-over hamper. Superhero and *Star Wars* posters line the eaves over the racecar-shaped bed—and then you see the disarranged covers are pulled over something human shaped, small.

No, you think. *It's a doll, a replica, made for the museum. It isn't some deranged human taxidermy, the preserved, stitched-up body of Mikey, with dead skin stretched over a small skull, grey fingers curled into claws, glass eyes in the sockets...*

Two things happen at the same time. The bedsprings in the room down the hall stop squeaking, and the thing under the covers shifts. You back out of the room and glance at the other door...which is opening. You hear muffled voices. You take the stairs two at a time, slide back into your seat, try to catch your breath.

Mickey comes down the stairs, her hair tousled, jacket wrinkled, face flushed. She blows the hair from her face as Quint casually descends behind her, a look of satisfied triumph on his face, a sort of pathetic swagger in his step.

"We should probably head out," you say, glancing at your wrist as though there's a watch there.

"Are you sure you don't want to stay?" she says breathlessly. "There's only a half hour left of the opening presentation, and a slideshow, and, and, and, *the rest of the museum.* There are things here you really should see. The chapel, for one, and Mikey's bedroom..." You're thinking of something polite to say, when she breaks the awkwardness with a smile. She shrugs and tears a swath from the bottom corner of the first page of her script. She writes something on it and hands it to Quint. "Thanks for coming," she says, and it's all you can do to keep from laughing.

"You dog."

"Shut up, man."

"What happened back there?"

"What do you mean, 'back there'?"

"You *dog.*"

You're on the green now, side by side on the walk, strolling slowly, Quint sipping from his coffee cup, the contents of which can only be tepid by now. The sun is high in the sky, everything tinged sepia, like the pictures of Mikey back in the museum.

"So, are you going to move to Mikeytown now? Rent one of those apartments above the shops? 'Cause suddenly you seem *verrrrry* comfortable here."

"I dunno, man," Quint says, scoffing. "Leave me alone."

"Oof," you say. "That's how it starts. Soon you won't be answering my calls. Your metalhead t-shirts'll be replaced with Mikey shirts." Something occurs to you. "Hey, Quint...did you wrap that rascal?"

He looks skyward, rolling his eyes and groaning.

"Soon there'll be little Quint-Mikey's running around."

"Man, that's the least of my worries. I'll be checking my pecker for spots for a month."

"Nice way to talk about a young woman who seemed very sweet."

"It's always a good idea to check in on the little fella."

The walk ends at a section of grass backed by a great display of gladioli, snapdragons, lilies, chrysanthemums, carnations, and roses, the front and sides roped off by heavy lengths of chain in red plastic sheaths attached to stone stanchions. "Check it out!" Quint says...and in the center of the green grass you spy a shadow in the shape of a boy, arms splayed, legs just slightly apart, as if his invisible body was leaping across the sky just above. There's no boy, obviously. You wonder how they achieved the effect. Darker grass? Spray paint?

A grave marker, long and low to the ground, reads

THE SHADOW SPOT
MICHAEL "MIKEY" RICHARD BERESFORD
INTERRED IN SHADOW
1981-1986 GONE BUT NOT FOR LONG
...*since death came through a man, the resurrection of the dead comes also through a man...*

"They just, like, darkened the grass," Quint says, echoing your own thoughts, but his voice betrays a filament of doubt. He steps over the rope and walks toward the shadow. The sun brightens in the sky. Quint's shadow looms over the boy's, fitting it with eerie accuracy. A whisper of warm wind blows back your hair and you turn. A massive shadow approaches, wide as your view can encompass, horizon to horizon, sliding down the mountain, darkening hillock and hollow, spilling over the line of buildings and washing across the green like the shadow of an invisible tidal wave. Along with it a hum rises in pitch and volume, like the quickening of the vibration of the planet in the gulf of space, like a tornado warning siren, like the wail of something living underground as it races to the surface of the earth to be born.

Quint is as still as a statue, his shadow and Mikey's shadow are fusing, blackening, charring, smoking. You clamber over the rope, nearly spilling over onto your ass, and circle around to face Quint. Something ripples in his eyes.

The treetops are whipping, and voices are calling one to another from the streets and buildings beyond the green. A car horn blares, and through the trees at the far end of the green you see two policemen running toward you, hands hovering over their service revolvers. They're grinning and braying laughter. Quint sees them too and he's up on his hands and knees and then standing, leaping back over the ropes and you're both beating feet to the car, faster than you've run in years, cheeks puffing, fists pumping, sneakers squeaking, and you look down and you have a shadow but Quint has left his behind, *no time to think about that now, no time, run, run, run,* and with relief you see no one's blocked the car in, and you're jabbing the door with the key, missing it, missing it, you hit it, you're whipping open the door, jumping in, unlocking Quint's door, and you're both in and you're off, the trees and houses blurring by on the sides, and sirens start up, a cacophonic chorus wailed in rounds, and the sky is black as midnight now.

Houses and yards and flags and trees blur in the streetlight glow, the road striped with shadows, and you're barreling, cars in the rearview mirror small, getting bigger now, closing in, gaining, and your foot aches from jamming down the gas.

You look over at Quint, and he looks queasy. His eyes are unfocused and he's holding his hands to his forehead. The car clatters over the fallen gate again, and this time, there's a loud popping sound and the car sinks just slightly. You hear the *chugga chugga chugga* of a flat tire. The car is bouncing now. You brake. Smoke pours from the undercarriage. You look up in the rearview, and the other cars are there...but they're stopped, just sitting there, headlights on, faces in the dashboard glow staring.

Quint brings his hands down from his face. Staring straight ahead, he looks terrified. His breathing comes in shallow, vocal gasps. He turns his face toward yours and his eyes widen. You see no recognition in them at all. "Stay back," he cries, and there's something wrong with his voice.

"Quint?"

"Let me go," he says. "Please just don't hurt me and let me go."

"Hurt you?"

His eyes fixed on you, he fumbles behind him for the door handle. He opens it, and steps out, backing away, watching you carefully, then turning and bolting. In the rearview, a couple emerges from a station wagon. Quint runs toward them, the faltering, fumbling run of someone trying out new legs. The pair, just silhouettes, fold him into an embrace. You hear sobbing. And chanting. More car doors open. A couple of men head your way, wrenches in their hands. There's only trees here, no house lights, no lights at all save the headlights. You look around for a weapon, bracing for their attack.

What's taking them so long?

They're putting the gate back up. A couple of pickup trucks pull up. Men get out. Wheelbarrows and cement blocks. Reinforcements. You drive out slowly, the damaged wheel protesting all the way. In Blackwort you're able to flag down a car and call Triple A.

You never hear from Quint again. His father's house is quiet, dark at night, the driveway empty of cars, possibly abandoned. In your dreams, you're still driving out of Mikeytown, headlights cutting up the darkness behind you, lighting up the inside of the car. Your eyes aren't on the road at all. Your hands aren't on the wheel. Your seat is turned toward Quint, its back against the side window. Quint's face is purple, plump, his eyelids swollen up like he's got golf balls under them. His lips are moving like he's trying to speak, but then you realize that something's pushing at them. Two small purple fingers appear and there's a *crack* like a tree snapping in two and Quint's head goes curiously wide. More fingers, small and purple, push their way through the horizontal slit of Quint's left eyelid. His eyes move farther apart and the skin above his nose splits. Something is back there behind a gap in the chalk-like skull, something alive, looking at you. You bounce up, your head hitting the ceiling of the car—a curb. The car swings sickeningly, spinning and jouncing, and you're hurled against your door, and finally you're stopped in a patch of mud in the front yard of an abandoned house. Quint is leaning against the passenger door now, legs together, body still. His head is split down the middle, twin bowls holding grey soup and gristle, and his shirt is all blood and something pale yellow. As cars skid to a stop behind and on all sides, you spot something on the floor among the snack bags and the crumped receipts. It opens its eyes and you wake up calling out for your friend.

Publication History

Monica in the Hall of Moths: *Uncertainties 3* (Swan River Press), 2018

Effigies of Former Supervisors: *Vastarien, Vol. 2 Issue 1*, 2019

The Museum of Laughter: *The WXXT Program Guide*, 2021

Dr. 999 : *Ashes and Entropy* (Nightscape Press), 2018

Oh the Beautiful Stink: *Vastarien, Vol. 3 Issue 2,* 2020

Provisions for a Journey: *Phantasm/Chimera: An Anthology of Strange and Troubling Dreams* (Plutonian Press), 2017

Call Me Corey: *Test Patterns* (Planet X Publications), 2017

The Dark Match: *Three Moves of Doom: Weird Horror from Inside the Squared Circle*, 2016

The Two-Wheel System: *Walk on the Weird Side* (Lovecraft Arts & Sciences), 2017

If He Summons His Herd: *Lost Signals* (Perpetual Motion Machine Publishing), 2016

Leeds 2600: *Terror in 16-Bits* (Muzzleland Press), 2017

The Long Lost Parent : *Strange Aeons #22*, 2017

We Pass From View: *Darker Companions: Celebrating Fifty Years of Ramsey Campbell* (PS Publishing), 2017

The Storefront Theater: *Letters of Decline: Four Tales of Job Interview Horror* (Orford Parish Books) 2017

Deep Into the Skin: *Tales from a Talking Board* (Word Horde), 2017

Go to the Devil: *Behold the Undead of Dracula: Lurid Tales of Cinematic Gothic Horror* (Muzzleland Press), 2019

Master of the House: *A Breath from the Sky: Unusual Stories of Possession* (Martian Migraine Press), 2017

Where Night Cowers: *Lost Signals* (Perpetual Motion Machine Publishing), 2016

Mikeytown: Original to this publication

Acknowledgments

S INCERE GRATITUDE TO my family and my wife, whose support has been unequivocal and fierce, especially in these last few turbulent years.

And to my friends for the same reasons.

And to the editors who found these stories worthy of publication: Ross E. Lockhart, Max Booth III, Scott R. Jones, Jon Padgett, Robert S. Wilson, Lynda E. Rucker, Tom Breen, Duane Pesice, Scott Dwyer, Joseph S. Pulver Sr., Scott David Aniolowski, Jonathan Raab, and Justin Steele.

And to my fellow practitioners of horror and weird fiction, and music, and visual art, and film, many of whom I count as friends, too many to mention, so many that to attempt to list them would be to accidentally leave out someone worthy.

Again to Tom Breen, my dear friend, colleague, and collaborator.

To s.j. bagley for everything.

And to my readers, by whose enthusiasm and support I am frequently overwhelmed.

And to Scarlett R. Algee at JournalStone. Truth: in early 2021, she dreamed she was typesetting a collection of mine in "some weird near-illegible blackletter." Here it is now, and in a legible font to boot.

About the Author

MATTHEW M. BARTLETT lives in Western Massachusetts with his wife Katie Saulnier and their cats, Peachpie and Larry. He is a full-time writer and a part-time purveyor of books and alcoholic beverages.

CPSIA information can be obtained
at www.ICGtesting.com
Printed in the USA
BVHW041704100723
667022BV00001B/62